# The Company We Keep

Also by Frances Itani

**Fiction**
*That's My Baby*
*Tell*
*Listen!*
*Requiem*
*Missing*
*Remembering the Bones*
*Poached Egg on Toast*
*Deafening*
*Leaning, Leaning Over Water*
*Man Without Face*
*Pack Ice*
*Truth or Lies*

**Poetry**
*A Season of Mourning*
*Rentee Bay*
*No Other Lodgings*

**Children's Books**
*Best Friend Trouble*
*Linger by the Sea*

Frances Itani

# The Company We Keep

A NOVEL

HarperCollins Publishers Ltd

Published by HarperCollins Publishers Ltd

First edition

HarperCollins books may be purchased for educational, business or sales promotional use through our Special Markets Department.

HarperCollins Publishers Ltd
Bay Adelaide Centre, East Tower
22 Adelaide Street West, 41st Floor
Toronto, Ontario, Canada
M5H 4E3

*www.harpercollins.ca*

Library and Archives Canada Cataloguing in Publication
Title: The company we keep : a novel / Frances Itani.
Names: Itani, Frances, 1942- author.
Identifiers: Canadiana (print) 2020022882X | Canadiana (ebook) 20200228854 |
ISBN 9781443457538
(softcover) | ISBN 9781443462648 (hardcover) | ISBN 9781443457545 (ebook)
Classification: LCC PS8567.T35 C66 2020 | DDC C813/.54—dc23

Printed and bound in the United States of America

LSC/H 9 8 7 6 5 4 3 2 1

There's a time to laugh and a time to weep . . .
But sometimes the two get muddled up.
—*Remembering the Bones*


Hold your collar, touch your toes.
Don't want to be in one of those.
—*The Lore and Language of Schoolchildren*

September

# The Notice

No one knew that Hazzley was emptying her house, one room at a time. An early riser, she'd been up since six, working on room two, Lew's office. She pulled at his desk, which refused to budge. She went around to the other end and shoved hard, hip against the side. Years ago, Lew had insisted on sticking felt pads to the bottom of everything. As long as there was no carpet, even the largest pieces would slide across the floor if she could get them started.

Carpets were already gone.

She stopped after manoeuvring the desk through the doorway and into the wide hall. She had emptied its side shelves the night before. She went back for chairs, a tall and narrow set of drawers and a low filing cabinet. Lew had been thorough; the filing cabinet, too, had pieces of felt stuck to the bottom.

The small items were easy. Her conditions, also easy. Do not

1

shift items from one place to another; that solves nothing. Get rid of it all. Unclog your space, give yourself some air. Think of the pleasure of living in an empty house.

Everything was lined up, ready for the truck. She leaned into the door jamb and thought of what Sal would say. "Mother, why is your furniture in the hall? Why are all the rooms empty?"

And Hazzley would reply: "I am clearing my life." Or should that be "cleansing"? Didn't matter; her daughter lived in another city. Not her decision. Hazzley suspected that if Sal pushed her to explain, she'd have to admit that what she was really trying to do was recreate a life—*her* life, the story of herself as she wanted to be right now.

AS PROMISED, Habitat for Humanity had its ReStore truck at the house by eight thirty. Two strong men loaded everything she'd pushed into the hall. She couldn't believe the size of one of the men. He must have been seven feet tall, maybe six-eight or -nine. He and his lifting partner were efficient and made the work look easy. Since the truck was half-empty, Hazzley told them to take the hall sideboard, too. At the last minute, she threw in a wingback chair. Men and truck were gone by eight fifty. She closed the door and stretched out her arms, did a forward bend, touched the floor with her palms. She'd better quit while she was ahead or she'd wreck her back.

She went to the kitchen, thinking of what lay ahead. The basement was the nightmare. If anyone thought of a basement as ballast for a house, hers would never fit the description. Her basement was emotionally fraught territory. At least she didn't try to fool herself. She just wasn't ready to face it head-on.

She had no plans to move out of her house, even though ownership was becoming . . . well, onerous. Simple as that. She called up the Latin: *onerosus*, meaning "burden." Indeed, yes. Burdens could be oppressive. The more she owned, the more "things" to look after. Things: exactly what she didn't want. Maybe she should tackle the dining room next. Furniture was bulkier, higher; she might have to call in assistance. ReStore again? How many times a year did she use the dining room, really?

Think of the pleasure of strolling from one empty room to another. Think of the pleasure of a journey through an empty house. A tear escaped onto one cheek, and she brushed it away. Come on, she said to herself. It's been three years. You like the idea of paring back. You use the kitchen, bathrooms up and down, one bedroom, your office upstairs. That's about it.

She reached for the mug she'd abandoned when the men arrived, but her coffee was cold and she dumped it down the drain. She stared out into the backyard. The leaves were turning red and gold; it was that time of year. Change went on outside the house, no matter what transpired within.

Maybe she needed a new idea, a different sort of journey. She sat at the long kitchen table, pulled a piece of paper toward her and reached for a black marker. Think, she told herself. Write things down. This is what you're good at. Think this through.

She went to the phone and hit the memory key for Cass's number. While waiting for her friend to pick up, she thought: *Change, to make or become different. Cambiare, Latin; changer, French.* Yes, change would definitely help.

MARVIN'S GROCERIES OPENED AT NINE. By ten, Hazzley was in front of the community board, which was fastened to the wall in a narrow space at the end of the checkout aisles. She had her sheet of paper in one hand and four red push-pins in the other. Although extra pins were scattered about the edges of the board, Hazzley had brought her own. She pinned her notice in a prominent spot and scanned the board, marvelling at the earnest business of information exchange. Never, until this day, had she posted anything. A few customers were usually standing around, taking photos with smartphones or scratching numbers and websites onto bits of paper. On this Thursday morning, no one but Hazzley was present.

The rules of the board, enforced by Marvin, were printed in bold lines across the top:

> *Notices must be dated and will be displayed for*
> *two weeks before being removed.*
> *Offensive or distasteful material will not be tolerated.*

Hazzley looked up to the inside window of the main office on the second floor and proffered a wave. She knew Marvin would be up there looking down. He waved back, and then quick-rapped the glass twice with his knuckles in a sort of solidarity gesture. Marvin had a wide head that Hazzley thought of as scrunched, the way heads looked on TV when the setting was slightly off. His jet-black hair, ungreased, stood up like wire. He was grinning down as if to reassure her that he enjoyed rising early to supply food to the neighbourhood. Sometimes he could be found in the aisles, supervising staff or assisting customers, but most days he was up there at his desk, managing, overseeing the space he'd inherited from his father, also Marvin, and that was now under his rule. He worked hard to earn loyalty and made it clear to customers that he was aware of big-box stores edging into the core of Wilna Creek. One new mall with a huge supermarket had opened on the far side of Spinney's Ravine. The mall satisfied high-tech workers in that area of the city, but it created competition. As for the noticeboard, Marvin viewed that as a responsibility to shoppers, whether they were loyal or not. He also believed that not every communication between humans had to flicker across a tablet or a lighted screen, or had to be tweeted, or needed a thumbs up or thumbs down. Despite the relentless march of technology, Marvin let it be known that as long as he owned the store, he would protect space for pencil and paper, pen and ink, thumbtack and push-pin.

Hazzley turned her attention back to the board. In a corner of one notice, someone had drawn a rainbow, along with a half sun and a few strokes of rain. The image made her think of the word "parsec," a surprise in the morning crossword. A couple of times a week, she was stumped by some such word. Parsec had something to do with astronomy, distance. She'd looked it up but knew she'd never use it in a sentence.

The aroma of baking bread wafted past, drifting from the rear of the store. In response, she closed her eyes and rocked on her heels, almost losing her balance. Once upon a time, she'd made her own bread. A different time in her life. Every woman of her generation grew up knowing how to make bread. If they didn't know how, at the very least they'd watched their mothers knead dough and lay damp towels over glutinous mounds that mysteriously grew rounder and higher. Hazzley wondered if she should take home a loaf of rye or a couple of blueberry scones. She heard a hissing noise and watched a sleepy-looking clerk in the vegetable aisle give a shake to a length of rubber hose as he aimed a spray of mist over the fresh produce. The young man hadn't bothered to comb his hair.

This week's notices included promises made by people who offered to look after children, teach yoga and fly tying, purchase military medals, form choirs or prayer groups, administer safe tattoos, predict the end of the world, practise meditation, provide instruction in ventriloquism, sell lotion guaranteed to soften cracked heels, exchange seeds, teach sermon writing, look after cats, run a boot camp, join laughter groups and divulge foolproof ways of making money. One notice asked for extras for Friday night poker. Another hinted at "discreet" services; Marvin must not have spied that. An index card advertised Sam the Man with

Truck. Some ads required severe editing. Half a dozen were posted by people who needed or offered the services of a handyman. She read one of these and laughed aloud: *Handy Andy, supplies own tools.* She was not taken in by that.

Her own notice was clearly written and direct:

### GRIEF DISCUSSION GROUP
*Weekly: Tuesdays 7–8:30 p.m.*
*Backroom at Cassie's (Cassandra's Café—38 Beamer Street).*
*First meeting September 18. All welcome.*

Cassie's was located two blocks from the grocery store. Anyone from the east side would know its whereabouts; anyone coming in from farms or suburbs on the west side could find it easily enough. In recent years, the café had become a popular drop-in place. Cass Witley, Hazzley's friend, was generous about allowing people to use the backroom, at no charge, for community purposes. During this morning's phone call, she'd assured Hazzley that the space was available Tuesday evenings. Hazzley, new to this sort of venture, booked the backroom for four weeks. Cass had told her she could use one of the round tables for the meetings. She had three, of different sizes.

Hazzley rechecked her notice for precision and inclusivity. She had slit fourteen tear strips along the lower edge, each printed with address, time and date of the first meeting. She did not include her personal phone number and email address because she wanted nothing to do with crank calls or lunatics. She had no firm plan for the meetings, but she would not schedule talks on how to do your own banking (for women whose recently deceased husbands had run the entire show) or how to boil an egg (for men whose late wives had fed them three squares a day). She would not invite earnest guest speakers who would expound with PowerPoint. She wanted nothing more than a quiet and uncluttered setting. Cass's backroom could provide that, along with coffee, tea, maybe a glass of wine—all of which could be purchased at the café. Hazzley envisioned honest men and women who would support one another, share conversation and companionship. She admitted to herself that her expectations were vague. Life's events would unfold. After four weeks, if participants wanted to continue, she would rebook the room and carry on.

She would also keep track of events in her journal, a practice she'd kept up for fifty years. She had never shaken the desire to write things down. For a long time, she'd been making her living by the pen.

She wondered what her daughter would say about this initiative. Once or twice a week, she and Sal exchanged emails, but for now, Hazzley wouldn't mention the notice. Sal, fifty-three, had moved to Ottawa decades earlier to work for Heritage, or whatever the department was called. Communications, or maybe Citizenship—Hazzley couldn't keep up with government name changes. Sal's husband also worked for the government, and from what Hazzley could see, they lived a hectic life. They had five children, two of whom attended university. The other three were in their teens. Framed photos of the five grandchildren hung in a row along the upper hall of Hazzley's home. She stayed in touch and tried to keep up with their lives. They sent emails and called her on FaceTime to tell her about a race won, a mark achieved, a pet that died, a disappointing argument with a friend. Hazzley loved them all dearly and wondered what they'd say about her partly empty house.

Well, she wouldn't mention that, either.

She stepped away from the noticeboard, forgot about buying bread or blueberry scones and left the store. She had to get home to finish an assignment for a popular science magazine. She was editing an article about bones, teeth and early tools discovered in a cave. She had a three-day window to deadline.

A wind had come up while she was inside. An outdoor geranium on display had tipped over, and crimson petals were trapped in an eddy between the front of the store and the parking lot. She tightened her jacket and stepped around petals that swirled about her ankles. Despite the wind, she was sorry she'd brought the car. She usually left it at home, unless there would be too much to carry. She walked most days, in an attempt to keep her heart (and brain, she reminded herself) healthy. She did the crossword every morning and dabbled at sudoku. She had a membership at the local gym—useful in bad weather—and stared at a muted TV screen while walking on the treadmill. She tried to stay abreast of the news and had learned multiple ways of averting her attention from American politics. She read the obituaries daily and was saddened by death—early death, any death. Too much cancer, too many accidents. She tried to keep her weight under control, knowing that many in her generation could no longer see their own feet. She was a strider, a fast mover. Lew had once referred to her as "fleet of foot"; she smiled, thinking of this. She liked to believe that she was wending her way through a life that was in no way sedentary, even though she spent hours at her computer while she worked at freelance editing jobs. She kept her hair dark and tidy, but she knew that despite her efforts, outside attitudes prevailed. People in their twenties and thirties had begun to address her as "dear." She ignored this. She felt strong and, if anyone had bothered to ask—no one had—ageless.

Nonetheless, she was putting on a bit of beef in the thigh. No matter how much effort she put into keeping fit, her body had begun to take its own twists and turns. Four weeks earlier, she and Cass, who was eight years her junior, had signed up for swing dance lessons. At the first class, Hazzley was not bothered by the fact that she was the oldest person there. She was happy to be with Cass, who had the most infectious laugh of any of her acquaintances. Cass loved dance, loved music, loved having fun. "I predict that you'll be the best dancer in the group," Cass told her. Hazzley sometimes wondered about the accuracy of her friend's prophesies. These were subtle, buried in conversation, unremembered until after the fact. Cass had always been amused by the name her mother had bestowed upon her—Cassandra—along with its mythical narrative. She'd been nicknamed Case, also by her mother, but that abbreviation was used only by immediate family and her partner, Rice. To everyone else, she was Cass or Cassie.

Rice was a jazz musician who occasionally performed at the café. He had not been interested in signing up for swing lessons. From Hazzley's point of view, Cass had a solid partnership, and a few dance lessons without Rice wasn't going to bother anyone. After dance class, Cass went home to Rice. Hazzley went home alone.

Well, she thought, I could always join the Friday night poker group that's advertised on Marvin's board. Or I could put a white sock over my hand and paint on a lipstick mouth, an eye on each side, and teach myself ventriloquism. Learn how to work around those seven difficult consonants—BFMPVWY. I know that much; I'd have a head start. I talk to myself anyway, so I may as well talk to a sock in a mirror with my lips partly closed.

What would she tell the sock? Ventriloquism was about deflection, wasn't it? Deflection of attention, change of direction.

One thing she could say for certain was that since Lew's death, she'd been as lonely as a person could be.

And what would the sock reply?

Before she started the car, she spotted the end table wedged into the back seat. She remembered that she'd run back into the house, earlier, and carried the table out. Another item gone. She felt lighter already. She'd drop it off at the Sally Ann on the way home.

Tonight, she would add this to her journal: *First step taken. Notice pinned at Marvin's. Now I'll have to wait and see what happens Tues. night.*

# Flock

G W E N

Gwen heard screams as she pulled up to the garage, but she sat for a moment and allowed the sun to warm her. Despite the wind, she left the car windows down. She loved the crisp air, summer's ebb, the perfect fall day. A maple tree on the next lawn had begun to scatter a few red leaves across the browning grass. The screams turned to shrieks, raucous and shrill. She got out of the car and fit the key to the front door. Abrupt silence at the click.

*Dead quiet means predator approaching.*

"Hey, Rico. It's me, Gwen. Remember?"

She kept up a foolish banter as she walked into the family room. From the farthest corner of his cage, Rico was taking her measure with what Gwen interpreted as hostile indifference. She wondered if hostility and indifference could coexist in a parrot— or in anyone, for that matter. She had invaded Rico's space, his home. Perhaps he was formulating a plan to extend and sustain the mood as long as possible. Small black pupils stared. Rings of white around the black. A white mask was fitted to perfection around the eyes and above the beak. Chain-mail hood of soft grey. She had not attempted to smooth a finger over those intricately layered feathers. *He will allow you to pet his head, but give him time—don't try right away. He'll learn soon enough that you are his source of food.*

He tried to press himself against the back corner, but he was already at the far end of the perch. His perch—one of several in the large cage—was thick, made of braided rope. In the short time since Gwen's morning visit, pellets and seeds had been scattered in a wide crescent over the tiled floor.

"Beady," she said. "Your eyes are beady." She, too, could be hostile—or indifferent. "And you've made another mess for me to clean up." This observation was unhelpful; he turned his back. She knew he was watching.

*Vision is his strongest sense.*

He began to examine every angle of the room except the one where she stood, but she knew he could see her. She went to the kitchen to get the broom.

This was her third day, sixth visit. Duties included preparing and providing food, as well as supplying him with fresh water. Visits were twice a day, every day. Her most important task was to converse with the parrot one full hour every morning and a second in the late afternoon. Rico needed to socialize. Rico needed *flock*.

He had not yet spoken. He'd created a variety of sounds—

certainly screeching when she approached the house—but no utterance had come close to resembling a human word. Cecilia Grand had told Gwen over the phone that he'd be talking before the end of visit one.

Cecilia, a stranger to Gwen, had failed to provide hands-on orientation, a distinct disadvantage. An emergency had come up; details were vague. Cecilia and her husband had a daughter in LA who was undergoing a crisis, and they were compelled to depart a week earlier than intended. That's what Gwen was told when she'd received a frantic phone call. The house key would be stashed under an upturned wheelbarrow at the side of the garage. The Grands had no choice but to leave for the airport before Gwen could get to the house to meet them or the parrot.

When Gwen had first replied to the ad by phone, she was told that she would be meeting the parrot and shown what to do. When the well-intentioned plan fell through, Cecilia, in emergency mode, had written instructions on both sides of a piece of foolscap and fastened the sheet to the fridge door with a magnet. Every detail of care was squeezed onto those two pages. A separate sheet on the kitchen counter contained a recipe called Rico's Chop. Gwen had never heard of a parrot's chop, but she was to prepare said chop and pack it into a plastic container in the fridge. With lid. To keep it fresh. Every three days. Fortunately for her, Cecilia had made chop the day she departed, so at least Gwen knew what it looked like in its prepared state. To make the chop, she was to choose from a long list of vegetables that included carrots, snap peas, Brussels sprouts, cucumber, radish—the list went on and on. Fresh herbs and cooked pasta could be added. No celery—strings too dangerous. And only 10 percent of the diet was to be fruit. Today was chop-making day. Vegetables were in the crisper drawers, money for extras in an envelope on the kitchen counter.

The parrot-sitting job was meant to last seven weeks, possibly eight. Gwen would be notified by phone as soon as the Grands had booked their return flight.

Was trust not a factor? Didn't they care about hiring a stranger who would be wandering in and out of their home for seven weeks? "I trust you," Cecilia Grand had said over the phone. Now Gwen wondered if she was the *only* parrot-sitter who'd responded to the ad. Well, of course she was. Maybe the Grands had skipped town and abandoned a parrot who'd become an unbearable responsibility.

Gwen reconsidered. Everything had sounded sane and reasonable during the preliminary phone call. Cecilia answered Gwen's questions and inquired about her previous work record. She asked for a work reference, which Gwen supplied. Cecilia might even have taken the time to check with her former boss. Gwen imagined the staff in the accounts section of Spinney's Office Furniture hooting with laughter over supplying a reference for her role as parrot-sitter. Don't be paranoid, she told herself. They probably don't give you so much as a second thought.

When Cecilia had called Gwen about the crisis and early departure, she'd said, "I'm truly sorry I won't be able to meet you to provide a proper orientation. But I can tell the kind of person you are just by talking to you. I know you're honest. I'm completely confident." Before Gwen had time to think up a reply, Cecilia rang off because she and her husband were short of time and facing a two-hour drive to the airport.

GWEN HAD FIRST come across Cecilia's ad on the noticeboard at Marvin's and had pulled off one of the tear strips for a lark. She'd taken it home and stared at the phone number. She imagined introducing herself to a parrot: *I am Gwen. Recently retired, age sixty-three.*

Maybe the job would not be entirely dull. Better than sitting at home imagining a replacement at *her* accounting desk in what used to be *her* tidy and familiar office. Better than thinking of the golden handshake and early retirement. Better than standing in the doorway of Brigg's clothes closet, wondering what to do with his as-yet-undistributed belongings.

How difficult could it be to talk to a parrot? The job was about conversation, companionship. She had snickered to herself when she first read the ad.

Gwen knew, or believed she knew, what her former colleagues thought of her. Nondescript, quiet, fair-haired-but-greying Gwen. Five-nine, thin—perhaps a little too thin. Hard-working, good at keeping books, never a problem with accounts. Honest as the day is long, her manager said during his final tribute to her. When it became known that she'd put in her notice, the fourteen employees on staff, including the drivers of Spinney's two delivery trucks, took up a collection and presented her with a painting: a tranquil scene of rolling hills and a placid lake. She thought it lacklustre as a piece of art. She wouldn't want to travel to or be inside that particular scene, but what could she say? Without faltering, she thanked her workmates for the gift. The presentation took place during a farewell dinner at an Indian restaurant called Spice. Over the years, the company had often used Spice for seasonal celebrations or promotions, and when paying tribute to departing employees. The group sat around an extra-long table in one of the restaurant's side rooms.

Gwen visited the hairdresser the morning of the farewell dinner, and the stylist convinced her to have ginger-toned highlights put in so she'd look her best. Both Gwen and the stylist were pleased with the result. At the restaurant that evening, after the presentation of the painting, Gwen choked on a lump of killer-hot green pepper during the main course and was forced to rush to the washroom, tears streaming down her cheeks. Janey, the company receptionist, followed to ensure that she was okay. But she wasn't okay. Her insides had ignited, her nose was running; she didn't want to go back to the table. She wondered why she'd bothered about ginger tones in her hair because grey continued to announce itself at the edges. She felt half-dyed, a retiring scarecrow with a head of straw.

After hacking and gagging and staring at her red face and brimming eyes in the mirror for more than five minutes, Gwen returned to the table. She couldn't exit the restaurant without walking past the room of colleagues. There was no escape. She sat down, nose still running, tissues bunched in one hand. She picked over the rest of her food. Her boss was telling an off-colour joke. After the punchline, he guffawed and looked over at Gwen and said, "You get me?" But she'd glazed over. No one at the table seemed to get the joke. Gwen, completely depressed, felt a headache coming on and began to count the minutes until she could leave.

The others, oblivious to her flaming esophagus, began to tease about what she and Brigg would do now that she was joining him for extended leisure time. They didn't know that he'd bullied her into retiring. He wanted someone to golf with, someone who would make the necessary arrangements and then travel with him so he wouldn't have to look after details. Gwen harboured an intense dislike of golf and would have preferred to stay with her job.

She retired in February. Brigg had a stroke in early March and died in late April. His rapid decline over that two-month period was unexpected, shocking. He was older than Gwen by seven years, and though they'd been married thirty-six years, she had never understood what he saw in her in the first place. Their sons—twins born on Halloween—returned for Brigg's funeral. They were both involved in high-tech work, and at the end of their university years, not used to being separated, they'd moved to the same town in the farthest corner of Texas, as far away as they could banish themselves. The grandchildren—each son now had one daughter—did not attend the funeral. There were mutterings about the children not wanting to miss school. The girls remained in Texas, along with the wives. Gwen and her sons were the only family members present to mourn. All told, a dozen people attended, including five men from the local golf club.

But Gwen and her sons had little to mourn. Arm in arm, in unbearable silence, the three followed Brigg's casket out to the hearse. They had done their grieving decades before. After the service and the mercifully short reception, Gwen returned to the house and had the twins gather up the golf clubs—every one—and drive them to the Sally Ann.

IN THE GRANDS' KITCHEN NOW, Gwen reviewed her parrot duties. Four items were capitalized at the top of the list.

*FOOD*
*WATER*
*FLOOR OF CAGE/CLEAN DAILY*
(*plastic gloves in box on kitchen counter*)
*CONVERSATION X 1 HR TWICE A DAY, A.M. & P.M.*
(*allow time for response*)

Beneath these items, the list went into an unreasonable amount of detail: *Wash pellet bowls and food dishes. Replace cage-floor papers. Monitor Rico's intake accurately. Wipe down cage wall weekly. It's important to wipe perches. Supplies are under kitchen sink.*

This was a cosseted parrot, accustomed to princely care. The back of the page contained threatening information in red about what Rico was capable of if he lacked companionship and satisfactory conversation.

*If he clings to the side of the cage and beats his wings rapidly, that means he's upset.*

*He'll work at keeping his feathers in good condition. If he's stressed or bored, he could start pulling them out.*

Plucking feathers was a true threat. Gwen hoped Rico would not become petulant and start plucking on her watch.

*Before you leave the house each day, turn on the radio, preset to CBC— soft voices, good mix of music and conversation. A parrot can DIE from loneliness. Turn off the radio during your visits to allow for exclusive interaction with you. On weekends, a favourite is Michael Enright's* Sunday Edition. *A good mix of human voice and music.*

*If you feel confident after a few days, let him out of cage for brief periods. You'll have no problem getting him back inside. He returns for food, treats and water. Remember that cage is home. He likes his home.*

*I've left new foraging toys in a basket. Change toys in cage as you wish. You'll know when he's bored. Some toys have a nut hidden inside. Add treats.*

Gwen dug into her shoulder bag and pulled forth a clump of tough-looking kale. She hacked off a two-inch chunk and fastened it to a metal clip. Kale is a treat, she reminded herself, though she was doubtful. She went back to the family room, kale in one hand, broom in the other. Rico was staring hard. Gwen understood that he needed to know where she was at every moment.

"Come on, Rico," she said. "I'm not so bad. You're a pretty boy, did you know that? A pretty boy. Look at those tail feathers. What a gorgeous red!"

He flipped his bird body and walked upside down toward her, his parrot toes easily grasping the top bars from inside the cage.

She changed her tune. "You're a dude, Rico. A real dude." *Rico is highly intelligent,* Cecilia Grand had written. *Challenge this intelligence!*

What did Cecilia know? Well, maybe he really was.

He continued to stare with his head upside down. No matter where Gwen stood in the room, she could be seen. Rico climbed down a bar of the cage sideways, as if to prove something. His entire body remained horizontal; he was still staring.

She stared back.

He righted himself and edged his way to the far corner again while she clipped the kale to a bar of the cage. He hunched, a sullen attitude. Muttered. She had no idea what a parrot's mutter was supposed to sound like, but she was certain that he had muttered.

Petulant bird, she thought.

"Show-off," she said aloud, hoping that teasing might get a response.

At the sound of the word "show-off," he righted himself and began to preen.

"Eat your treat, Rico. I went to Marvin's on the way here so I could buy one piece of kale—just for you. Tomorrow, I might bring broccoli."

She remembered that on her way out of the store, she had torn a strip from a notice on the community board. *GRIEF DISCUSSION GROUP.* There wasn't much information on the tear strip—only location, time and date. She felt for the strip in the pocket of her cardigan. The first meeting was to take place the following Tuesday at Cassandra's Café.

Gwen had been to Cassie's—that's what everyone called the place. Long ago, Cass—well known in town—had taken over the old Belle Theatre, Wilna Creek's earliest movie house, so that she could prevent its destruction by developers. She and her partner, Rice, had transformed it into a flourishing live theatre, and after several decades, they sold it to a trio of actors who had new energy to invest. When Cass and Rice gave up the theatre, they purchased the café. Less work, less responsibility, they told everyone. They could close the café for weekends when they felt like doing so. They could take off for a week or two and drive away from the place. Cass didn't have to schedule performances a year in advance. She didn't have to collaborate with half a dozen or more people the way she'd done for every production while she'd managed the theatre. All this had been written up in the *Wilna Creek Times.*

The previous December, Cass had held a sixty-ninth birthday party for herself at her own café. She took out an ad in the paper and invited patrons to drop by for a piece of cake. Gwen didn't go because she had no one to go with. Brigg would have had no interest. She didn't bother telling him she'd like to go.

Now a person in town—man or woman, no way of knowing—was organizing some sort of discussion group about grief. The group would be meeting in Cassie's backroom. Gwen weighed the decision, considered Brigg, considered grief. Maybe she would show up. After the first meeting, she could make up her mind about continuing. She hadn't been part of a discussion group since university days. She'd certainly never joined any sort of club. During Brigg's illness—to distance herself from his anger and constant demands—and later, after his death, she had begun to stop in at the café to sit for long periods over a drawn-out latte while reading a book from her late mother's library. With time to herself, she was beginning to discover the contents of that library. She'd started with Arthurian tales translated from Middle English, recalling a day when her mother had held out a book and said, pointedly, "Gwen, this is not a translation. This is an exciting story that happens to be told in an earlier version of your own language—English."

For whatever reason, excitement or scholarship or both, her mother had committed herself to the Arthurian legends. After Gwen's father died—from a lingering war wound in the late fifties—her mother continued the research and became an accomplished and renowned scholar.

Cass never bothered Gwen at the café. Never asked her to move or give up her table. Gwen associated that welcoming place with losing herself in the adventures of King Arthur.

She had inherited her mother's books, some of which she *did* consider to be translations. Gwen had studied mathematics and accounting at university and was not skilled at reading Middle English, though she loved to read and had plowed her way through excerpts from *The Canterbury Tales*. Even those required frequent checking of footnotes. A first-year scan course in English literature was the only arts class she'd taken during her time at university. She'd forgotten the details of the *Tales*, but remembered Chaucer's bawdy humour.

She'd never finished sorting her mother's books. Some were packed in boxes, some displayed on shelves along the hallway at the bottom of the stairs. Brigg had been all for selling the lot to a second-hand bookstore. He had pressured, for a time, but Gwen dug in her heels—one of the few times she had. Those times—of defiance—could be counted on the fingers of one hand. And now, out of nowhere, into her thoughts dropped the word "roundheels," causing a noise to erupt from her throat, a half snort. With a cold, old shudder, she shook from her mind one memory that represented all memories: the number of times she'd half suffocated under Brigg's heavy, lumpy body. Who else would have endured what she had endured? Did that mean she was weak? Spineless? She laughed aloud, and Rico squawked.

Again, she felt for the strip of paper. What sort of grief would she talk about among strangers?

"Woe came upon the people," she said to Rico, recalling a line from an Arthurian tale. She tried to envisage a group of wailing strangers. She would be expected to say something. Wail along with the crowd. Or maybe there'd be no wailing; maybe there was a possibility of laughter.

She would become still and listen. Perhaps she would become friends with someone. A person who, like her, had been cast adrift. Someone with a heightened awareness of this new lone state. Gwen didn't know which had been more upsetting: her retirement or Brigg's death, which had made her a widow. The two events were muddled and inseparable.

Janey, from Spinney's, had shown up at Brigg's funeral and she referred to his passing as an unfortunate "off-time" death. Gwen nodded and accepted Janey's hug, but she'd never heard the term and looked it up later on the web so she could be sure of its meaning.

*Off-time death: Not expected, premature. Before the expected time.*

Brigg was not yet seventy at the time of the stroke.

Along with Janey, three others from Gwen's former office attended the funeral to express condolences. Gwen genuinely appreciated their presence, but seeing her former workmates made her realize that she missed the office routines as much as she missed the routines of marriage, despite Brigg.

There was no one to tell things to.

For instance, she would like to tell someone this: Two nights ago, after her first visit to Rico, she had a dream about walking along the paths of a city zoo she had been taken to as a child. What was different was that the visit took place now, at her present age. She felt like a child but saw her adult self standing before the glass wall of a large aviary. The expansive enclosure was roofed and filled with trees and shrubs and roosts and loops of thick rope. As she walked past, winged creatures inside stared out at her. One bird laughed uncontrollably.

What could such a dream mean?

Brigg would have dismissed her imaginings—or maybe not. He might have been interested. She had no way of knowing; he was dead and couldn't be asked. Since his *off-time* death, Gwen no longer had to think about being ridiculed. She no longer had to listen to the detested handbell clanging demands while its echoes bounced off the walls. Brigg insisted on having the bell atop his bedcovers after the stroke. It had to be placed in exact position, beside his left hand, the one he could move. She listened to the barbarous *clang-clang-clang* all through March and into April, the interminable and desperate days leading to his death.

And there was something else. He made a noise at the back of his throat, a staccato mechanical sort of sound he did not seem to realize he was responsible for: *click-click, click-click*.

She reminded herself that she no longer had to respond to calls in the middle of the night when he shouted from his bed. *Click-click, click-click*. She tried many times to convince herself that he was gone. She kept looking over her shoulder despite willing herself not to. She did not present her back to a door—any door—though she knew he would not return. She tried to stop listening, stop waiting for the handbell to announce his anger, clatter his demands. She'd moved into one of the spare rooms during his illness, but her sleep had been constantly interrupted. After his death, she stayed on in the spare room, not wanting to return to a space they'd once shared. Why had she allowed the bullying? She had no answer.

Instead, she put effort into convincing herself that she no longer had to be alert to mood, or prediction of mood, every waking moment. Not until the visits to Rico began. Rico, she decided, was a moody bird. But she was not afraid of Rico.

If the Grands did return home at the end of seven weeks—or eight—she wouldn't tell them about her zoo dream. Except for the two phone calls she'd had with Cecilia Grand, and except for being inside their house every day, Gwen had no idea what kind of people the Grands were. Even if she did recount the dream, she would not disclose that Rico, with his parrot-sized brain, was the impudent bird directing his laughter at her.

"You're a piece of work, Rico," she said aloud, and he perked up and cocked his head to the left. In real life, he was anything but laughable. She wondered if he could create the sound of a laugh, and at that very moment, he laughed—like a human! The sound was unmistakably male, a deep, hearty laugh, but with a sort of buzz, as if the sound had been filtered through a partially clogged horn.

She swept up the seeds with the broom and returned to the kitchen to get water—*bottled, never tap!* Rico watched intently. When she filled the container at the side of his cage, he edged away. He didn't like her near; that was easy to see. He didn't like her putting fresh food out for him, but after it was in place, he settled and began to eat. He was nervous. He didn't know her well enough. That's what she told herself. *The African grey is a beautiful bird, but it can be skittish.* She looked at the curve of his beak. Black, not really black, more like smudged charcoal. She caught a glimpse now and then of a coal-black tongue. Was the tongue perfectly curved to fit within the beak? From the side, the half mask that circled his left eye was a swirling white nebula, indistinct around the edges but with a vigilant black pupil at its centre.

She sat on a chair in front of his cage and heard her throat make a chirring sound. One of Cecilia's instructions had explained that Rico liked to hear insect sounds. What sort of insect? How was Gwen to know? An insect sound wasn't exactly conversation.

"Ch-ch-ch-ch."

Rico hopped over to a different perch.

"Ch-ch-ch-ch."

No response. He chewed away at the kale.

She decided she would bring Rico something from home. Maybe she would read to him. That might get him talking. Maybe he'd enjoy listening to a soft and steady voice. If she read aloud, maybe he would show some respect.

ON THE WAY HOME, Gwen drove back to Marvin's. She needed margarine. She needed a loaf of bread. She needed food. Nothing with seeds; nothing chopped or shaped like pellets. After she'd made the insect sounds, Rico had pecked at his seeds with renewed vigour and scattered them widely, creating another mess that required cleaning up. For her own evening meal, Gwen wanted human food in large pieces. She chose a salmon steak and dropped it into her grocery basket. She would eat a baked potato cooked whole. She contemplated lolling in front of the TV, and hoped there would be no news items about temperamental birds that might pluck their own feathers.

She meandered through the produce department, selected broccoli and decided she would take a chunk to clip to a bar of the cage the next day. She had the feeling that Rico preferred fruit, but she had to stick to the vegetable–fruit ratio prescribed by Cecilia Grand. *Total diet: 50 percent veg/10 percent fruit/40 percent pellets.* Halfway through the list of possible foods, Cecilia had underlined: <u>NO PITS, NO APPLE SEEDS</u>. Maybe red palm oil took care of whatever it was that more fruit would supply; Gwen was to add palm oil to Rico's chop and treats. Or maybe a diet heavy in fruit caused diarrhea. Could parrots have diarrhea? Gwen couldn't think why not. Maybe there was a special word to describe parrot droppings, a word similar to "mutes." Isn't that what hawk feces were called? Falcon feces? She muttered the word "mutes" to herself.

Marvin was at the cash, having stepped in for an evening employee who was on supper break. Gwen exchanged a few words with him, paid for her food and passed the noticeboard on her way out. She paused when she saw that two more strips had been torn from the notice for the grief discussion group.

So. Other people were grieving. She hoped she wouldn't know anyone who turned up at the café. Cass would recognize her, but Cass wouldn't have posted the notice. The city was large enough that the attendees could be complete strangers to one another.

Maybe she wouldn't go at all. She didn't want to be part of any sort of group confessional. Woe to the people, indeed.

She cast a glance at other notices and inspected the array of fonts and coloured inks, each attempting to draw attention. What would it be like to brandish her name publicly in outrageous fluorescent capitals? Her full name, stretched across the length of the board.

G-W-E-N-D-O-L-O-E-N-A.

A name she used only on official documents, such as passport forms. Brigg had believed her name to be outlandish. At the beginning, he had teased; later, he'd scoffed.

Gwen knew that her late mother had been fanciful at the time of her birth. She'd become pregnant at thirty-nine, and Gwen was her only child. She'd named her after Gwendoloena, wife of Merlin the Magician, even while writing serious articles declaring that Merlin's stories were not a true part of the earliest Arthurian legends. Her mother had published a respected paper about the Arthurian portion of Layamon's *Brut*, a Middle English poem known as *The Chronicle of Britain*. She loved any story of Arthur, and especially loved the language of the *Brut*.

If Gwen's mother hadn't approved of her daughter's marriage, she'd never said as much. She'd died long ago and wasn't around for support while the twins were growing up.

Gwen stared at the board again. Other people seemed to have lives that were whole, fulfilled—but did they really? She wondered if she had always been on the fringes of that sort of experience. Who on earth did she used to be? How far back would she have to go to find the Gwen who was buried in the past?

She had several days to think about joining the discussion group.

The wind was gusting when she left Marvin's. She stopped to straighten a potted geranium that had tipped over on its side. Crimson petals were blowing about. She crossed the parking lot and slid the groceries onto the back seat before climbing into the front. Fragments of grey clouds swept across the grizzled sky.

# Carry Tiger

CHIYO

Chiyo stopped at Marvin's on the way to her evening tai chi class. She paid for a tin of olives and a plastic container of arugula, and stuffed both into her backpack next to her energy bars. After class, she would make a salad, add tuna and olives, chop in a bit of celery, green onion. Before leaving the store, she scanned the noticeboard at the end of the checkout aisles. She was thinking of her mother's illness, the diagnosis of leukemia, the treatments, the long, slow death at home. When her mother had stopped leaving the house, Chiyo became responsible for errands, necessary and unnecessary. Sometimes, for Chiyo, coping had been a matter of walking out of the house for no apparent reason. No reason except to get away from her mother.

"Anything of interest at Marvin's?" her mother would say the moment Chiyo returned home. The question—posed in a way that demanded an answer—set Chiyo on edge, an edge she willed herself to control.

Her mother had become thin and weak during the last months of her life, and she was unable to walk more than four steps on her own. Caregivers came and went. Despite her weakness, she'd been resolute about keeping up with happenings in the community and news of the world. The TV in her room was permanently set to the CTV news channel. She also wanted "Marvin's store news," even while expressing shock that the citizens of Wilna Creek freely posted personal information in a public place. Chiyo teased about this, knowing that her mother bristled. Mock anger, Chiyo thought now. Maybe I couldn't tell the difference between real and mock. Real anything. Mock anything. Maybe I still can't. My mother filled herself with anger, or others did this for her. Old anger from way back, long before I was part of the scene.

As a young girl, Chiyo's mother had been forced to move, with her parents and more than twenty thousand other Japanese Canadians, to one of the many inland camps in the mountains of British Columbia, close to the Fraser River. This had happened in early 1942, several months after the bombing of Pearl Harbor. Her mother had carried her childhood anger about this betrayal of democracy, this injustice, into adulthood. The anger had never been resolved. Too late for resolution now. Or maybe, maybe she was at peace.

During the final three months of her mother's illness, Chiyo carried paper in her backpack so that she could copy out some of the notices on Marvin's board. These gave her mother something to think about, or rail against, or laugh at—whatever mood happened to fit. There were always notices about some guy supplying his own tools, but Chiyo ignored those. On days when she couldn't be bothered stopping at Marvin's, she invented notices in hopes of satisfying her mother's curiosity.

*Rare-looking snake with colourful markings rescued from apartment toilet. So far unidentified. Ophiologists? Care to advise?*

*Will babysit your child for $25 per hour, with the proviso that I am permitted to use your sewing machine during work hours.*

*Learn twenty-one ways to cook with stale bread.*
*Will add an excellent recipe for head cheese.*
*(My recipe does not use head of a pig.)*

*Found: Wedding dress, hacked to pieces, Booth Street,*
*corner of King.*

The last was a jibe at her mother. But really, Chiyo's inventions did nothing more than set her own trap. Day in, day out, her mother lay in bed with the door ajar so that she could see into the kitchen. From there, from her sickbed, she was aware of the outside door opening and closing. Her dulled eyes watched, no matter how quietly each person arrived and departed. She monitored Chiyo as she left in the morning and returned in the evening. Before Chiyo could remove her shoes, she heard her mother's voice, weakened from the effort of straining against illness. The hoarse whisper rasped across the kitchen: "Anything of interest at Marvin's?" Gradually, to conserve energy, the question was reduced to "Marvin's?"

Chiyo was expected to reply. She had no choice, no excuse. Marvin's bulletin board became the main topic. Pretty much the only topic, if she didn't count caregivers' schedules, bathroom routines, medications taken, food that her mother did or did not eat. The truth was, her mother's world had shrunk to a pitiable state, and Chiyo had been trying to prevent shrinkage of her own.

Even when her mother was well, she wasn't an easy person to live with. She pried. Disapproved. Assumed the right to comment on Chiyo's every act, her every friend. She commented on Chiyo's appearance.

"You should eat more. You're too skinny. So much exercise makes you look like that."

"Like what?"

"The way you look. Skinny, like a giraffe neck."

At other times: "Have you been eating too much? Your stomach isn't flat anymore. That can't be healthy."

"When the stylist cut your hair this time, he finally got it right."

What was that supposed to mean? All the other times, he'd got it wrong?

Never a real compliment.

Chiyo was often out because she was booked to teach at regular times in a city-run gym in her area. She taught classes for Parks and Recreation three mornings and three evenings a week:

stretch and strength, Pilates, yoga, tai chi. Sometimes she held extra classes on Saturday afternoons. Before and after class, she occasionally scheduled clients who engaged her as a personal trainer. For those meetings, she drove to a YMCA/YWCA gym located in the new shopping mall on the far side of the ravine. She knew that while she was out teaching, her mother was probably at home rifling through her private belongings. She didn't bother to hide the fact that—until she was too weak to do so—she regularly inspected her daughter's dresser drawers and closet shelves. Post-cards from Leonard were scrutinized, but he knew enough not to send private letters when travelling.

Chiyo had been involved with Leonard for six years. Her mother disapproved from the beginning—in the same way she disapproved of anyone else Chiyo had dated. Her mother wanted her to produce a marriage certificate, grandchildren who would crawl around the kitchen linoleum and who could be shown off to her friends. But her mother's friends had fallen away in the final year.

When Leonard used to come to the house, her mother—still well enough—made a point of getting to the door first.

"It's *him*," she called back over her shoulder, her small stature blocking the doorway by half. She refused to say his name. At the time, she didn't know that Chiyo had every intention of marrying Leonard. But the relationship hadn't turned out that way.

"Your name might mean eternal," she said to Chiyo one morning, "but you're running out of time if you're going to have a child." She spoke as if her words were etched onto a blade to be twisted as only a mother could. "Child-bearing years do not last an eternity."

Chiyo had no reply. She did not fight her mother, but her body flinched from the wound. She didn't shout: *Do you think I'm unaware of my own biology?* She was forty years old, and if she was ever to have a child, it would have to be now. But she had not been brought up to shout at her mother. She'd been raised to maintain silence. Respect elders. While her mother's voice yammered on in perpetual staccato, with each beat sharply detached from the next, Chiyo diverted her inner attention to tai chi. *Bend bow to shoot tiger*, she said to herself, and her body responded as if it had at that moment created the move. *Strum lute with both hands.* Music calmed her. She thought of the *shakuhachi*, the haunting echo of rich tones through bamboo. The music of monks.

Leonard was out of her life. Now she was seeing Spence, who lived in an apartment nearby. Chiyo had stayed on in the house, which was left to her in her mother's will. She had no siblings; her father had died of chronic lung disease related to the repeated bouts of pneumonia he suffered throughout his childhood in the camps. According to family lore, his health never truly recovered after the years he'd spent in an uninsulated tarpaper shack in the mountains. His lungs, weak in childhood, became weaker in adulthood. He died four years after he married, when Chiyo was a toddler, almost three. She held wisps of father memories: a word uttered softly, a movement, a facial expression, the sensation of safety and abandonment inextricably entwined.

The bungalow that was now Chiyo's was cramped and poorly planned: a crowded kitchen, two squared-off bedrooms, a front door that opened directly into a living/dining room, no coat closet at the entrance, a boot mat prominent by the back door. Not much had been done in the way of modernizing, but despite cracked linoleum, chipped paint, an outdated kitchen, Chiyo enjoyed the independence of living on her own. Since her mother's death in April, she no longer reported to a parental inquisitor who followed her every move. Spence, easygoing Spence, made no demands and was as independent as Chiyo. Sometimes he stayed overnight or for a weekend, but by the beginning of the week, he was back in his own apartment. Monday mornings, after his departure, Chiyo expanded her spirit. Her right arm extended high while she reached for the sky; her left arm pushed low. *Stork cools wings.* She occupied her own widening space and inhaled deeply.

NOW SHE SHIFTED her backpack over her shoulder. The arugula container knocked against her scapula. Film, she thought. Bette Davis, she thought. Bette as Charlotte in *Now, Voyager*. Charlotte had been locked inside a pattern of bending to the will of a controlling mother. Claude Rains had also starred in that film. Rains had a way of frowning with intensity, the implication being that *his* thoughts were superior, intelligence reaching into him from some far-off source. Paul Henreid was Charlotte's love interest. Paul had a high forehead and carved profile that expressed sorrow even if all he did was turn his head to the side. It didn't matter that

Bette Davis shared the space with men who were cast in roles that portrayed them as having chiselled profiles and superior knowledge. She ate up the screen, and there was nothing her co-stars could do about it.

Chiyo found it easy to identify with Charlotte. Five months after her mother's death, she did not feel kindness, compassion, love each time she thought of her.

I can face that, Chiyo told herself. I can face that shortcoming in myself, now that she's gone. I can face the fact that I was a disappointment, that I did not produce grandchildren. My mother worked hard to raise me after Father died. She provided for the two of us in this house. She fought like a tiger to support, clothe and feed us both. She spent her entire childhood in a mountain shack. She never forgot the chill that drilled into her bones in the camp in winter. The experience affected her outlook for the rest of her life. For her, the world remained as it had always been: an unforgiving place. But I did not live in the camps. I have to be free of my mother's experience. For once. For the first time. Even though I loved her.

Chiyo felt tears welling. She remembered how her mother's body had shrunk during illness, her limbs so thin they curled to her torso, leaving not so much as a dent in the mattress. She'd become weightless; Chiyo had no trouble lifting her into the tub to bathe her during her final days. Her mother had looked at her from the soothing water and cried. She had looked at Chiyo with love.

*Carry tiger to mountain.*

Chiyo reached into her pocket for a Kleenex and dabbed at her eyes. Her attention was caught by a sheet of paper newly posted on Marvin's noticeboard:

## *GRIEF DISCUSSION GROUP*

Meetings were Tuesdays at seven. Chiyo had no classes Tuesday evenings and was free to attend. She tore a strip from the bottom of the notice and shoved it into the pocket of her windbreaker. She checked her watch and headed for the store exit. A teacher should not be late for her own class. She stuffed her damp Kleenex into a garbage container on her way out, and lowered her head to the wind.

# An Act of Love

Tom dropped his son at departures and headed home, a two-hour drive. Will had told him not to bother coming inside and then stood at the curb, luggage in hand, until his father drove away. What was different about today? Tom had always gone into the airport and stayed until Will was ready to go through security. Maybe his son was concerned about putting him to extra trouble—having to drop him off, park the Jeep in the lot, find him in a crowded lineup at a check-in counter. Maybe Will thought his father was getting old. Or maybe he wanted to work on his laptop while filling in the time before boarding. Simple as that.

Tom switched on the radio and scanned channels until he found music he liked. Joe Cocker was singing "With a Little Help from My Friends." Will had stayed four days this time, tacking the visit on to the end of a business trip in eastern Canada. Now he was on his way home to his own family in Edmonton. Will worked in IT, a troubleshooter, on the road half the year. Tom wondered what that sort of job did to—or for—Will's home life, marriage, health. The job brought in plenty of income, that was certain. Probably more than Tom earned buying and selling antiques for Rigmarole, the shop he'd owned for half a century in Wilna Creek's south end. At Rigmarole, some years had been better than others. Sales depended on what he could find to buy and sell. Collectors' items slipped in and out of fashion, the swing of the pendulum ever a consideration. Even so, loyal customers showed up at his door when they wanted to sell, or called when they had an estate to get rid of or were searching for a special item.

Tom had made a pretty good living picking, unearthing, swapping, selling a wide range of curiosities. He'd also begun to tell himself that he would sell the business someday soon. There were two other antique stores in town now. One was more of a junk shop, but both were competition. He'd also heard that a consignment shop might be opening. Even more competition. Still, he loved the hunt and the interaction with collectors. Every piece he acquired had its own provenance; his job was to track the information, set a value. He was challenged by the work and didn't want to quit while his knowledge was ever-expanding. The thought of retiring, of separating from his business, was not a simple matter. Even though the reality was that young couples were not much interested in antiques. They wanted dishes that could be put through a dishwasher. They were not attracted to heavy claw legs, bone china or early pine. But for the time being, there was enough business to keep the shop going. He wasn't being forced to make a decision to find a buyer. Not yet.

As he drove, Tom hummed along with the music and allowed his mind to drift over memories of airport arrivals and departures of the past decades. He and Ida used to enjoy travelling together. Every few years, Ida had taken an extra trip on her own to visit her sister in Medicine Hat. In the early nineties, at the end of one of Ida's visits west, Tom closed his shop and arrived early at the airport to pick her up. She'd been away for two weeks and he missed her. He'd vacuumed the house, and bought yellow freesias for the dining-room table and arranged them in a Satsuma porcelain vase shaped like a lantern—an exciting find he'd come across while she was away. At the airport, he checked the arrivals board and drank coffee and still had a half hour to wait. He stood idly and watched people crowd around one of the luggage belts. Two flight numbers lit up the signboard, and the belt creaked and wheezed and began to circle. A group of eight or nine welcomers—until then, they'd been off to the side—came close and began to chant. From their hoots of laughter, Tom could tell that they were practising so they could sing out when the person they were greeting appeared. Because of their numbers, they were brazen and gleeful and raucous. When the inner door finally opened and the arrivals streamed toward the moving belt, one recognizable passenger strode ahead of all others. He carried a worn leather briefcase, had no luggage to pick up and headed directly for the taxi exit. The man was no other than Peter Gzowski, the popular host of the CBC Radio show *Morningside*.

The welcoming group was taken by surprise to see this well-known figure, and to their credit, they rallied quickly. As their own expected traveller had not yet appeared, they began a loud, laughing chant and substituted Peter's name:

*Yay, Peter! Yay, Gzowski!*
*Yay, yay, Peter Gzowski!*

Peter, with a grin, kept his stride. He gave a wave to the group of strangers and carried on, knowing that the welcoming party wasn't for him. Nonetheless, there had been a feeling of cheer in the place because of Peter's response.

At the time, Tom had laughed good-naturedly along with the others. Now, in the car, he was wondering what it would be like to experience an impromptu reception like that. Out of the blue, a surprise, his name called out with affection. Tomas Ollery wouldn't exactly fit into a rhyme, but his schoolboy nickname could be used and sung unabashedly:

*Yay, Tom! Yay, Olley!*
*Yay, yay, Tom Olley!*

What nonsense. Why would any group be at an airport to greet him? There was no fame attached to being Tom Ollery. There would be no one to chant if he arrived from some unknown place. A place he couldn't imagine going without Ida. But Ida had died. She'd been dead for eleven months.

THE YEAR HE AND IDA MET and decided to marry, 1963, they were twenty-four years old and had nothing but each other. Ida had moved to Ontario from the West. She'd earned a science degree, but the only work she could find in Wilna Creek was a job as typist and desk clerk for an independent laboratory. Tom had a brand-new degree in history and English and was employed by what was, at the time, the town's only bookstore. He wanted to set up some sort of business of his own, but he hadn't figured out what that might be. His job at the bookstore began in April; the wedding was planned for June. He and Ida found a partially furnished apartment in an old three-storey house that had been divided into units, one per floor. Their unit was the least desirable because they had last choice, the others having been rented out. After the wedding, Tom and Ida moved in, sandwiched for almost three years between upper and lower. The couple below thumped their ceiling any time he and Ida played a record on their turntable after nine thirty in the evening. The couple above had twins who tramped like a pair of perpetually roaming bison, up and down the outside stairs that led to the top apartment.

Tom and Ida loved the place because it was their first. The landlord had left in the unit several pieces of furniture original to the house before it was divided: a tall pine cupboard with narrow doors; an oak bookcase that had belonged to a judge; a Duncan Phyfe–style dining-room table, which Ida covered with patterned oilcloth and converted to a kitchen table; a bronze sculpture of a pair of geese about to take flight. The geese, modelled after the Canada goose, were almost life-size and were set on the floor in one corner of the living room. Tom bought a second-hand bed and a new mattress, and Ida's parents contributed a rug. When Tom and Ida entertained, they sat with their guests on throw pillows scattered about the rug in the living room. On his days off from the bookstore, Tom attended auctions and began to visit second-hand shops in villages and towns surrounding Wilna Creek. He found a sturdy set of Bavarian dishes with a fawn-coloured rim, a chimney cupboard, an Eastlake-style chest of drawers for the bedroom. Before long, he and Ida had all the furnishings they needed and more. Nothing matched, but they didn't care.

Ida liked greeting people and didn't mind typing lab reports. She also liked her colleagues. She stuck with the job for three years, until just before Will was born. By then, she and Tom had scraped together enough money for a down payment on a house. They found one that had been built in 1898 on a corner lot, purchased it without fanfare and decided to take their time fixing it up. Before they moved out of their apartment, Tom negotiated with the landlord to buy the judge's bookcase and the pine cupboard. The landlord threw in the bronze geese as a housewarming gift.

Once they were in their own place, Ida made the decision to stay home with the new baby. She and Tom worked at stripping wallpaper. They painted ceilings, patched holes, levelled floors— always some project on the go. Tom resigned from the bookstore and opened his own shop, buying and selling used furniture, pressed glass, Depression glass, uniquely designed tables, bridge lamps and, once in a while, rare books. Ida had an eye for antique jewellery. She suggested the name Rigmarole for the shop because it reminded her of a rag-and-bone man who used to come door to door during her childhood to collect used clothing, cast iron, bits and pieces, odds and ends.

Tom was able to earn enough from the business to support the family. Ida missed her full-time job, and she and the baby began to accompany him to estate auctions. Some days, Ida looked after the shop while Will slept in his carriage in a quiet corner. On those days, Tom drove up and down country roads, exploring barns and attics. He'd been advised by a lifelong collector, one of the town's old-timers, that when he was out scouring the country-side, he should keep a lookout for potted geraniums on window-sills. *When you see a geranium, knock on the door.* Sure enough, whenever Tom approached farmhouses with geraniums on sills, he came away with bevelled mirrors, pressback chairs, vintage rockers and occasionally a piano stool with ornately carved legs or an organ that had been stowed in a back shed for generations.

Prior to their marriage, Ida, always frugal, became determined to sew her own wedding dress. She was discreet about asking Tom what he planned to wear, and he told her not to worry, everything was in hand. The truth was, he had no plan. Two weeks before the ceremony, he walked into Wilna Creek's only thrift store—run by the Salvation Army—a place where he'd earlier come upon a pair of brass lamps. He searched through rows of clothing racks and discovered a smart pair of tuxedo trousers, stripe down the side. He draped these over one arm and made his way to the opposite side of the men's section, where he found a tuxedo shirt and, after that, braces hanging from a hook against the back wall. He found a jacket to match the trousers—differences not detectable. His entire wedding suit cost twenty-two dollars and seventy-five cents. The volunteers discovered a suitable tie in a sagging cardboard box filled to the top with castoffs, and they threw it in for free. They rounded off the total to twenty dollars because they'd entered the mood—*and* the search—when Tom explained that the clothes were for his wedding day. Everyone in the store was jovial that day, especially Tom, who was always exhilarated by a bargain and a find.

He did not breathe a word of any of this to Ida. The day of the ceremony, she was so impressed with his appearance, she believed that for her sake he'd been saving secretly for months. He didn't reveal the origins of his pieced-together outfit, but whenever he thought of it, he had to grin. He knew how snazzy he had looked. Absolutely snazzy. Photographs confirmed this. Ida never did find out.

That same wedding suit was now encased in a plastic garment bag at the far end of the bedroom closet, where it had been shoved along the rack, past the tweed jackets and comfortable trousers he'd worn throughout his working life. What was he to do with a wedding outfit now? He didn't have the shoulders he'd once had;

he knew the jacket would sag. He should donate it back to Sally Ann so someone could claim it as vintage clothing. Some young guy could wear it to his own celebration. So what if fifty-five years had passed since Tom had picked out the items second-hand?

Although his son frequently urged him to visit the family in Edmonton, Tom had not left town since Ida's death, except for his volunteer work. The year he turned seventy, he'd begun to close the shop one day a week so he could drive for Wheels of Hope. If some other volunteer driver had to cancel, Tom sometimes took on an extra day in addition to his own. His job was to transport people to and from their appointments at the Greenley Health Centre, an hour's drive away. Passengers were those who could no longer handle a vehicle, didn't own one in the first place or were too ill to manage their lives. All required cancer treatments or diagnostic procedures that were not available at the hospital in town. Greenley was a teaching hospital comprising various specialties that the Wilna Creek hospital didn't have.

Tom kept up the volunteer work after Ida died because he was used to being around people. The past two weeks, he'd had only one passenger on his list—though he could comfortably manage three in the car, and often did. Depended on who needed what and which days appointments were scheduled. The sole passenger of his recent trips was a man named Dave who lived at the Haven, the local seniors' residence. During the drives to Greenley, Dave kept up a running commentary about life at the Haven. Dave was built like a barrel and had a short, thick neck and a big voice.

Tom recalled some of their conversations. "We call ourselves inmates," Dave had told him. Tom was beginning to feel as if he knew the inmates, though he'd been inside the Haven only a few times. Mostly, he sat in the car in the parking circle by the front door, waiting for his assigned passengers. "A lotta memories bottled up in that place, for a lotta people," Dave said, though he didn't say if the memories were good or bad. Tom figured that could mean both.

Dave had more to tell. "I have to get up early to go downstairs because two copies of the paper are delivered to the main lobby for residents. Can you believe this? People fight over the bleeding paper to get to the obituaries. As for me, I'm up at six, shower, get dressed, wear a tie. I'm not one of those unwashed men who make everyone hold their breath and stare straight ahead in the elevator while waiting for the door to open. When we go to the dining room, we have designated tables—groups of four, groups of six. If someone has a problem with seating, well, they can request a move, but generally we get along okay. If not, we can take complaints to the management, ha-ha! Every Friday for lunch, we have haddock and fries. A woman at my table—her name is Rose—picks up her fries with her fingers and eats as if she's going to stab the back of her throat with every chip." Dave was laughing out loud, and Tom couldn't help but join in. "She snaps her brassiere straps in the elevator. I don't think she realizes what she's doing, but the rest of us notice. Rose plays a helluva hand of bridge, though; I'll say that for her."

Dave liked to read and he'd always liked poetry, even when he was forced to learn whole verses in school when he was a kid. He and Tom had a couple of long conversations about Seamus Heaney; about Patrick Lane and Lorna Crozier; about Percy Bysshe Shelley's heart, which had been pressed between the covers of a book after his body was cremated on the beach in Italy—true according to Marchand, the biographer Tom had read on quiet days in the shop. Dave wondered about the story of the pressed heart. The two discussed Byron and his great love, Countess Teresa. Tom admitted that he sometimes dabbled at poetry himself, and had been doing so for decades. Especially when he'd needed a change after spending hours at his desk in Rigmarole on days when few customers appeared. Ida had never encouraged Tom any time he'd discussed his poetry with her, but he didn't mention this to Dave. Nor had he ever sent a poem to a magazine to see if it would be accepted for publication. Still, he'd filled one notebook and kept another, partly filled, in the top drawer of his desk at the shop. Soft and black, its cover was imprinted with an illustration of the planets. The notebook was old enough that Pluto had not yet been relegated to dwarf-planet status.

Dave's response, when he'd learned that Tom wrote poetry, was to admit that the poems he was most partial to were "The Rime of the Ancient Mariner" and Joyce Kilmer's "Trees."

"I never did get a college education," said Dave. "But in high school, I had an English teacher who taught me to love poetry. Because of her, I've been reading it ever since. Everyone thought

I should be playing football, but I wanted to study poetry, drama, literature. I'm a reader. There isn't one inmate who shares my love of verse. Not that I can find, anyway." He carried on, and recited for Tom:

*I think that I shall never see*
*A poem lovely as a tree.*

*A tree whose hungry mouth is prest*
*Against the earth's sweet flowing breast.*

"Oh yeah, and the last verse."

*Poems are made by fools like me,*
*But only God can make a tree.*

"That's all I can call up for the moment."

Tom was thinking of how Joyce Kilmer had been killed during the First World War. He didn't say that to Dave, who, in a chilling, rattly voice, suddenly came up with Coleridge:

*He holds him with his glittering eye—*
*The Wedding-Guest stood still,*
*And listens like a three years' child:*
*The Mariner hath his will.*

Dave gave a hearty laugh and challenged Tom to recite some of his own verses, but Tom wasn't in the mood. They were silent for a while, and Tom recalled, but to himself, a stanza he'd written earlier in the year. Last New Year's Day, in fact. Ida had been buried three months by then. He'd been feeling down when he pulled out his notebook. The poem was not to be shared. Not with anyone. Not even Dave, who loved Kilmer's tree poem.

*What are we to do with all this pain?*
*How do we overcome longing*
*Admit our losses and stop stop stop*
*Our high-pitched laments?*
*I've begun to find notes*
*In my own handwriting:*
*"How many days must one go without hope?"*
*Can't be helped; look up there*
*Even the inner curve of the moon*
*Has been chewed.*

Tom figured if he recited his poem out loud, Dave would laugh. Or maybe not. Didn't matter, because Tom wasn't prepared to take a chance that day.

There was something else he hadn't mentioned. Since Ida's death, he'd begun to write his poems at the back of the planet notebook, working his way through the pages from right to left. It was as if he'd begun to compose in Hebrew or Arabic. He decided this was a symptom of missing Ida, his *Ida affliction*. He'd been turned back to front: What was there to understand?

53

HE WAS APPROACHING the town's outskirts now and thought of the slim pickings in his fridge. Will's four-day visit was over and the fridge was empty. His son, a tall fellow, had always been a big eater, especially during his teen years. At the end of Will's every visit, the cupboards were bare. Tom thought of his own teen years, and the summers his mother insisted they spend with her parents in Nova Scotia. Aunts and uncles and cousins had been invited for a family supper during one visit, and at the end of the meal, one of Tom's uncles told him: "You cleaned your plate, son, and that's good. But I'd rather pay your board than board you." Everyone laughed, and Tom had not forgotten the remark.

He drove directly to Marvin's, picked up canned salmon and tuna, a bag of frozen peas, a loaf of freshly baked bread, a half chicken darkly roasted and ready to eat, three blueberry scones, a container of potato salad and a bar of dark chocolate. He added a copy of the daily paper to his grocery cart. Since Ida's death, he'd begun to pay closer attention to the obituaries—something he hadn't bothered about before—though he hadn't let on the day Dave had mentioned them. Tom wasn't morbidly interested, but he did read the mercilessly compressed details of people's lives with more than a little sadness.

He paid for the food and his paper, raised a hand to Marvin (who was at the upstairs window) and checked the community board on the way out. One notice attracted his attention:

### *GRIEF DISCUSSION GROUP*

What was that about? He didn't stop to consider. He detached a tear strip from the bottom edge and tucked it into his wallet.

HIS HOUSE, THE CAPACIOUS OLD HOUSE—too big for one person now—into which he and Ida had moved three years after they married, was a few blocks from Marvin's store. As he approached, he saw the Danzigers, neighbours from the cul-de-sac at the end of his street. He knew they were heading out for their early evening walk. The Danzigers were in their nineties and had lived on the street forever—long before Tom and Ida moved to the area. Mrs. D was wearing a scarf over her head and tied under her chin, and she was bent low over her walker, butting her head against the wind. She wasn't able to be out without the walker anymore because her gait was unsteady. Mr. D was stumping along beside her, supported by his cane, which he brandished in greeting when he recognized Tom's Cherokee. Tom returned the wave and manoeuvred his Jeep into the narrow garage he'd erected in 1979. Most of the structure was put together from old barn boards he'd been given by a man known to everyone as Mott. For generations, the Mott family had farmed two miles past the outskirts of town. Tom had picked up more than a few antiques from Mott descendants.

Building the garage had been a project of pride for Tom. He slowed the Jeep now, aimed it straight ahead and watched for the green tennis ball suspended from a string tied to a ceiling beam. The moment he saw the ball thump against the windshield, he braked. He'd come up with the tennis-ball solution after ramming his first car into a workbench he'd installed across the back wall of the garage. As there was little room to spare, the swinging tennis ball saved all subsequent vehicles from minor scratches and dents. He scooped up his groceries and entered the house through the side door.

He was sorry Will hadn't stayed longer. His son was good company and there was never any loneliness when he was around. But when Tom was alone, as he was now, his own footsteps echoed. An inner voice reminded him that he was hanging on by a frayed thread. Sometimes the same voice asked: *What's the point?* A question that was never answered.

Ida was the one who'd kept up most of their social contacts. She had organized outings and entertainments. After her funeral service, friends and colleagues came back to the house to support the family. Will and his wife and children circulated, shaking hands and accepting expressions of sympathy. Women busied themselves in the kitchen. Tom noticed that his male contemporaries sat around the edges of the living and dining rooms, rheumy-eyed with drink. One of them mentioned that he'd started up a branch of the Fountain Pen Society, and he invited Tom to join. They needed a few more members before they began to meet at one another's homes. Tom hadn't owned a fountain pen for thirty years, and though he could see the interest in old pens—why would that be any different than an interest in old watches?—he declined. The main reason was that he couldn't imagine himself taking part in discussions about nibs, pens and inks. Actually, he didn't know what the members talked about, but he couldn't work up enough enthusiasm to find out.

During the weeks that followed the funeral, wives left casseroles and tins of date squares at the side door. Whatever they baked was cut into tidy pieces. The phone rang for a while, but gradually these efforts ceased. Neighbours continued to greet him. Acquaintances and regular customers dropped in at Rigmarole to express condolences. But his present life was not his easy, routine life, with Ida looking after most household decisions. The two had relied on each other, and he missed that. He had a flash of memory now about travelling with Ida through a small village in Greece, more than a decade ago. Four old men were sitting in a row on a wooden bench at the edge of the village square, observing activities from which they were excluded. The four kept up a rhythmic clicking of worry beads. Tom did not want to become one of those excluded old men clicking his worry beads.

He dumped the food onto the kitchen counter and turned on the radio. He needed human voices near; what they were saying wasn't relevant. He went to the pantry to put the tins away and glanced at his reflection in an oval mirror Ida had bought at auction. She'd hung the mirror from a nail on the back of the pantry door so she could do a quick check on hair and lipstick without having to leave the kitchen, especially when they were expecting company.

The person he saw was a tall man with shadows under his eyes, a blotch on his left cheek where a menacing-looking mole had been removed several months earlier, a thick head of white hair, glasses that needed cleaning. For a moment, he thought his Nova Scotia grandfather was staring back—Grampa William Murray. It was Grampa Murray who had taught him that fishing season didn't officially start until the alder leaf was the size of a mouse's ear. It was Grampa Murray who'd walked him around the boundaries of the farm so they could keep watch over fences, fields and soil conditions. When they arrived at two apple trees at the far end of the property line, Tom was told to check the fruit for size and ripeness. If an apple was picked, his grampa took a salt shaker from his shirt pocket because you'd never eat an apple without sprinkling a bit of salt on the tart flesh after the first bite.

His grampa also tried to teach him to shoot, but Tom didn't want to hunt animals. He wondered what his late grandfather would have thought of the news report earlier this year about a goose that had fallen from the sky after being shot. The dead goose dropped plumb down, directly onto a hunter's head. A bizarre story. The hunter was severely injured, and he wasn't even the one who'd shot that particular goose. Maybe Grampa Murray, if he were alive, would have drawn a moral from the tale; he had often read Aesop's fables aloud during those summer visits after the war. In his will, he left Tom a beloved book of poetry called *The Casquet of Gems*, published in Edinburgh in 1885. The final poem in the book was by Robert Pollok, a man whom Grampa Murray had spoken about sadly because Pollok died before reaching his thirtieth birthday. The poem was about Byron, part of a longer work titled *The Course of Time*. Because of this verse by Pollok, Tom had, in turn, come to admire the work of Byron.

*He touched his harp, and nations heard, entranced.*
*As some vast river of unfailing source,*
*Rapid, exhaustless, deep, his numbers flowed,*
*And oped new fountains in the human heart.*

Tom loved the line "And oped new fountains in the human heart." He had grown up without a father, but he'd never stopped wishing for one. Every moment he spent with his grandparents was special. On arrival in Nova Scotia, he attached himself to his grampa's side. In 1945, when he was six years old, he'd met his father, once, but that was a separate memory. One he could recall in intimate detail but didn't indulge often, and wouldn't now.

He glanced back at the pantry mirror again and tried to smile, but the smile was forced. Ida had told him decades ago that he wore every tale of woe on his face. After hearing that, he made an effort to hide his natural expressions. He didn't want to be held accountable—even to Ida—for every emotion he experienced, past or present. Ida was one of those persons who believed that truth should and would be told on every occasion. But truth was a strain, and he had kept more than a few private thoughts to himself.

One of his truths now was the heaviness that had burdened him the past year. As months went by, the weight had become more leaden. He didn't know what to do about this and assumed there was nothing he *could* do. There was no one around with whom he could share these thoughts. Ida had been taken from him swiftly, unexpectedly. He'd had little time to prepare. He could not have predicted what his life would be like after she was gone. How could he have known that the initial feelings of grief would go on and on? What he felt, when he admitted this to himself, was a disturbing sense of upheaval. A sense of being tossed in a fathomless sea, a sea of memory and shadow. Sometimes he was certain that Ida needed him, that she was calling his name from another part of the house. Sometimes, without thinking, he answered and called back.

And that was not all. There were moments when he had the distinct impression that she was in the house, just beyond his peripheral vision. He turned his head quickly, as if he might catch a glimpse of her now.

There was no one there.

Well, what about this discussion group? He unwrapped the chicken, grateful that it was still hot, and removed the lid from the potato salad container. He sprinkled pepper—no salt—over his food and sat at the table. After Ida died, he had moved into her chair, not wanting to stare at her empty place. He felt better doing that, and Ida's chair afforded a view out the side window. He told himself he was seeing what she would be seeing if she were alive. He thought again of the notice at Marvin's and removed the strip of paper from his wallet. He stared at the date, time and place. Next week at Cassie's, Tuesday night. He and Ida used to stop in there after a movie or a play. They had enjoyed sitting together over a cup of coffee, or occasionally a glass of wine, discussing the performance they'd seen.

Maybe he would go. He'd been listening to CBC Radio at Rigmarole one morning and had heard about meetings at death cafés: groups of people who met for coffee or tea and discussed ideas and fears and beliefs in hopes of becoming comfortable with the topic of death while making the most of their lives. He'd also listened to a program about grief walks on a talk show. Over the years, with the radio on in the background, he'd acquired knowledge he wouldn't have been able to invent. Perhaps the meeting at Cassie's next week would be a death café. There might even be cake; that's what was uniformly served, according to the people interviewed on CBC. He hadn't had a decent slice of cake since the weeks following Ida's death, when food was dropped off at the side door.

He looked out the window just as a plastic garbage bag blew into the large V of the oak at the edge of his yard. The black bag snagged on a ridge of bark and began to flap and flutter as the Danzigers came into view, returning from their walk. The wind was now at their backs, but the two had slowed to half their previous pace. Something wasn't quite right. Tom looked again and realized they had made a switch. Mr. D was now bent over his wife's walker, and Mrs. D was walking with the support of her husband's cane.

For reasons Tom could not explain, one eye began to water. He was witnessing an act of love.

He wanted to be loved. Or even liked. Love would be a bonus. He asked himself, Isn't that what everyone wants? Ida and I loved each other in comforting ways. We were together many years. The emptiness of this house is too much to bear.

He looked at the strip of paper again. A discussion group about grief. Well, maybe on Tuesday evening he would walk over to Cassie's and see what was going on. His attendance wouldn't hurt anybody, would it? Maybe he would just go.

# Facing Up

By late afternoon Saturday, the sky was awash with charcoal clouds nudging one another, shaping and reshaping until they merged into an edgeless mass. Addie leaned back in her living-room chair, feet raised on the jute ottoman she'd put at the top of her want-to-keep list years ago, when she and Tye split. She was listening to Beethoven's Ninth and rose reluctantly during the abrupt silence that followed the tumultuous "Ode to Joy."

She put away the CD and thought about Vienna, and about Beethoven in his fifty-fourth year. He was on stage the night of the premiere, but because of his deafness was uncertain of the moment he should turn to face the audience after the final note. A woman close to him on stage came to the rescue and gave a signal, hoping no one else would notice. Trying to save him from embarrassment but wanting him to know that the audience was applauding wildly behind his back.

Joy. Beauty. Music saves me, Addie thought. Music saves us all. I could not get through a day without listening to music of some kind.

She pictured Beethoven, entirely deaf while composing his magnificent final symphony, but never hearing a note except in his internal imaginings. Imaginings that, for him, would not have been silent at all. His interior creative self. Would the Ninth be the same if he'd been able to hear? This would always be unknown. Every time Addie listened to the final feverish note, she wanted to sit upright, fill her lungs with . . . well, song, actually. Yes, song. When she thought about this, she realized that she hardly ever sang.

She went to the kitchen to make tea and returned to the armchair. Her ankles were definitely swollen, thicker. She was putting on weight. She looked over at the Montreal letters, which were in chronological order atop a pile of books. The first had arrived eight months ago and was about the lumps. She knew the words by heart. At the time, Sybil was refusing to text or email. She refused to use her iPad while she was an in-patient after surgery. She wanted nothing to do with smartphones. What she did want was to articulate her thoughts clearly; to do this, she wrote them out in longhand. Now, all these months later, she had access to computer and phone but was too weak to use them or even to care.

At the beginning of August, Sybil had been moved from her apartment in Montreal to her mother's home in Greenley, Ontario. She wasn't as far from Addie now—only an hour from Wilna Creek. Sybil had other family members in Greenley besides her mother: a married brother and his wife, a niece, an uncle. Caring people who could be relied on to provide solid support. But Addie was Sybil's closest friend. She and Sybil were each other's de facto family.

Sybil's mother and brother had recently begun to turn to Addie for decisions that had to be made, asking questions that were impossible to answer. Today, before Addie drove back to Wilna Creek, Sybil's mother had stopped her on the front step and pleaded: "How much time does she have left?" Addie did not want to reply. How could she know? Being forced to contemplate her friend's death was difficult enough. She hugged Sybil's mother on the doorstep and the two cried quietly, being careful that Sybil, in her bedroom down the hall, wouldn't hear.

Addie held power of attorney. She and Sybil had appointed each other the year they turned forty. Now they were forty-nine. Neither of them had anticipated this. *This* being the blatant, real and obscene fact that one of them was dying.

Addie had casual friends, but no one as close as Sybil. Not counting Tye. The marriage was over, but she and Tye kept in touch occasionally by phone. He worked in the field of bioethics. She had met him in Montreal. Her friendship with Sybil had also begun there, but that was before she met and married Tye.

Thirty years ago, on their first day of university and while standing as two strangers in a slow-moving line of students, she and Sybil waded through registration procedures on the McGill campus. It was a sunny September day, a day filled with promise. After the first half hour, while inching forward and making barely discernible progress, they agreed on a plan for lunch. The two had been friends ever since. Reliable, loving, lifelong friends. Sybil worked her way up to becoming a professor in the nursing faculty several years after graduation, and she continued to teach, deriving enormous satisfaction from her job. Addie studied administration in health services. After completing her studies, she stayed on in the city. When her marriage broke down, she made the decision to relocate; she needed a new start. She responded to an ad and moved to Ontario, accepting an administrative position at the Wilna Creek Hospital. Eventually, she became the unit manager responsible for the large and newly expanded Danforth Wing.

Addie had always been comfortable around hospitals, even as a teenager. Her late mother had trained to be a nurse in a hospital school, but after graduate studies, she'd worked as a psychiatric nurse on the locked wards of one of the old Victorian-era institutions—of the kind that were probably no longer in existence. When Addie was in senior high, she sometimes met her mother after school so they could drive home together. Her mother was part of a large family, and Addie still had aunts, uncles and cousins in Quebec and New Brunswick. Sadly, no one made much of an effort to stay in touch now that her mother was dead. Some individuals were key to keeping families together, and that was a fact of life. Addie's father was not one of these; he had remarried and moved to Spain, and was now living in Sitges.

Addie's marriage had lasted sixteen years. She was single now, though she'd resolved to keep Tye's surname after the breakup. One less change among many at the time. Tye's full name was Thierry Levesque. The superintendent in their first apartment, a Portuguese immigrant who'd recently arrived in Canada, always pronounced the *s* in her married name. She had never corrected him. Indeed, she sometimes thought of herself as the former Madame Levesk.

She unfolded the first letter from Sybil. This was the announcement of the illness that would soon end her friend's life. Addie knew she should throw away every one of these sad reminders, but so far she had not.

*Dear Addie,*

*Have you ever had the feeling that you're going through something that can't really be happening? Not happening to you?*

*Well, that's the way I feel at this moment. And since this letter has to be written sometime, the time might as well be now. Remember the lump I mentioned a while back? I told you that I would see about it, that it would be a routine investigation. But it was not a cyst, as I'd been told to expect. The lump was cancerous.*

*This is happening. To me. Right now. I am being forced to face reality.*

*I'm sorry to be sharing this, but you have to know the facts at some point, and there isn't going to be any good time to pass on the news.*

*January 9 I discovered the lump; two days ago I was in the OR* having my left breast removed. I am on the ward now, and in the best hospital for the surgery. Half the nurses here are people I trained myself. I am treated the way one hopes to be treated—if one is unlucky enough to be here in the first place. I'm not experiencing physical discomfort. I dress myself in my own clothes every day. I don't wear a gown on the ward. I have already begun exercises. The staff—including the cleaning staff—believe me to be an imposter. I cry a bit. I'd like to scream, but not here. That's the first thing I'll do when I'm back in my apartment. I don't want to upset the other patients. I'll be home soon, as they don't keep patients long, not here—or anywhere, for that matter.

I'm cheered somewhat because things are looking positive. Having gone from the initial belief—self-created—that I had two weeks to live, I have now accepted a brighter prognosis. Now discussion is about possible spread: lymph, liver. Or not. Chemo or no chemo. Radiation or no radiation. That news is yet to come. I'm trying to be hopeful. That's what I mean when I use the word "positive."

My mother insisted on coming to Montreal and has been staying at my apartment, but I have encouraged her to go back to Greenley. She wanted to be present while I was undergoing surgery, and I understood her need to be here. However, I want time alone when I'm discharged.

I'll be remaining here and won't be travelling to Greenley, or even to Wilna Creek, for a while, but I will later, during my recovery. For now, for the first time in years, I can report that I have time to read. I asked my mom to bring a couple of books from my apartment, and she showed up on the ward with One Hundred Years of Solitude by Márquez and a biography of Hans Christian Andersen. I admit that I sat in my chair weeping over a badly written biography of the great Dane. At least I learned things about the man, but there have to be better accounts of his life than the one my mother found. As for Márquez, his novel has been buried in my to-read stack for three decades. I hope I have enough time left to finish the tome because I'm enjoying the saga of the Buendía family. I know you gave up on me ever taking the time to read it, but I have become a woman of leisure. Yes, I've quit my job. The dean told me she would hold my position in case I change my mind, but I've decided to leave permanently. This has not been an easy decision. I have always loved working with students and patients, but now I want to take advantage of opportunities I've passed up because I've been so busy in the profession. I'm calling this an early retirement.

Next step? Maybe I'll have to face chemo. I'll let you know as soon as I have results.

Don't you love receiving cheery mail like mine? If you think this letter is gloomy, look at it this way: my situation is a thousand times more positive than it appeared to be even a week ago. Dear friend, I am going through the sense of loss and fear that we have recognized many times in so many others. I'd have phoned, but the spoken word fails me for the moment. I'll keep writing until we can talk face to face. If I can manage, I still plan to travel to Denmark with you for our holidays in late spring. Don't jump to make reservations yet. I'll let you know when I've broken free of the muddle, which at the moment is a guessing game at best.

In the months that followed, many letters were exchanged between Addie in Wilna Creek and Sybil in Montreal. Sybil continued to communicate only by letter; writing to Addie was therapy. Chemo had been necessary, and the effects were brutal. That was followed by what Sybil labelled her "good life" stage, which lasted two months. But the disease was aggressive. There had been no trip to Denmark. During her own vacation time, Addie travelled to Montreal and stayed with her friend for the three and a half weeks they had planned to be in northern Europe. The treatments Sybil endured did buy her extra time—a little more than half a year. But inevitably, her apartment had to be given up. She had moved back to her hometown of Greenley, back to her childhood room in her mother's large bungalow. Desperation was setting in. Every weekend on her days off, Addie, though fatigued, found herself driving an hour each way, to and from Greenley. Sometimes, she made extra trips after her day's work.

She realized that Sybil would have to be admitted to hospital before long—this time to the cancer ward of the Greenley Health Centre, the palliative care wing. Complications of care were becoming too much for Sybil's mother, too much for everyone. Sybil's mother was in her early eighties. Addie was worn out from helping while holding down her own demanding job. She was worn out from driving back and forth.

Sybil was giving up, breath by breath, what had been, until the past year, her firm grip on life. Her body, once strong and fit, was failing. During today's visit, Addie had tried to offer comfort, hope. But how could she offer hope when they were both aware of what was happening? Aware of the hopelessness. One of them was on an out-of-control journey toward death. While driving home, Addie cried most of the way. That, too, out of control; the state was called grief. The feeling was despair, a heaviness lodged behind the eyes. Much of the time, she felt as if an invisible mask had been tied in place, holding back the light.

She remembered how she had studied stress and its effects on the body. One of the psych courses she and Sybil had signed up for together was called Health Effects of Stress and Stress Management. They'd also studied Spanish. They wanted to learn an extra language beyond French and English and often took vacations together, so they opted for Spanish.

Addie had no difficulty remembering Sybil's capacity to abandon herself to helpless laughter. She could also be entirely practical. "C'mon, Addie. Let's not create stress by anticipating. Let's not get worked up before something happens. Because maybe nothing will happen. If a problem comes along, we'll lay out the options and choose a solution."

Sybil had propped her up when she and Tye separated, and Addie had been grateful to have someone close to talk to. With their give-and-take friendship, neither she nor Sybil had ever had to lie on the couch of a professional.

The stress now, however, was the real thing for both. Addie knew that her stress level could not be placed on the same scale as that of her friend. She also had to look after her own well-being while watching Sybil go down. Otherwise, she'd be of no help to Sybil or her family. Nor would she be able to carry on with her own work. Problem-solving abilities were not useful at the moment.

For weeks, Addie had been helping with the physical care of her friend in Greenley, which meant that she was spending precious little time in her own fifth-floor apartment in Wilna Creek. She cancelled delivery of the *Wilna Creek Times* because papers were stacking up unread. She had no hope of keeping up with local news, but occasionally she flipped through a city paper left behind in one of the hospital waiting rooms. She began to pay attention to obituaries, and read through these with a deep, knowing sadness while studying photos of the deceased and imagining their lives. She'd recently learned, during a coffee-break conversation, that several of her colleagues carried laminated cards in their wallets with instructions for their own future funerals and those of their partners. The funerals were prepaid, every detail worked out in advance. She sat in astonishment while her colleagues cheerfully compared boxes they'd ticked for various pâtés and specific sandwich fillings for receptions that would not be enjoyed by them. They'd be present, but inside an urn or a casket—also preselected.

Addie was not one of these preplanners who could whip out a funeral card from her wallet. Nor was Sybil, she was certain. Addie was not executor of Sybil's will; that duty had been assigned to Sybil's brother. But she was responsible for some of the decisions being taken now, during Sybil's illness, because of the power of attorney.

In the meantime, she made attempts to keep herself in balance. She had little time for physical exercise, little time to make proper meals. Before falling asleep at night, she flicked on the TV. National and world news slipped by without any involvement or say-so from her. Any news apart from reports of Sybil scarcely mattered anyway.

Realistically, apart from work, all Addie now had time for in her shrunken world was a series of tasks: laundry, change of towels, change of sheets. On occasion, a quick run of the vacuum through the rooms of her apartment. She was fatigued, preoccupied, sick of being in a car that was constantly on the move between two points on a road map. And—she realized suddenly—she was hungry. How could she think of food while sharing her friend's last days, weeks, hours? Earlier in the day, Sybil's mother had urged her to stay for dinner, but Addie had found herself making excuses. She could not sit at a table eating while Sybil was down the hall in her bedroom, propped against pillows, taking sips of fluid through a straw, coughing, short of breath, trying to stay alive.

Do not indulge in melodrama, Addie told herself. She folded the letter she held in her hand and picked up the one beneath it.

*I am not trying to "stay" this disease. I am out for a cure. You will know what a setback it was for me to learn that the last test result was discouraging. Instead of moping, I'm focusing on what is within my control: diet, exercise, mood. I'm doing my best to stay in balance. Trying to mete out my strengths so I can call upon them when I must.*

*What I'm missing is <u>laugh therapy</u>. I underline these words because laugh therapy will happen during your visits. Oh, Addie, my friend, we need to laugh. I can't wait to see you.*

Addie pushed aside the rest of the letters and got up to check through her kitchen cupboards. Not much to inspire. Her weight gain since her breakup with Tye had been slow and gradual. She'd been eating all the wrong foods and knew she'd have to make a correction, but she didn't have the energy to solve that issue. Not now. She needed food, any food, and would worry about losing weight later. After Sybil. That was as far as she could take the thought.

She looked out and down from her kitchen window and began to watch a woman who lived in the building facing hers, but two storeys below. The woman, who had carrot-orange hair, was placing dishes on a patio table in the sheltered part of her balcony. A setting for two: plates, napkins, a bottle of Chianti. The woman stood back and considered. She disappeared into the interior darkness of her apartment, returned with a watering can and sprinkled a hanging plant, a lobelia of the deepest blue. Around the corner of the building, same level, another woman—out of sight of the first—chain-smoked on her balcony while standing at the railing. Smoking was not permitted inside Addie's building or in the building across the way, and the smoker could be seen outside in all weathers. Some mornings, she was out there shivering in black-and-blue-checked pyjamas, huddled against the cold, a blanket draped over her shoulders, quick desperate puffs pulled into her lungs and wisping outward into the frigid air.

Addie put on her jacket, took the elevator down to the indoor parking garage, got into her car and drove to Marvin's. She bought pasta, fresh tomatoes, herbs and green onions. She would make a decent meal for herself. She chose a green pepper and was reminded that this was chili-sauce weather, though she had no time to start putting up jars of preserves. Her mother used to make chili sauce every fall when Addie was a child. On those days, always a weekend, the kitchen was filled with an expanding aroma that took the breath away: tomatoes, apples, cinnamon, onion and celery, allspice and cloves, vinegar and cayenne, all simmering in a cauldron-like container on the wood stove—later, on the electric range.

Addie passed the bakery shelves and selected a Black Forest cake. Eat now, worry later. At the checkout, she added two bars of dark chocolate. On the way out of the store, grocery bag in hand, she stopped by the noticeboard. One notice looked fairly new, though several strips had been removed:

### GRIEF DISCUSSION GROUP

The first meeting was to be held the following week, Tuesday evening at Cassie's. Addie tore off a strip and dropped it on top of the green pepper in her bag. She didn't want to discuss academic or analytic stages of grief. She didn't want to turn to colleagues at her own hospital for help. But she did want to talk. Or listen. Yes, if she could listen to others, that might help.

Good decision, her administrator's voice echoed in her head. And then she heard Sybil's voice chip in, too.

Good decision, Addie.

# Talking Heads

The meeting was called to order by Hazzley, who was self-consciously aware of Cass watching. Her friend had deliberately positioned herself at the front counter and was facing the glass partition that separated the main section of the café from the backroom. Hazzley frowned and Cass looked down, pretending to tot up receipts. The partition was partly covered with trailing ivy, but not covered enough. Cass, now grinning ear to ear, stared at Hazzley and raised her eyebrows as if sending a message: *Get going. Get the group moving.* Hazzley did not return the grin. She was hoping new customers would storm into the café and occupy Cass's attention.

Hazzley did not want to be anyone's leader. But she was the one who had posted the notice; she was responsible. Four people had showed up, for a total of five. Once again, she glanced in the direction of the partition. On the other side, Cass was nodding to herself, biting her bottom lip. Another message? Hazzley wondered for a moment if Cass should be the one running this group. Over the years, she had accumulated her own list of people to grieve. Hazzley was relieved to see her friend disappear in the direction of the café kitchen. She felt free to give her full attention to the group.

Three women and one man tilted slightly forward in their chairs. There was an undercurrent in the room. The tension of strangers. Of expectation. Of strange expectation. Give it up, Hazzley, she told herself. She'd been standing as the others came in, but now she sat at the round table Cass had set up. A slender vase of cosmos, wispy pinks and mauves, adorned the centre. The most elegant of fall flowers, in Hazzley's opinion.

She noted that the man was close to her in age, probably in his seventies. He was tall, had soft pouches under his eyes, looked familiar. He had thick white hair and long slim hands, and he wore a tweed jacket and sat with arms folded across his chest. His glasses needed cleaning, but his gaze was direct and he was taking in the details around him. Hazzley had seen him around town; she couldn't think where. She saw sadness in his face, but she saw strength there, too. In fact, she sensed strength from more than one of the people now looking at her.

Two of the women appeared to be younger than Hazzley's daughter, Sal, and this surprised her. Had she been expecting widows her own age? Widowers?

"Shall we start by introducing ourselves? Say a few words?"

The man, seated to her left, responded instantly, as if he'd been lit like a firecracker. He removed his glasses and rested his arms on the tabletop.

"My name is Tom," he said. "From Tomas with no *h*. My wife, Ida, died eleven months ago. She died quite suddenly. Had a heart attack and died in hospital within two days of being admitted. I didn't have time to adjust, to prepare, to think about the possibility of losing her. But I've had plenty of time to think ever since. I guess I can say that I was glad to see the notice at Marvin's. Almost a year now, I've been grieving. I live on my own. I'm the owner of Rigmarole—it was the first antique shop in town. You can find me there four out of five weekdays and sometimes Saturday mornings. The shop is half the size it used to be and definitely more manageable. When I first opened the business, I bought the adjacent property, a long narrow space that used to sell electrical supplies. I joined the two by knocking out a wall and putting a doorway between. Now my shop is back to its original size, and the wall is sealed again. The other property has been taken over by a printing business. Once a week, usually a Thursday or a Friday, I drive for Wheels of Hope and take cancer patients to the Greenley Health Centre for treatment. I'm fine—I tell myself I'm fine." His voice dropped. "I read, write a bit of poetry, meet with friends occasionally, but . . ."

He was thinking of a long-time customer named Kay. After Ida died, Kay began to arrive at his shop with small gifts of food sealed with plastic wrap, served on a china saucer so she'd have to make another trip to collect the dish. A slice of this, a slice of that. He never knew when she might come through the door. One day, she carried in a wedge of what she laughingly told him was "hopeful pie." He remained polite, recognizing the message that new life begins, but he offered no particular hope in her direction. What Kay didn't understand was that a person was missing from his life and there was nothing he could do, no action he *could* take, even though he felt he should force himself to move toward pseudo-optimism and usefulness. Kay did not realize the depth of aloneness she was trying to penetrate.

He nodded, more to himself than to the others in the group. He'd surprised himself, and probably them, by mentioning his poetry. He tried to cover up now, before anyone could comment, and spoke directly to Hazzley.

"How far along are you on your grief walk?"

Hazzley was stumped by the question because she'd never heard of a grief walk, which raised all sorts of images, including a memory flash of being with Lew in Cyprus decades earlier, hiking in a rural area, and stumbling across a single-file procession of villagers following a casket carried by four men. The mourners were making their way to the local graveyard, which could be seen on a hillside not far off. She and Lew stepped off the narrow dirt path and waited, their heads slightly bowed, while the procession passed. They were in no way acknowledged by the mourners.

She recovered quickly. And was able to place the man the instant he mentioned Rigmarole—an antique store she'd wandered into a few times. It was on a street that Hazzley knew because the bookstore she frequented was located in the same block.

"I guess I haven't thought about grief in quite that way," she said to Tom. "Shall we continue? Carry on introducing ourselves and maybe say a word about why we're here?"

The other three were staring at the tall stalks of the cosmos and looked as if they might change their minds about being present. And Cass—was she hovering near the doorway?

"Why don't I go next, then?" Hazzley said. "Since I'm beside Tom with no *h*. I've been in your store, Tom. I bought a reflector for an old gas lamp from you; that was years ago. It was one of those wall-mounted sconce types. I think the reflector is made of mercury glass."

Tom was nodding. He remembered the reflector.

"Anyway, I'm Hazzley, everyone—my name was supposed to be Hazel, but that's another story—and I'm the one who posted the notice at Marvin's. I'll come right out and tell you frankly that I've been lonely. My husband, Lew, died three years ago. Sometimes it seems he's been gone thirty years instead of three. But there are days when I'm convinced that if I look through the kitchen window, he'll be out there in the backyard, raking up leaves. There are days when I can hear soft scraping sounds as he rakes."

Several people were nodding. This, they understood.

"I carry on. I have things to do. I work part-time as an editor. I freelance from home and love the work. But there are things that are undone. Unfinished, incomplete." Her words slowed. "And maybe never will be complete." She thought of the two rooms she had emptied. She thought of the boxes in the basement, hidden away under a tarp after Lew's death, cardboard boxes filled with empty bottles, the flaps taped shut. She had not dealt with those. She had never talked about the boxes—not to Cass, not to Sal, even though Sal had been aware of her father's drinking. Hazzley could not bring herself to load the car and drop the boxes off somewhere. Or put them out on the curb. Or drive country roads until she saw a sign for a garbage dump. Or hire Sam the Man with Truck to haul them away. Many times she'd imagined a man arriving in a truck, the expression on his face when he looked at the boxes and heard the rattle and immediately understood the quantity of liquor that had been consumed.

She gave up on this train of thought and stretched an arm toward the woman to her right. Poised, younger. Shining black hair recklessly gathered into a spray held by a single elastic. Asian descent, Japanese Canadian, maybe?

"My name," said the young woman, "is Chiyo. The name is supposed to mean 'a thousand years,' or maybe 'eternal.' I've been told it dates back to the seventeenth century. My parents were traditional when it came to naming. My dad died when I was young, but I remember a few things about him and I try to hang on to the memories. It's my mom who recently passed away. That was April, five months ago. Losing her has been difficult because, well, she's my mom. We relied on each other—we've always lived together."

My mother is gone, she was thinking. Disappeared, forever.

How does that happen? How am I supposed to deal with that? With a person's disappearance? Despite the logical answers. Dust to dust. You speak to a person one day—engage, laugh, cry, whisper, shout, love or not love—and the next day you never see that person again. Nor does anyone else.

She carried on. "I'm a fitness instructor. I conduct classes for city programs, and those include tai chi and yoga. That's how I earn my living. But even when I'm working, I can't stop thinking about the steady stream of caregivers who were in and out of our home at all hours during the final stages of my mother's life. She died in her own bed. I'm forty years old—I'll soon be forty-one." She added that, as if someone had instructed her to reveal her age.

What Chiyo's memory was hauling up was the difficult period during which she had shouldered every responsibility on her own—without caregivers—long before outside help was approved and granted by the health system during the last months of her mother's life. By the time her mother was deemed eligible for nursing-care hours at home, Chiyo was worn out. One morning, a nursing supervisor arrived and announced that she was there to do an assessment of the home situation. She handed Chiyo a form—a full page of questions—and asked her to fill it out, ranking her feelings about any stress she might be under. Chiyo studied the eight questions while the woman stood quietly by her side in the kitchen. Chiyo was aware of the bedroom door ajar behind them, could feel her mother's eyes watching.

*4. Do you experience frustration while caring for a patient?*
*7. Do you feel alone and unsupported while carrying out your responsibilities?*

One question addressed degrees of anger. Another asked her to rank her feelings about interference. Did the patient's illness interfere with other aspects of her life?

Leonard. Her classes. Her students. Clients. Her life. Trying to get to a movie once in a while so that she could stay sane. Leonard had fallen away, but Spence had come into her life. Thank heavens for Spence, who could make her laugh, feel loved and wanted, who made her feel beautiful. Thank heavens for tai chi, which helped her to meditate, keep her energy level up.

When she looked over the questionnaire that day, she found herself holding back laughter. Laughter or rage—the two at that moment were interchangeable. She stared at the supervisor and handed back the form.

"No. I won't be filling this out," she said, and the woman, to her credit, did not push.

*A soft answer turneth away wrath,* Chiyo thought at the time. She had not forgotten the proverb, learned one summer during her teens, when her mother had insisted that Chiyo accompany her to a Bible study group held in the basement of the Anglican church they attended. Chiyo didn't want to be in the study group, but her mother overruled.

What would the supervisor standing in her kitchen have done, in any case, with the high-ranking score Chiyo would certainly have totalled up? Anger, stress, frustration. Her score would have revealed outrageous and even dangerous limits. Was anyone prepared to help Chiyo in her caregiving role? No one on the horizon that she could see. Everyone was too busy filling out forms, going from one house to another, complaining about having to keep track of heavy caseloads. The supervisors and coordinators who arrived to do assessments were weary and overworked. Not one of these women—all were women—returned a second time. Burnout must have been high. They were reassigned at a rapid rate, becoming faceless as they replaced one another. Each handed Chiyo a business card for contact information. Chiyo stacked the cards in a teacup. Meanwhile, the caregivers themselves—a more stable group than the supervisors they reported to—carried on with varying degrees of efficiency and self-preservation. One excellent caregiver to whom Chiyo's mother had taken a liking took three weeks off to return to the Congo, where she was born, but she disappeared inside her homeland and never showed up again on anyone's radar. The agency was at a loss to explain what had happened to the missing employee.

Of course, the physical care had been focused on Chiyo's mother. As it should have been. Chiyo was a casualty of a different kind.

She looked at the faces around the table; everyone seemed to be waiting for more. Her thoughts were tangling. She was the youngest—she could see that. Would the others understand? Could she even articulate how complicated her relationship with her mother had been? Aware of her vulnerabilities, she decided she'd said enough.

"Thank you, Chiyo," said Hazzley. "At forty you're half my age, more or less. Well, not quite. I'm seventy-seven. And not in any rush to meet my next birthday, coming up in November."

"Likewise," said Tom, who knew the feeling. "I just turned seventy-nine. I'll be eighty next year. If I can hold off the cele-brations—if there are any—I will definitely try."

The woman beside Chiyo began to speak softly but did not offer up her age. She was tall and thin, wore no makeup, had ginger tints through the natural grey in her hair. Hazzley thought she might be in her early sixties. Attractive as she was, she wore drab browns and beiges, no jewellery, no other colour. Her back was hunched; she looked down at the table, glanced up and then down again.

"I'm Gwen. I'm happy to meet everyone."

Happiness was not what Hazzley was seeing. The woman looked as if she might bolt. Indeed, she kept eyeing the doorway as if a predator was expected. Hazzley succeeded in making eye contact, and after that, Gwen fixed her gaze on Hazzley's face and scarcely blinked while speaking. The word "fragile" scurried its signal through Hazzley's mind. *Easily broken, of delicate frame or constitution.*

"I saw your notice that windy day last week," Gwen went on. "Objects were flying through the air: branches, leaves. Road signs tipped over."

Others were remembering. Tom thought of the black bag lodged in the oak. On windy days, the flapping plastic resembled a huge crow with one ragged, beat-up wing. Perpetual motion that yielded no results. The crow was too high for him to dislodge; he'd have to get out the ladder. He'd written a few lines in his notebook on one of those windy days:

*Leaves falling, the sway*
*Of earth now felt and seen.*
*Is this all we have come to?*
*All we have been?*

Hazzley was thinking of geranium petals, an eddy of red swirling about her ankles. She held her gaze steady on Gwen and saw the tightness of her jaw, the neck and facial muscles.

Gwen carried on. "I decided it would be good to talk to people who've had similar experiences. That's why I'm here. My husband's name was Brigg." She looked over at Chiyo. "He, too, died in April. He had a stroke—a devastating stroke. And. Well." Gwen had lost track of her thoughts. After a pause, she started up again. "The meaning of the name Brigg is 'dweller by the bridge'—Old English." She said this with a straight face, perfectly serious, but Hazzley, watching her, sensed irony, or humour, or the threat of humour beneath the surface. "I haven't dealt with Brigg's clothes," said Gwen, making a sudden U-turn. "In his closet, you know. Five months and I haven't been able to force myself to the task."

Tom interjected. "Ida's, too," he said. "On shelves, in drawers. Winter boots, ankle boots in the front closet, shoes on the rack. An old church hat with a navy-blue veil. I keep promising myself to get the job done." He said this wistfully. He was thinking of Ida in hospital the day before she died. Propped against pillows, the head of her bed raised, her skin pale and cool, the low and steady hiss of oxygen administered by means of a nasal cannula. He held her hand and she said, "I'm thankful, Tom. I'm content with the life I've lived. I feel blessed that we've had so many years together." Ida had grace; in that moment, she'd been filled with grace. He wanted to weep. Then and now.

Gwen acknowledged Tom, and continued. "I'm retired now, but I used to work at Spinney's, the office furniture business over by the ravine. I'm an accountant. I was the company bookkeeper there for years." A memory darted in: She'd been sent by the manager to take a three-day computer course in the mid-nineties. The class was small, about ten people. The man at the desk beside her in the classroom moved his mouse around like a toy truck. He was in his fifties and thought he was amusing her. He whispered, for her benefit, "Vroom, vroom."

"I'm sure I've seen you at Spinney's, Gwen," said Chiyo. "I bought a desk there last year. And a two-drawer filing cabinet. You look familiar."

"I came out to the sales floor occasionally, though most of the time I was in the office," said Gwen. "I miss work," she said, abruptly. And added, lest the others think her cold, unforgiving,

"And I miss Brigg. I loved him." She had no explanation for blurting out that unnecessary and untrue piece of information. She stopped because she could think of no further admission to make, true or false. She looked down at the table again, silent.

"Thanks, Gwen. We have one more person to hear from," said Hazzley. She looked across the table at someone she was sure she'd seen at Marvin's checkout. A woman in her forties who looked as if she'd willingly sit down with strangers and listen to their long-drawn-out life stories. A woman who would know how to impart wise counsel about matters of the heart and soul.

Addie sighed audibly and smiled.

"I'm Addie," she said. "I work at the hospital in town—I'm unit manager for the newly expanded Danforth Wing, a busy job. We've probably passed each other in a hospital corridor at some time over the years. I seem to have been there forever. Well, not forever, but it feels that way. I applied for the job after deciding it was time to leave Montreal. I graduated from McGill years ago. I'm not a nurse, but my mom was. She was heavy-set and she was tough. She had to be tough because she worked in a psychiatric hospital in Quebec—one of those sprawling Victorian buildings that were erected on fenced-in grounds and housed hundreds of patients on locked wards. So many men and women lived out their final days in those places."

What did that have to do with grief? And what did her mother's weight have to do with anything? Was she stalling? Why was she startled by the fact that each of the others in the group had spoken about someone who had died? Now that she'd mentioned her mother, maybe the others assumed she was here because of losing a parent. Her mother had died years earlier of complications from what had begun as a blood clot in her leg. She'd had excellent care in Montreal, and Addie had been with her as much as possible, but her mom died suddenly, while supposedly recovering. Now Addie's father, at seventy-eight, lived comfortably with his new wife in Catalonia, year-round. Addie loved him and saw him every two years. She still grieved her mother, but . . . she was losing track of what she'd intended to say.

"My dearest friend," she said. "Sybil." She could think of nothing else to say without the entire story of the past eight months pouring out. "Breast cancer." She heard something like a sob coming from herself and felt a hand on her shoulder. Chiyo, the young woman to her right. The personal trainer. A brief but reassuring touch. Soothing.

"She was a professor of nursing and worked in Montreal, but after she had surgery, she quit her job and moved home to Greenley, where she grew up. She had to move back in with her mother. She and I were friends from our first day at McGill, when we were just starting out."

"It's terrible to lose a good friend," said Chiyo.

Hazzley added, "I'm so sorry, Addie."

What had just happened? Her closest friend was dying, not dead. Addie lowered her head, horrified at the mistake, at describing Sybil in the past tense. She could hardly correct herself now, could she? *When you lie, quote a distant witness.*

"Sounds as if we've all dealt with the illnesses of our loved ones—some for short periods, some long," said Hazzley. "Short or long, the stress of this takes its toll."

What have I done? Addie asked herself. I didn't actually say that Sybil has died. Everything else I said was true. If she were only here, in Wilna Creek. But that would be selfish, to move her away from her mother and her family. And Greenley's hospital does have palliative care, which we don't have here. She's going to need that type of care—all too soon. And now the people around this table believe she's dead.

The others were staring. Had Addie said any of this aloud? She didn't think so. So many rapid thoughts, like eyelids moving in REM sleep. The way you hear of events flashing before your eyes during your final moments. Was that a myth? She refocused. The people here had lost someone important in their lives. They were present because they wanted to discuss death, feelings, reactions to loss, ways of coping. They were wondering how *she* was coping.

Some people know when to remain silent, she told herself. Others blather. I'm an internal blatherer. But I'm not invisible.

The dark place behind her eyes suddenly shifted and allowed a flicker of light. She felt her strength quicken, revive. "You know," she said, "when I'm having difficult moments during my days off, I clean my apartment. Stow my thoughts in some neutral space where I don't have to deal with them while I push a vacuum around. Sometimes I listen to music while I dust. Put on a CD and turn up the volume. The *Emperor Concerto* is great for dusting. Keeps my thoughts from dwelling on the mundane or the miserable."

The others laughed.

"I'm with you," said Chiyo. "I do the same. But not while listening to classical music. I call up movie soundtracks. Spaghetti westerns." Ocarina, she was thinking. *A Fistful of Dollars. The Good, the Bad and the Ugly.* A slow, mesmerizing dance. "I flick a soft rag; dust motes float and settle in the air while I listen. That's what I do."

"I stare out the window a lot," said Tom. "At home and at work. I keep the radio on for company—both places." He thought of mentioning the black notebook partially filled with poems in the desk drawer at his shop, but he didn't. He thought of demoted Pluto on the cover of his notebook. He thought of the way he was now writing back to front.

Hazzley was thinking that dusting to the music of Beethoven was something she might try. Cleaning house was, after all, a soulless exercise: repetitive, boring, necessary once in a while. Sometimes, after vacuuming, her back ached, despite her efforts to stay fit. Someday she might hire a person to help. By then, half the rooms would be bare, so cleaning wouldn't amount to much. For now, dusting to Beethoven sounded good.

Last spring, when Hazzley was visiting her daughter, Sal had taken her to a rehearsal at the National Arts Centre. Sal was a donor and entitled to bring a guest. Alexander Shelley was conducting the *Emperor*; Emanuel Ax was soloist. The two men had their sleeves rolled up during rehearsal, and Hazzley marvelled at the movement of hands, fingers, arms. Normally, you wouldn't see this sinuosity of limb at a performance because the men would be in formal concert dress. What surprised her was the way Shelley's arms created swanlike curves through the space around him. Hazzley had seen Bernstein conduct half a century ago, and he'd performed in a similar way, his body weaving unrestrainedly, from the tip of his toes upward. Hazzley had settled in, wanting the music to go on forever.

At that moment, Cassie entered the backroom with an order pad and pen. "Coffee, tea, wine?" she said. "Whatever you'd like to drink. On the house for your first meeting—a welcome to the café, though I guess most of you have been here before. Hazzley . . . well, I've known her a long time. She's a regular, a bad apple."

"Cake?" said Tom, but Cass shook her head. *None left.*

They all gave their orders except for Addie, who declined. She was depressed by the misunderstanding and wasn't certain how to go about correcting it. She had nothing more to say about Sybil anyway. Except that she was alive, just barely. She also had nothing to offer about her personal life, about the topic of her own marital status or her separation from Tye. She and Tye were kinder people when living apart. Each of them considered their friendship— though it was fragile—to be an accomplishment. No bitterness. When together, they were sometimes capable of making each other miserable. Having thought of Tye, she was ready to divert.

"Tell us about your name," she said, turning to Hazzley. "You were saying that was a bit of a story."

Hazzley had begun to relax. The others were no longer angular shapes bent over the table. They were less tense, sitting back in their chairs, waiting for Cass to bring on the drinks. Hazzley had observed Addie's expression after the long moment of silence. Understanding diversionary tactics, she stepped up to the rescue.

"I was born in England, second year of the war," she said. "We stayed in London, Mum and I, except for a short period when I was sent away to a safe place in the country. I was so unhappy, I came right back to my mum. Dad was off being a soldier, but he managed a two-week leave, which somehow coincided with my November arrival." Her eyes widened as she spoke. Addie, relieved of the need to fend off questions about Sybil, noted that Hazzley's pupils were hugely dilated. Some people had large pupils naturally, but Addie couldn't help wondering about a harmful flash of light searing the retina.

"My parents decided to name me Hazel. My gran—on Mum's side—was born in Hazel Grove in Cheshire, up in the northwest. At the time of my birth, my mother worked at the Victoria and Albert Museum on Cromwell Road in London. She was one of the workers who'd helped pack up hundreds of items that were transported to areas not so likely to be bombed. Some were sent as far away as Cornwall for storage. The museum closed in 1939, but only for a short period. The public wanted it open, although even the objects that remained had been moved to the basement to keep them safe. The war dragged on and the museum was used as a shelter, eventually as a canteen. But Mum worked right up until two days before I was born. While she was in hospital—childbirth at that time meant seven to ten days in bed, a practice that would now be considered barbaric—she sent my father to register my birth. An elderly male clerk at the registry office asked for the baby's name, and when my father said 'Hazel,' the clerk said, 'Oh, come now. You'd best rethink that. You can't be naming your child after a nut.' So my father changed the spelling—added an extra z, switched letters around, added a y. In that instant, I became Hazzley. Mum was not impressed, but she didn't bother going through the paperwork required to change my name back to what it was supposed to be. My father was soon to return to his unit, and they were trying to spend every moment together after she came home from hospital."

Cass returned and set down a tray that held glasses, white wine, Pellegrino, slices of lime. She went out again to make a decaf latte for Gwen.

Hazzley carried on. "I didn't arrive in this country until the early sixties. Lew was a Canadian studying history in London. We were both history students. I had a job at the Victoria and Albert Museum, same place my mum had worked. She had taken me there many times when I was a child, and I was captivated by the place.

"Lew and I married young, and I quit my job in England when I left for Canada, though I was sorry to let the job go. Lew helped set up the museum here; he was an advisor and became a jack of all trades behind the scenes. We're lucky to have a museum in this city. It was still a small town when we first arrived. Lew was happy at his job and that kept him busy, along with his readings of Conan Doyle. He belonged to a group dedicated to keeping the works of Doyle in the public eye, and he prided himself that he owned most of Sir Arthur's books in first edition. Took a while to collect them, but he was a man of patience. Well, he was patient most of the time.

"While he was getting set up in his job, I began to edit articles for a history magazine. I did that for a long time, working from home in an upstairs bedroom that I converted to an office while raising Sal—she's our daughter. After many years, the magazine shut down, and I branched out. I edit for a national magazine now. Occasionally, I receive requests from history journals. It's all free-lance, but the people who do the hiring get to know who's out there and who's willing to take on a job. After Sal grew up, Lew and I began to travel to different parts of the world. We returned to England several times."

She paused for a moment. "Now here's something I remember with a good deal of clarity. Shortly after we arrived in Canada, Lew saw a magazine ad in which a man was measuring his wife's height so he could buy her a new ironing board. The wife in the ad, wearing a dress and frilly apron, was looking all perky and delighted. After seeing the illustration, Lew picked up a tape measure one evening and recorded my height. I had no idea what this was about; I'd not seen the ad, and Lew told me he needed the measurement for a surprise. He arrived home from work the next day with an ironing board over his shoulder. I needed the ironing board but was not pleased when he showed me the ad. He might have thought he was giving me a ticket to a land called happiness. Let's just say it was decided then and there that he would iron his clothes and I mine.

"I only hope young women today have some idea of what went on in my generation. Even soap ads told you how to behave. Oh, yes, you might win your man, but how were you going to keep him? You had to use a special brand of soap, that's how! Well, never mind the soap or the ironing board. Things worked out. I did miss my parents after we left England, and I persuaded them to visit us in Canada—twice. But I've never regretted moving to this country. Now my parents are long gone. As is Lew," she added, and realized that his name spoken aloud was a sinker at the end of a line, its weight dropping through a deep dark pool, but undeniably attached.

Talking heads, Chiyo was thinking. *My Dinner with André*. We need a court jester to prance into the room. Someone who can juggle or perform a balancing act. Maybe this is part of a parallel world we're experiencing. *This* being the group around the table. Maybe the entire meeting is taking place in the future, or we're on some sort of timeline and the meeting took place in the past. Maybe we've all met before. Maybe I don't know what I'm talking about.

"I remember those ads of the day," said Tom. "My Ida didn't have much use for them. She always tried to carve her own path."

Hazzley poured a glass of Pellegrino and listened to small talk around her while the others sipped at their drinks. She thought of the empty bottles again; she had to get them out of her basement. Why had Lew become addicted during his last years? Was he so very desperate after his retirement from the museum? She'd asked herself the question many times. She could have asked him directly, but she hadn't. Why? Because he'd created an atmosphere of silence around the subject. Because he'd ensured that most of his drinking took place after she went to bed. Because at first he'd tried to hide the evidence of bottles and corks and bottle caps, and those efforts were so childlike, so amateur, they were laughable. But never could he hide the odour of alcohol exhaled all night long into the air of their bedroom.

She raised the subject of his drinking once, and he resisted angrily. Resisted the suggestion that he had a problem, and that drink was killing him. And then, suddenly, because she, too, flared up in anger, his resistance collapsed. His arguments fell apart and he agreed. Humbly. Mumbled that, yes, he had a problem. She was so taken by surprise, she could go no further. She asked him to seek help and he said he would, but took no action. In the weeks and months that followed, she told herself it was his problem to resolve. But he wasn't strong enough, did not have the will; she knew that then and she knew it now. The self talks the self into taking action—or not. The self is capable of tricking the self. Lew died an alcoholic, his liver damaged over a period of years. An earlier death than he should have had.

She had loved him, deeply. But in countless ways, she was glad to be free of him because of the drinking. Free of his inability to cope with his own life. She did her best to ward off thoughts about sharing the blame. Why should she take the blame? As a result, no blame was ever laid. He drank, he drank too much, he died. She was lonely and aware of the possibility that her life might not get any better than it was now. She had Sal; she had Cass and a few other friends. She had as much work as she wanted, but . . . perhaps there would always be a but. Cass had known that Lew drank, but she had no idea how much, especially as his drinking took place at home. As for the bottles, they remained hidden. Boxed. Out of sight.

A few nights earlier, Hazzley had leafed through pages of her old journal and noticed an entry from that period of her life. A time when she had not felt worthwhile. To herself or to anyone. *Oh, human frailties*, she had written. *How they penetrate the head and heart and soul.* What she understood now but was not able to consider at the time was that Lew, too, had not felt worthwhile.

But this group. Was there something in the air when they finally adjourned? Called out their goodbyes? Every one of them said, on parting, "See you next Tuesday."

HAZZLEY JOINED CASS at the front counter. Business had picked up, and they had only a few moments together. Cass was wearing a calf-length skirt, a multicoloured gypsy sort of top. Around her neck, miniatures of dual theatre masks hung from a cord of dark

99

leather: tragedy, comedy. She had never completely broken ties with the theatre she'd once owned in town. She twisted the cord between her fingers as she spoke.

"The quiet one," she said to Hazzley. "The tall one with ginger hair. Tinted. More butterscotch than ginger. She's been here more than a few times—likes to read for hours. She has a glint in her eye, even though she presents a serious front."

"You're astute, as always, Cass. But *glint?*"

"You know what I mean."

Hazzley did know. Gwen had told the group that her husband died in April. "She's fragile," Hazzley said. "Beaten down, maybe. I'm going to keep an eye on her."

"Last few months, she's been coming in here carrying a book," said Cass. "I thought she was on the lam because she kept glancing toward the door as if someone might charge in and drag her out. I leave her to sit for hours over one coffee. She doesn't stand straight, never assumes her own height. She tries to erase herself, become invisible. There's beauty there, a kind of hidden beauty she isn't aware of. Even so, she's contained. If you think of contained as someone who's about to take flight. Sometimes I look over to check on her, but she has already slipped out the door and is gone."

Hazzley considered this. "What about the others? Do you think they'll return?"

"I predict they'll all return."

"They said they would. What about Tom? Did you have a chance to speak to him?"

"He'll be back," said Cass. "Tweed jacket and all. He and his wife used to come in for a glass of wine after a movie. Sometimes they came to listen to jazz when Rice was playing. I knew Tom's wife had died, but I hadn't seen him for a while. Now that he's alone, he rarely comes in. And don't concern yourself about grief walks. I've never heard of them either. I'll surprise him with cake some week, to please him. He might have thought you were starting up a death café. What about the one called Addie?"

"She works at the hospital, in administration. Manages the Danforth Wing."

"I wonder if she knows the history, that the wing was named after my great-grandfather. Think of the life span of our family in this town! Next week, I'll ask if she's aware of the connection. You know, I always wished I could have met my great-grandfather. I'm only consoled by knowing how lucky I was to have my great-grandmother in my life when I was growing up. She and my great-grandfather were madly in love—everyone said so. Do you remember me telling you what she used to say to my mother and me? *Be not ignorant of any thing in matters great or small.* She found so many ways of fitting that into conversation. Especially when she knew one of us was about to make an important decision. She was bloody wonderful, that's what she was. I had her in my life for twenty-two years."

Hazzley had met Cass's mother, but not her grandmother or great-grandmother. She also knew about the family connection to the Danforth Wing, but she hadn't thought of that for a while.

The hospital had expanded over the years. The new section now accounted for about half the total space.

All in all, it was obvious that Cass had been eavesdropping during the introductions. Listening intently. She'd certainly heard more than a few fragments. Fine. Hazzley could forgive her that. It was a public meeting, after all. Public to the participants. In any case, she couldn't get along without her friendship with Cassie.

# Rigmarole

TOM

A new customer had begun to visit the shop. He'd been dropping in over the past month, so far not to buy but to comment, look around, chat with Tom. He entered now with assurance, pulled up a chair and sat near the front desk. He positioned his chair so that he could keep an eye to the doorway. He did not present his back to the entrance, nor was he face on; he maintained a kind of sidewise position.

The man's name was Allam. He did not mention a surname. He might have been Egyptian, Lebanese, Syrian. Arab, of some sort. He had dark but greying hair; he was muscular, heavy-set, about Tom's height. He spoke English as if he had learned it from a dictionary.

Allam was vague about personal details. He could address many topics and might have come from anywhere, and for those reasons, his name suited him. His name meant "learning," "having knowledge," he told Tom. His parents valued education and wanted their children to be learners. His father and mother came from a small village, and when Allam was ten, they moved to the city. He didn't say which city. He addressed Tom by his full name, with emphasis on the second syllable: Toe-*mas*. During his first visit, he had examined and then pocketed one of the business cards Tom displayed on a calling-card tray at the entrance. The tray was shaped like a lotus-leaf, Victorian silver, a favourite of Tom's. When he'd had the cards printed, he'd used his full name, Tomas Ollery, and added the short form (Tom) in parentheses.

"Toe-mas. Do you know that Egyptians are eating twenty-two pounds of dates per person in each year? Imagine someone in this country eating so many dates!" The word "pounds" came out as "bounds." *Twenty-two bounds of dates per person.* While Tom was catching up, Allam tipped his chair back and laughed. Rubbed at his chin. His skin was dusky-coloured, creased. He was probably in his early sixties, hard to tell. He had what appeared to be a two-day beard. Allam never seemed to work in the morning, or to be expected anywhere. Only some days, in the afternoon—if he happened to be in the shop—did he dodge out the door, always at the same time, twenty minutes before three. No explanation for these quick exits.

"Toe-mas. The scarlet ibis, have you been fortunate enough to see one? Brilliant red, magnificent. Along north regions of Venezuela. Beauty like that should be protected. The beak is a wonderful curve, a marvel. There are other ibises, close to extinct now. Bald ibises. Some few are found where once I lived."

When asked if he had lived in Venezuela, Allam gave a quick shake of the head and made a sound like *mmph*, which could have meant yes or no. Tom would like to see the scarlet ibis. Somewhere, anywhere. He and Ida had never travelled to South America. Nor had they been to Trinidad and Tobago, where, according to Allam, the scarlet ibis was the national bird.

Allam wandered through the shop, lifted objects, turned them every which way, inquired about provenance. He was curious, appreciated the worn splendour of old things. He inspected three railroad watches in a display case. He spoke knowledgeably about the jewellery business but did not elaborate.

What was clear was that Allam, like Tom, wanted to believe that the truly beautiful objects were those that had been cared for lovingly—a hundred, a hundred and fifty, two hundred years in the past.

Early on, when he'd started up his business, Tom had convinced himself that he could tell which objects had been possessed by caring owners. There was an intimacy to acquiring something others had owned and loved. A sense of personal history passed on. Each owner had been a custodian, a temporary guardian. Each object had been entrusted to someone's care. The nineteenth-century dough box, for instance, purchased during the summer. How he wished Ida were alive to see it. Table height. Solid pine. Thick legs squared by an artisan who had taken pride in his work. The lid—almost the length of a door—was thick and heavy, with smoothed, rounded corners. With lid removed, the box—more like a table, really—was deep, and Tom was certain it had been in the daily service of someone who'd baked bread for a family with a dozen children, and extra farm workers, too. No nails pounded in, thick boards held together by rounded wooden pegs. How many hundreds or even thousands of loaves had risen inside the dough box over time? He was reluctant to sell the piece and considered bringing it home. For now, he had a discreet sign on top: Not for Sale. By keeping it in the shop, he could share its beauty with others. If he did decide to sell, he knew it could be used in several ways: for objects stored, objects secreted away. And certainly as a dough box, if anyone baked that quantity of loaves anymore. He watched Allam run a hand over the surface. He watched him admire the grain of wood, the polish, the overall perfection.

"Rig'ma'role," said Allam as he returned to the chair by the desk. He spoke with precision, articulated as if each consonant was a word of its own. "I am liking the name you choose for your shop, Toe-mas. I once had a dream of creating a sign in a shop window that would read 'Master of Complications.' Lives have complications, you know that. The people want to discuss, sort problems, stay alert. Always, it is necessary to stay alert." Again, he did not elaborate.

Tom, sensing tragedy, did not ask. He knew little of Allam's background, but wondered if he might be interested in coming to

Cassie's to meet the others. It wouldn't hurt to offer information.

"Earlier this week, Allam, I attended a discussion group. A meeting—small group. Five people turned up. Four women and me."

"For what was this meeting?" Allam looked wary but curious.

"Have you been to Marvin's Groceries?"

"Sometimes. At back of store, someone makes bread. Almost like a real baker, but not."

"There's a bulletin board for notices. Near the exit."

"Notice of what? I have never paid attention to this board."

"Not everyone uses his phone to plan activities," said Tom.

"I have a phone. I use it for phone calls only. What is on this board?"

"All sorts of things. Take a look next time you're there. Events going on in the community. Advertisements. Offers to help, a variety of items. Occasionally I check to see if an auction or estate sale is coming up."

"I will look next time I go to the shopping."

"The five—we all shop at Marvin's—well, we all saw the same notice on this board and came together to talk about grief. We met at a café called Cassandra's. The meeting was not sad. We weren't there to be morose."

"'Morose' is a good word, Toe-mas. Much of the world is morose. What do five people together say about not being morose?"

"I suppose each of us told a bit of our own story. A small piece of the life pie. None of us knew each other beforehand. There were good feelings in this group."

"Did someone read aloud? A fable? An invention of the mind? A story, a poem?"

"No. Though I suppose some stories might have been inventions of the mind." Tom again thought of, but did not mention, the poems in the drawer beneath his hand. "We spoke about people we've lost in the past. Recent past. We spoke of different things, not only loss." He smiled while considering fables, inventions, what was real, what was not.

Allam was silent, also looking inward. He glanced toward the door, always checking.

"People are bringing their pain to this group? They speak aloud their pain?"

"Not exactly. Everyone was friendly, informal. And kind. We'll be meeting every Tuesday, seven o'clock. If you'd like to come, I'll bring you along. The meeting is open to everyone."

"I cannot next week. But for weeks after that, I will think abou-t," said Allam. And left the *t* sinking through the air as he departed.

# Memory Vault

CHIYO

Chiyo, too, was thinking. She had decided that she would return. She might be the youngest in the group, but Addie was around the same age. And she liked the idea of there being no hard-and-fast agenda. Everyone seemed reasonable about expressing what came to mind, nothing rehearsed. In some instances, details erupted sharply. In others, a shade was drawn, whatever veil there was to hide behind. Topics changed quickly. And yet, grief underlay everything.

We have the ability, she told herself. The ability to experience sadness. Maybe not exclusive to our species, but it does help to make us human. And there's something hopeful about people getting together to share. Who can possibly know how profound the experience of grief can be except those who have grieved? I suppose that includes almost everyone. From the smallest child who loses a pet, or whose best friend moves away.

She was sitting at the kitchen table, checking through release forms for her private clients, tabulating her hours for the city, preparing paperwork from a printed list of names for a tai chi class that would begin in December, after the present one finished. The maximum number she accepted for tai chi at any time was sixteen, and the city required that the planning be done well ahead so space could be booked in advance.

Her mother had once looked over Chiyo's shoulder when her papers were laid out over the table, drawing her finger down the enrolment list and commenting on various names—everyone unknown to her.

"You could be sued," she'd warned. "People will sue over anything."

"You've been watching too much television," Chiyo told her. "But don't worry. My students are aware of the risks. Private clients have to sign a waiver. Any classes sponsored by the city are covered by insurance." Not to mention, she was thinking, the extent of her own preparation: the certification required, the hours she put in to stay current every year, the updating of skills—first aid, CPR/AED. Did her mother think she wasn't qualified?

She had wondered, at the time, why her mother spoke in the manner of someone giving orders. Orders, demands, complaints, needling behaviour. That was the way she talked to her daughter— but never to her own friends. Chiyo tried to remember if this was true. She had been so accustomed to hearing her mother address her a certain way, she was surprised at the momentary insight. Would her mother have been aware of the differences in the way she spoke? Would she have understood that an alternative existed? Probably not. Insight had not been her mother's strong suit. She didn't sit around contemplating the possibility of change.

She counted on me to comply, Chiyo told herself. She dumped her mother–daughter expectations on me when I was young— really young. I learned to be compliant before I knew what the word meant. Maybe my own insight has been compromised. What I *don't* want to be is compliant.

She stood up from the table, and as she rose, she recognized a man's name at the bottom of a sign-up sheet she'd posted in the city gym to advertise the upcoming class. She would add these extra names to her master list, which meant the class was now full. The name she recognized had been scrawled in red ink, hurriedly, an afterthought: E.L. Hopps. How could she forget? Hopps—who insisted on being called just that—was a man in his late thirties who had once engaged Chiyo as his personal trainer. His first name was Eldon, he had told her, but he didn't like the name, so he answered to Hopps. He insisted on exercising to music—had to be Miley Cyrus—but couldn't follow a beat. Chiyo worked with him for months and finally gave up. She couldn't prevent herself from assigning silent descriptions to her client: manic, frenzied, frenetic.

But Hopps's name suited him. He had ruddy red cheeks and orange hair that stuck straight up. A huge forelock fell over one eye whenever he hopped up and down. It was unfortunate that he was oblivious to instruction as well as to rhythm. Chiyo had always expected him to topple over, but that hadn't happened. Now, several years later, his name was on the sign-up sheet for tai chi. How would someone that frantic be able to engage in a meditative exercise? She would have to see.

Don't count on anything, Chiyo warned herself. Maintain zero expectations.

Already a challenge and the class had not begun. And now, having considered Hopps, she thought of how everyone these days seemed to need slowing down. In her various classes, she found herself using adverbs like *mindfully, carefully, deliberately, gently*—all the while speaking in her low and steady reassuring voice. Each instruction was geared toward staying safe, respecting the body's limits while exploring its possibilities. She wondered if she should be exploring a new vocabulary, too.

There was also Maria, who frequently signed up for classes. Participants often returned, keeping fit by repeating or mixing classes of their choice. Maria, strong and lean, danced to every move no matter what the class, no matter what the exercise, music or no music. She was incapable of being still. If she was lifting weights, she danced. While stretching, she danced. Her feet tapped a double beat to everyone else's single. If other participants were stationary, Maria was wiggling around. But Maria also had grace. She listened to people; she cared. And why would Chiyo attempt to suppress anyone's natural dancing talents? No reason at all. So Maria danced through every session.

Chiyo stacked her papers and set them aside; Spence was

on his way to pick her up. They planned to go to the repertory theatre to see Wim Wenders's documentary *Pina*. Thankfully, Spence loved film as much as Chiyo did, and both were glad that after half a dozen years, *Pina* was finally coming to Wilna Creek. Chiyo had long ago purchased the DVD, but she wanted to see it on the big screen. She had huge admiration for the late choreographer's company, Tanztheater Wuppertal, the innovative use of space, the grit and beauty of movement. Pina Bausch understood emotions, but it was her use of the playful and absurd that most attracted Chiyo. Male dancers often wore dark striped suits too large for them and baggy pants, a sort of zoot-suit look of the forties that included snap-brim fedoras. The women wore bunched-up dresses, ill-fitting loose lingerie, heels or pumps with straps. Sometimes, men and women exhibited bizarre tics or swept their arms over their heads repeatedly. The work was visceral, spectacular; the absurd insistently reared its head. For Chiyo, the end result was a glorious display of creativity.

Another element of the dance was the way men and women sometimes relinquished their sense of balance. They tipped over, fell sideways or forwards or back, deliberately, occasionally violently. Usually, but not always, someone was there to catch them: someone who ran ahead, or behind, or alongside. But the fallers continued to fall. Repetition was paramount, and for Chiyo, this was a message about life itself: persistent patterns. Occasionally, the fallen stayed down. There was something semi-comic and vulnerable about the dancers after they fell, about their inability to get back up. At the same time, expressions of the tumbled body postures evoked deep sadness.

Later, after the film, Spence would come back to the house with Chiyo and stay the weekend. Chiyo smiled to herself. She would be glad of his company. She looked around the kitchen as if her mother might be standing in a doorway, peering inside her thoughts.

Only months ago, she could not have imagined bringing Spence home to sleep in her bed. Now each left clothes in the other's closet, supplies in the bathroom. None of this had gone on while her mother was alive.

DURING THE FINAL DAYS of the illness, Chiyo made up her mind that her mother was not going to be alone when she died. She could see that her mother was terrified. As part of the care plan, a doctor visited daily. Two caregivers alternated shifts, also daily. Chiyo was the "extra," and took few breaks. She cancelled some of her classes. She learned that a whole new category of help existed for her mother, whose needs now fell into a zone called end-of-life care. The caregivers' shifts sometimes overlapped, and this arrangement removed a bit of weight from Chiyo's shoulders and allowed a few hours of sleep here and there. The people who came and went were not nurses—not exactly—but they'd been trained by nurses to give specific types of care. Chiyo's mother wanted to remain in her own home and so she did, as had been arranged. During the forty-eight hours preceding her death, she drifted in and out of lucidity. She was weak, piteously so, but strong enough—her will was responsible for this—to raise her head an inch or more off the pillow. Always to ensure that Chiyo was present and could be seen.

What Chiyo was seeing was her mother's repeated feeble attempt to plead with two hoarse and desperate words: *Help me!* The words falling silently from her lips. Or rasping from her throat. The desperation was frightening to witness.

The doctor told Chiyo to prepare for the possibility that she might not be at her mother's side at the precise moment of her death. "The act of dying is private," he said. "I've seen dozens of cases where family members take turns sitting at a patient's bedside for weeks. The moment the person 'on duty' steps out into the hall . . . well, that's the moment the loved one departs. It happens again and again. Don't be disturbed if this is the case with your mom."

Chiyo vowed that she would be there, though she could hear what the doctor was saying. Were escorts waiting on the "other side," watching for that split second of privacy? Who? Whom? How could the timing be as intentional as he had implied? Was there a wall holding back an invisible world? No wall at all? A world that shifted and couldn't be seen?

Her mother died at eight forty in the morning. Chiyo had stepped into the kitchen to rinse a glass and refill it with fresh water. The doctor had left moments before, promising to return in the late afternoon. Both caregivers were present: one about to depart after the night shift, the other receiving the night report as her day shift began. The report took place while the two sat at the kitchen table discussing the notes in the chart.

Chiyo's mother had never come to terms with the fact that her life was ending. She died in her room with several people in plain sight. No one was with her at the moment of death.

The doctor was recalled before he had a chance to start up his car. He filled in the essential paperwork, notified the funeral home and told Chiyo a hearse would arrive within the hour. Chiyo sat with her mother's body, but after several minutes, the caregivers respectfully sent her from the room so that the body could be cleaned, prepared, dressed in clothes Chiyo had chosen from the closet and bureau.

When Chiyo went back to the room—these were the last moments she would ever have with her mother—the first thing she saw was a long strip of brown cotton bandage, two inches wide, looped under her mother's chin and tied in a clumsy knot above her ear, on one side of her head.

This was the image locked in the memory vault. The one Chiyo could not banish.

Her mother's face was peaceful. Her life was over, her body still warm. But the oversized knot of brown bandage at the side of her head was incongruous, discordant. Chiyo felt herself slipping sideways, the room unnaturally askew. Inhale, she told herself. Exhale. Call upon your training. Stay upright. You know how to focus. Go deep. Still the mind.

Why had her mother's jaw been tied? Would it have fallen open in death? Did her dentures not fit—for she did have dentures. Was there thought to be impropriety if a dead person had an open mouth? Chiyo didn't know. Nor did she know if she'd have been more upset if her mother's jaw was slack and drooping.

All she knew was that this was her last vision of her mother. The vision had nothing to do with love, which was what Chiyo had been expecting to feel. There was no room for love because it had been squeezed out by sadness, haste, the grim image now etched in her mind. The hearse drove up to the bungalow, and two quiet-spoken, efficient young people—a man and a woman in their twenties—arrived with a stretcher and wheeled her mother away in a body bag.

Sometimes this last vision swept in unexpectedly and lodged behind Chiyo's eyes: the brown-coloured bandage holding up her mother's chin, forcing her mouth closed for the first and last time. Not the mother she had known. The image refused to give way to something kinder.

She should have untied the knot and pitched the bandage into the garbage. But she did not. The caregivers were competent and had been through this procedure many times. Chiyo had yielded to them because they were supposed to know what they were doing. She should have spoken out.

What she wanted now was a reminder of her mother's beauty. Her mother was attractive in her younger years and remained so as she aged. There were photos in an album, not from her mother's childhood in the camp in British Columbia but taken during her thirties, forties. Chiyo decided she would find a good photograph and grace it with a frame.

SPENCE WAS AT THE DOOR and Chiyo greeted him with eyes brimming. She didn't have to explain. He knew she would share when she was ready. If ever.

She grabbed a thick wrap to throw over her shoulders, and they drove off in Spence's car. Heading for Pina. Heading into art. Chiyo wanted to lose herself in a landscape of wonder and desire, of sensuality and surprise. All of that along with the almost haughty dignity of the dancers, a dignity that paralleled the equal representation of abandonment and indignity. And of course, the flat-out absurd.

# *Irresolutus*

## HAZZLEY

In the final months of his life, Lew had become far too thin. Changes progressed quickly, transformation taking place before Hazzley's eyes. The disease began to ravage his body as if intent on leaving permanent marks. All of those marks now stored in Hazzley's memory, even though Lew had been dead three years.

There had been little outside activity in her own life during the last six months of his illness. Hazzley continued to go to the gym, but infrequently. She walked the streets of the neighbourhood, bought groceries, saw Cass occasionally, accepted a few articles for editing but also turned some down. She stopped inviting friends to visit and spent much of her time alone in her study. It was as if she were the person consumed by illness. Sal arrived for a short visit, and both parents were happy to see her. Sal was as concerned as Hazzley. Lew could still get around, but he was unable to reverse direction and wanted no interference. When he went out, it was to buy what he needed to drink. Much of the time, he was silent. He made no attempt to return the bottles. That effort seemed beyond him.

One of the low points during this period came when the Greenley Orchestra made its annual visit to the Belle Theatre in town. Hazzley and Lew had always enjoyed the yearly concert, especially as Wilna Creek didn't have an orchestra of its own. Hazzley purchased tickets weeks ahead, unsure if Lew would be able to attend. One way or another, she was looking forward to surrendering to music in a darkened theatre. She wanted to be at one with her thoughts. She wanted to forget about illness and about watching over Lew, whether he was beside her or not.

Every year, a group of women who called themselves Widows Rallying attended the concert, dining out at a local restaurant before arriving at the theatre. Hazzley knew two of the women. A dozen or more widows made up the group, and they met weekly at some restaurant or other, or at a gallery or museum, at openings or exhibitions. They took bus trips together and did charitable work and rotated shifts at the hospital, wheeling carts of books around to wards or helping in other ways as volunteers.

The night of the concert, Lew was unable to attend and Hazzley had to make her way to the Belle alone. When she took her seat, she immediately realized that she was four rows behind the widows, who took up an entire row of their own. In the ten or fifteen minutes before the curtains opened, there was a good deal of chatter and laughter coming from their row. Hazzley tried to ignore them, tried to ignore the fact that they were having a great time. She knew that if she were honest with herself, she would like to be sitting in that row, surrounded by women who were taking pleasure in being together. A part of her longed to give over to laughter and communal spirit, if only for one evening.

But she could not. Lew was not dead. She was not a widow and did not belong. She could only look on. She tucked her chin down and pulled her collar up, hoping she wouldn't be noticed. She was relieved when the lights went down and a concerto began. When the concert was over, she left quickly, knowing that the widows would be on their way out for a drink or a coffee somewhere, possibly at Cassie's.

Alone, on her way home, Hazzley could not push away the feeling of wistfulness, the feeling that she had assumed the role of permanent outsider. Outsider or enabler, she thought, grimly. Or both. She could not shake the desire to be out having fun with others who were completely alive.

After Lew died, she did not join the group because by then she had neither the energy nor the desire. There were too many things to deal with, though she knew well enough that the widows supported one another through their individual ups and downs.

TWO AND A HALF MONTHS before Lew's death, Hazzley made the decision to travel to Toronto. She'd been invited to edit two articles on the topic of Swedish settlement in the western provinces after 1870 for back-to-back issues of a national history magazine. The writer, a Swedish academic, would be flying to Canada. The managing editor—a reliable friend to Hazzley—phoned to ask if she would consider coming to Toronto for a couple of nights to meet the man in person. That way, any editing problems could be worked out face to face. There *were* issues, Hazzley was assured, mainly because English wasn't the writer's first language. Considerable money had been invested by the magazine, and the articles were important. With a bit of diplomacy and expertise, the editor continued, Hazzley could effectively clean things up. The Swedish writer was planning to visit other parts of the country and would be going on to Saskatchewan to visit relatives after his stay in Toronto. The editor believed it would be a good idea to take advantage of his presence and get the job done to everyone's satisfaction.

Hazzley travelled by train and planned to tack on a few extra days. She decided that she would visit the new Aga Khan Museum, which had been open more than a year. She would also walk to the Gardiner Museum and take her time over the exhibits, whatever the display. She would shop along Bloor Street and treat herself to a new skirt or sweater or coat—anything, didn't really matter. She would stay a total of six nights. But what she wanted most was to get away by herself. Have long, slow breakfasts at a decent hotel. Read the daily paper for hours. Be sure to slip a novel into her briefcase. She pushed aside her rising guilt. Lew would have to be left alone. Sal promised to phone every evening from Ottawa.

Lew insisted that he'd be fine. "Go ahead," he said. "There isn't a thing I can't handle on my own."

When Hazzley called Cass to tell her she'd be in Toronto, Cass had said, "Good. I'm glad you're going off to the big city." And added, mysteriously, "Who knows? You might have an adventure."

They'd both laughed.

"Just wait and see," said Cass.

From the Toronto train station, Hazzley hired a taxi and checked into her hotel at Bloor and Avenue Road. The magazine staff had booked the Swede, whose name was Meiner, at the same hotel. Hazzley met Meiner in the lobby the evening of her arrival. He was in his late sixties, perhaps four or five years younger than she—a tall man, heavy-set and fair-skinned, with brownish hair and a neglected greying beard. A bit rumpled, perhaps, but energetic and entirely comfortable with himself. In a large family he would be everyone's favourite uncle, she decided. Or great-uncle.

Hazzley was drawn to his personality and glad of his cheerful company. Glad to discuss research and language. Glad to be in any situation that could remind her of the existence of a world outside her increasing isolation at home.

The two sat for a while in the lobby and exchanged information. They met later in the main restaurant of the hotel, which was on the top floor, overlooking the city. They agreed to work in the business centre on the mezzanine level the next morning after breakfast. After dinner, Meiner would drop off revisions she had not yet seen; he told her he would bring them to her room.

While at the table, over dessert, he reached across a saucer of profiteroles, picked up her hand, held it in his two large ones and told her he would like to sleep with her. Hazzley was semi-amused and slightly tipsy; she began to laugh. They both laughed, but he assured her he was serious. He escorted her to the door of her room and told her he'd be back with the revisions. Twenty minutes later, he appeared wearing a deep-pocketed overcoat over a hotel bathrobe. He had his manuscript in one hand, a bottle of Veuve Clicquot in the other, and a long-stemmed glass in each of his deep pockets. Meiner lived large.

Hazzley invited him in, not really believing they would have sex. *Irresolute*, she was thinking, mainly of herself. *Showing or feeling hesitancy; sixteenth century—must be Latin—irresolutus, not loosened.*

She wouldn't know what to do, anyway—so much time had elapsed since she and Lew had been intimate. Since his heavy drinking began, she reminded herself. Since we stopped going anywhere. Since we stopped travelling, discussing, having fun, having SEX. She banished Lew from her mind.

She and Meiner did not discuss the editing until the next day, but they did spend the first night in her bed. "Never mind Saskatchewan," Meiner told her. "Never mind the Qu'Appelle Valley or Manitoba or the million Swedes who immigrated to North America. We'll deal with those hearty souls after breakfast in the morning. Hearty or hardy? What should I say?"

"I think you could use either." Hazzley was laughing.

"Ah! Either way, then, let us—you and me, no other Swede allowed, even on paper—enjoy ourselves this night."

Hazzley slipped into a robe in the bathroom, tried not to examine herself in the mirror, changed her mind, saw that this was a slimming mirror, a flattery mirror, and realized that the body she was looking at was the one she used to own. It's okay, she said to the mirror. I'm not fooling myself. But it doesn't hurt to look at what used to be. She removed her watch from her wrist, stowed it in her cosmetic case and wondered what to expect. Hazzley, she told herself, you don't have to be passive about this.

Meiner's body weight sank into the mattress and she rolled toward him. That was the beginning of the pattern that unfolded each night they were in Toronto. Meiner sent word to his prairie relatives and altered his dates, extending his hotel reservation to match hers. Three years later, Hazzley had to ask herself if the encounter had truly happened. Sex with Meiner was the only sex she'd had outside of marriage, and it was also the most satisfying she'd ever had. Or had she forgotten sex with Lew? Either way, Meiner caressed her, loved her—made her laugh. He smelled of a soap she could not identify, not perfumed, not unpleasant. That first night, after making love, they sat in bed, propped by pillows, and finished off every drop of the champagne. They talked and talked and talked. Were they both starved for conversation? Meiner told her he adored her spirit. He told her how certain he was that sex and life experience added up to the best combination. They slept in each other's arms, one of Meiner's heavy legs slung over both of hers. When they awoke in the morning, facing each other across hotel pillows, he said, "*Herregud!* Look where we are!" They laughed and made love all over again.

At the end of their time together, with no feeling of remorse or regret on Hazzley's part, they said goodbye. Hazzley did not ask herself: What have I done? There was no inquisitor around to examine her behaviour.

Would she and Meiner get together again? Maybe, maybe not. Since that time, they had exchanged an occasional friendly email, but they did live on different continents.

After meeting Meiner, feeling alive again, fully reminded that she was a sensuous human being, she returned to Lew. During the train journey home, over coffee and an unappetizing croissant that was squashed flat in its cellophane packaging, she looked out the window at the dregs of Canadian Shield and considered how life was so much more complicated than one could ever imagine in childhood. Just as well; otherwise, no one would want to grow up. Her childhood had begun during the war. She was a war baby and might not have survived. She remembered— or thought she did—the outrageously loud noises outside her London home, her mother's steadying voice within the terrifying darkness of an underground shelter. And then she was sent away to the country, to a stranger's home, but she was lonely there. When she returned to London, she remembered that during daylight hours, her mother set pots of fat outside the front door for collection. For grease? For the machinery of war? What else?

She looked around the coach and began to wonder what her fellow passengers would think of the nights she had just spent with Meiner. The two young women a few rows ahead, for instance. Checking their phones every few minutes, laughing and chatting too loudly, exchanging confessions and gossip for everyone to hear. They would look at her—at the thin skin of her wrists, at the outer corners of her eyes, at the thickness of her thighs—and they'd think she was over the hill, beyond sex. Truth to tell, she had no idea what young women thought today. She used to be more in touch. At one time, she believed she did know what was going on around her. Now she was uncertain. When had certainty abandoned her? She knew her own age group, yes. But two generations younger, what did they think—or think about? And what about her teenage grandchildren? There would be no room in their minds for considering a grandmother who'd had a six-night affair in her hotel room. They would be as unenlightened about her generation as she was about theirs.

She glanced at her imperfect outline reflected in the window and saw herself in her favourite wool cardigan, purchased decades ago in Edinburgh at the Scotland Shop. She was comfortable wearing this, a soft grey-blue, more blue than grey. Her face in the window seemed soft, too, her cheeks flushed. She thought of Meiner with true affection, and then she tried to think of nothing at all. She knew she had no answers for anything but history and grammar, the tools she needed for work. She unfastened her briefcase and opened her journal and propped it on the fold-out table. She wrote: *I feel wickedly satisfied, powerful and good. I wanted the sex.*

WITHIN A WEEK of returning home from Toronto, she resolved to make an effort to reconnect with friends. If Lew noticed a difference in her behaviour, he remained silent. Hazzley decided to invite four of their long-standing mutual friends, two couples, for lunch. Lew agreed to this, though she'd expected him to balk. Neither of them knew he would be dead within weeks.

"You'll have to help me look presentable," he said. "Iron a shirt, maybe? Take out the wrinkles?" He seemed to have renewed energy. Both felt the promise of festivity in the air.

Lew had always ironed his own shirts—since those early days of marriage, when he'd lugged home the ironing board—but Hazzley did the ironing that day without complaint. Lew chose a pale-blue shirt from his closet, no tie, something that would be loose and comfortable on his too-thin frame.

In the morning, he made a conspicuous effort. Rose early. Washed and shaved. Got himself into trousers and the blue shirt. Took some time to manage the buttons, all but the top one, which he left open. Sat on a chair; pulled on his socks, reached for his shoes. And in a wash of memory, suddenly began to talk about Hazzley polishing Sal's soft leather shoes when Sal was a baby and beginning to take her first steps. "It was Sani-white . . . something like that," Lew said. "Smelled a bit like chalk. Liquid in a small bottle. You shook it and put it on with a dauber, or should that be dabber? Little ankle-high shoes with laces. After you stroked the white polish over the surface, you set the shoes on the kitchen windowsill, up over the sink, to dry."

Hazzley's memory was stirred by the image. She smiled at Lew and made a mental note to check "dauber/dabber" later, at the end of the day. For now, she had tomatoes to marinate, basil to pick, a quiche in the oven.

It was only when their guests came through the front door that Hazzley realized how shocking Lew's appearance must be to others. She turned and saw what they were seeing as they greeted him. She could read the reaction on their faces. And if *she* could, so could Lew.

The heartbreak was that all of his effort showed. The ironed shirt. The looseness of it failing to disguise his gaunt frame. The unusual brightness in the eyes. Even his hair looked as if some outside agent had patted it down, forced a part with a wet comb.

He had scrubbed himself up for company and he looked the part.

Everyone sat in the family room, and Lew did his best to uphold conversation; he responded politely to queries about his health. Persiflage, Hazzley told herself while tasting balsamic in the kitchen. Light raillery, banter. He was holding court in the armchair that had always been his: the blue upholstered chair in which he read the evening papers and reread the stories of Conan Doyle. It was where he sat to listen to the radio, drink wine and whisky and ice-cold limoncello and any other alcoholic drink he could lay his hands on. That was his corner domain. She thought of champagne; she thought of Meiner in bed, his heavy leg slung over hers. *Herregud!* She felt a flush of warmth through her body. *We did what we did.*

She called everyone to the table.

Lew poured wine for himself during the meal. At first, Hazzley was shocked, and then not. Why *wouldn't* he drink? He drank every day and would not be capable of abstaining because of the presence of friends. She considered this from his point of view. He did the drinking; she had unintentionally assumed the chore of lugging the empty bottles to the basement because he no longer did so. They never spoke about this. Lew knew that he was at risk of suffering withdrawal. Hazzley looked around at their friends and said to herself, Try living with an alcoholic. This is what it's like. Something else takes hold and we move forward as if there's no other path on this journey.

Lew had been in withdrawal before: sweating, hands shaking, jittery, nauseated, anxious. The first episode had been so frightening to witness that she had backed away, gone out to the street, walked for a while, arrived at the gym, got herself onto a treadmill and stared at captions on a soundless TV. During an on-screen message promoting safety, Hazzley watched as a heavy-looking box fell from a shelf. The caption across the bottom read "Clatter, thud." Yes, Hazzley said to herself. Those are the sounds of being unsafe: *clatter, thud.* She jacked up the speed of the treadmill so that she could expend more energy. She increased the incline to 2 percent. When she was ready to leave the gym, she returned home and found Lew asleep on the floor of the bedroom, an empty glass close by on the rug. She wondered how he had managed to get up the stairs. She covered him with two blankets, and he woke up in the same spot in the morning, dressed in the clothes of the day before.

But the day they were entertaining their friends, the energy Lew had mustered in the early morning flagged all at once halfway through lunch. His shoulders drooped, the sacs under his eyelids became puffier, his eyes shone more brightly. His body was limp, his ankles beginning to swell. Misery showed on his face. The guests hurried through dessert, departed soon afterward. Lew walked upstairs to the bedroom, hand on the wall to support him along the way. He lay down in his clothes, this time on top of the bed. She covered him with a fleece throw, and he closed his eyes.

But earlier in the day, Hazzley had felt the current of success, however brief, that had sparked between them. Maybe during the planning, maybe in the moments before their guests arrived, or when everyone was seated around the table. She recognized the feeling for what it was: a revival of their old selves, the Hazzley and Lew who had existed a half century ago.

# Escape

GWEN

G wen heard the customary shrieks from outside.

The moment the key touched the lock, the house fell silent. Every day, same pattern. *Predator on doorstep. Predator sucks air from room.*

"It's me, Rico. Who else?" She removed her jacket and walked through to the family room. "Look! I brought something for you. But not to chew. If you chew these pages, you're off to bird camp. Permanently. You've heard of bird camps, right? They're out there, so be warned."

She pulled several clipped-together sheets of paper from a folder and held them up to the bars of the cage. A bit too close, because Rico dodged and scurried back. Never turning away completely, because he was the scrutinizer of *her*: messenger, feeder, conversation provider, companion of sorts.

He continued to stare hard. Head and neck hunched defensively so that two eyes looked out from under the tight-fitting grey hood.

She stared back, trying to create an expression that might appear friendly. Relaxed her eyes, relaxed her jaw, smiled—but the smile was tight, she knew that. Would the parrot intuit how much effort this took?

Rico came forward slowly. Tilted his head to the left, looked up, down, to the side.

"Sorry if I startled you. I'm getting used to you, too." She laughed. "I have the advantage, we both know that. I'm big. Bigger than you. And I can leave this house. Though I don't mean to rub in the facts."

Oh, beady-eyed creature, she thought. And wondered, not for the first time, if he could read her mind, or if she was mad to consider this.

Well, what about Sugar, the cat? When Gwen was a child in the late fifties, her mother had told her the story. Sugar's owners were embarking on a permanent move from California to Oklahoma. The cat, who was supposed to accompany them, leaped from the car's open window moments before they were to depart. To the family's great sorrow, Sugar had to be abandoned because she couldn't be found. After an amazing fourteen-month journey on her own, across varied terrain—desert, mountain, untold bodies of water—Sugar showed up one day at the family's door in Oklahoma. Fourteen months! Family films had been made of stories like Sugar's. Psychologists from parapsychology labs had become involved and interviewed pet owners whenever such an account became public news. Early experiments had been conducted in an effort to discern telepathy between animals and humans. Sometimes clairvoyance, sometimes telepathy *and* clairvoyance.

And what about Beautiful Jim Key, the famous horse known to be of high intelligence? He'd known the alphabet, numbers; he'd solved simple math problems and toured widely, and his feats had included a performance in the presence of President McKinley. Reputable people—psychologists, scientists—had tested animals like these and published their results.

Gwen wondered what would happen if she were to let Rico out of his cage while conveniently leaving the family-room window open. Would he fly after the Grands and locate them with accuracy in Los Angeles? Who knew? Maybe he could transmit telepathic messages to Cecilia Grand, or vice versa. A kind of telepathic radar.

"Someday, Rico, when I'm certain-sure you'll hop back in, I'll let you out. But I don't plan to open a window. In case you *are* reading my mind. Or Cecilia's."

She changed the water, cleaned the bottom shelf of the cage, added pellets to the food dish, sat on the arm of an upholstered chair several feet from the cage and looked over the pages she'd brought with her.

"The story is taken from a scholarly paper written by my own mother, Rico. Late mother, who loved me, and I loved her. It's about Arthur fighting Colgrim. Warring. The trade of kings—that's how war is described. Dryden said so, though you won't know Dryden. But think about that for a moment. *War is the trade of kings.*"

Rico continued to stare.

"Or tyrannical despots," she added. "But King Arthur is a man—was a man—about whom tales were sung and stories told, invented, reinvented, written, copied, enjoyed for almost a thousand years. Maybe he existed, maybe he didn't. His actual existence doesn't matter when you're privy to a sentence like the one I'm about to read. It was written by a priest whose name was Layamon. The priest was learn'ed, Rico. A clever man who wrote things down. And Arthur was clever, too. He sat his knights at a round table so that no one was below the salt. No one above the salt, either; everyone equal."

She glanced over at the parrot. "Okay, here goes. From Layamon's *Brut*. This is about escape, Rico, make no mistake. You might not understand. But it helps." She heard both sadness and apology in her voice. She stood the way she imagined an orator would stand before a crowd. "Up caught Arthur his shield, before his breast, and he gan to rush as the howling wolf, when he cometh from the wood, behung with snow, and thinketh to bite such beasts as he liketh."

Rico turned to one side and bobbed his head. She saw the white circles, the black pinpoint pupils.

"Maybe your owners don't read aloud? Maybe they don't read at all. I don't see any books around, do I? You've probably never listened to an Arthurian tale—any tale, for that matter."

Rico dropped to a lower perch and stilled as if waiting. No display of agitation. She turned a page. He cocked his head upward and investigated the ceiling as if he wasn't a part of this at all. *Not my scene.*

*Social interaction is vital!* Cecilia Grand had underlined.

Did he want something? He didn't seem to be in a hurry for seeds or pellets or treats. The water container was full. Could he be enjoying the sound of a reading voice? Gwen decided to continue.

"Woe came upon the people," she said, and set the pages down. She was thinking of the group at Cassie's.

Woe was what everything was about these days. Perhaps each person in the group was acquainted with a different version. Her woe was her life with Brigg. She had lied about him to the others. They probably thought she was someone who had buried herself for years in a dingy office at Spinney's, and maybe she had. But she liked the group, the people who were part of it. She just wasn't entirely comfortable there. Absolutely no one had mentioned the way grief could pursue: a scythe whipping through the air, closing in on the wounded. Was she the only one? She would not be able to explain this to the others. Her wounds. And maybe what was in pursuit was not grief at all.

She plunked down in the chair and began to cry.

Woe indeed.

She had occasionally dared to talk back, but only when Brigg pushed too far. From the time they were first married, he had doled out household expense money as if she were the hired help. He didn't want her to work, so she quit her job before their wedding—she'd been working as an accountant for a car dealer in town, her first job after university. Brigg insisted that he needed her at home. He wanted her to run the house and raise the children they both hoped to have. But she was quick to learn about his stinginess. He had no realistic idea of the cost of feeding and clothing two adults, paying utility bills, keeping fridge and cupboards full. He announced soon after they married that they wouldn't have joint bank accounts because he would write cheques for whatever she needed. All this was, at first, said in a good-natured way, a joking sort of way. And part of her had believed him. She wanted to believe that he knew what he was talking about. What did she know? She had never been married before. Maybe that was the way he'd been brought up. The husband controlling the money, the bank accounts.

But then he began to push hard, to bully. When he came home from work in the evening, no matter where she was, she felt his will as it roiled and swelled within the walls of the house. After their sons were born, Brigg told Gwen he would not increase her household allowance because she needed to learn thrift. A few months later, he accused her of stealing bills from his shirt pocket before she put the clothes into the washing machine. Money she hadn't bothered to return.

There had been nothing in his shirt pocket. She was outraged at the accusation and fought back. But he fought harder, until she began to wonder if the bills had been there after all. Maybe she'd washed them away in the rinse water. But no, that wasn't possible. Without fail, she checked every pocket on washdays.

"Keep this in mind," she told him in anger. "Your last shirt won't *have* any pockets. Keep that thought in your miserly mind."

Maybe that worried him. Maybe when he conjured the image, he imagined himself in a shroud. If so, he hadn't let on.

For Gwen, the episode was a beginning: a turning point that had taken a long while to be met head-on. Her will began to clash with Brigg's—she experienced this almost physically—but in brutal silence. Neither would back off. Confrontation was always on the verge, about to happen. For Gwen, it was like being one of two rival actors on stage, each locked in a role that could not be viewed by others but was known intimately by both players as necessary to their own death struggle. The most crucial action was yet to come, the climax inevitable, no matter how long it might take.

She bided her time and put her energy into raising the twins. The year the boys turned six, she began to read professional ads in the *Wilna Creek Times*. She applied to Spinney's for a full-time job as bookkeeper. She was hired immediately and arranged after-school daycare. Her salary was her own. She opened a bank account in her name only. Brigg didn't stop bullying, but he couldn't force her to stop working. Instead, he made fun of her; to him, her job was a joke.

But the situation had changed: she no longer had to ask him for money to buy underwear for herself or the boys, or for twenty dollars to go out for dinner and a movie with a few women who got together occasionally after work. In those days, it was possible to partake of a meal and a movie for twenty dollars. She wondered if Brigg had enjoyed humiliating her, enjoyed forcing her to ask for money during the boys' preschool years. He'd been successful, in part. She never invited friends home; she learned to rely entirely on herself. Gradually, whenever she went out, she went alone.

WHEN SHE CARRIED in Brigg's clothes to have him dressed for the casket, the director at the funeral parlour made no comment about the shirt pocket. Maybe he didn't notice that the opening of the pocket had been stitched across—trouser pockets, too, also jacket. She'd sewed them all up tight. She could hardly have brought in a shroud, though she'd have preferred to see Brigg wrapped in one. He went to his grave without a single pocket; she made sure of that.

In any case, what did she care about what the embalmer thought—the embalmer or whoever it was who'd dressed Brigg's corpse? The people who work in funeral parlours must have plenty of inside stories. Gwen wondered about the topics of their conversations at conventions and family vacations. What, exactly, was discussed?

"Arhh," she heard.

Or maybe the sound was *hargh* or *haw*.

"Haw," she said back. "Haw bloody haw."

"Haw," Rico said. "Bloody haw."

Gwen started to laugh. She laughed and laughed while Rico stared. He began to run back and forth on his perch. Finally—

perhaps intentionally, to staunch her outburst—he attempted to create the noise of the gasps she was making between breaths.

Then silence.

"You might save me, Rico," she said. "You might save me yet."

She lifted herself out of the chair and began to scoop up her belongings. She hadn't laughed like that for a long time. She couldn't remember a time when she had truly laughed. She was still laughing when she went to the radio and tuned in CBC again, volume low.

"So long, bird."

"Save me!" Rico shouted, in his beaky, birdy voice. And abruptly turned his back.

As she was letting herself out through the front door, she heard him laughing like a parrot maniac in a voice that sounded uncomfortably like her own.

October

# Stories, First-Hand

A side chair appeared in the shop. Tom knew Allam had carried it in because Allam was the only other person to know
where the extra key was stowed. He had mentioned previously
that he might bring in something Tom would find interesting.

Tom inspected the piece and understood that this was not
just any chair. Victorian or perhaps pre-Victorian, cane seat,
papier mâché backrest, wooden legs, unusual beauty. Slight
scarring at the rear of the backrest. Tom liked the scars, part of
the provenance. A touch of expert repair work had been carried
out to reinforce the back. This long-ago repair had been supple-
mented by a thickness of ancient leather, which added extra support. The most striking features of the chair were feather-like
designs within the curves, inlaid mother-of-pearl, highlights of
gold leaf, delicate hand-painted leaves and flowers—the whole
being lacquered, or "japanned." The chair was solid, fabulous.

Tom immediately thought of a couple who might be interested: a man and woman who loved objects from the Victorian era, that long period of history that spanned so much of the nineteenth century. The same couple often purchased mercury glass, as well as vinaigrettes—each with a special hallmark—from the Georgian period, the 1830s. Those small secret boxes fit tidily into the palm and were fashioned from sterling silver, with a fine layer of gold inside to keep the interior surface from corroding. Plain on the outside, beautifully intricate on the inside, with a pierced grille under which tiny pieces of scented sea sponge had once been placed. Tom seldom came across vinaigrettes, but when he did, he acquired them for the same two collectors. As for the papier mâché chair, he'd never seen one of this quality except in photos.

Allam came in moments after Tom turned the Open sign on the shop door.

"You have the chair," said Allam, a new edge of propriety in his voice. "A work of beauty, yes?"

"But you haven't paid for it, surely?"

"Not yet, Toe-mas. If you find a customer, we have an arrangement? I pay my source, you pay a commission—is that what you say? The owner told me the chair could come here to your shop. You are trusted in the town."

"Indeed. But where . . . ?"

"I walk in the city, Toe-mas. It is how I know this place; I am a walker. I make my way through streets and alleys. Old sections that are new to me. New sections—you call these developments? So many things are young in this country. But there are old things inside homes, things that come from far away. I get to know where people are, where they work, where they live. I go to coffee houses. I set"—he corrected himself—"I *sit*, listen. I try to learn more English. Sometimes I do not know expressions. 'See you,' a man said to me one week ago at a coffee shop. I did not know this man. I did not know his meaning. I was on my way out after drinking coffee. I asked myself, Does he watch me? Am I followed? I worried for two days about what he was seeing until I understood that for him he was saying goodbye."

"I would never have considered that," said Tom. "If you need an explanation for any other turn of speech, let me know."

"Turn of speech is good. I like that, Toe-mas. Also I tell you that I continue to learn English in a warm room of the library. Some mornings I read. Then I walk more. I stop at a business. I talk to merchants, owners. If I mention your name, they know right away about Rigmarole."

"I could have a ready customer for this chair, Allam."

"Good. A man? Woman?"

"Both—a married couple."

"If they want this chair, perhaps they also want a tray, papier mâché. A scene after Chinese, maybe Japanese. That detail is not of importance. It was made in England, not China, not Japan. It tells the story of a procession. Some revered person—perhaps a dictator. Yes, dictator for certain; when I see one, I know. He sits on a platform, a lion throne, and others fan him with big leaves. There are musicians—a flute player, drummers—men who carry gifts. I think you will like the tray, Toe-mas. It is black and gold except for green robes and sashes. Sky is black. Dying sun is made of golden rays. And"—Allam paused here, for effect—"the tray can be used. Cared for. As in the past. Which makes it beautiful."

"Bring in the tray and I'll phone the couple to see if they're interested. They might as well see the two together."

"Tomorrow I will return to the owner of the chair and I will ask for the tray."

"And Tuesday evenings? Have you thought any more about joining the group?"

"Yes." This with no hesitation. "Until now I have not been free, but I will come soon. I thought about what you told me. I am interested." A pause. "To know how things happen."

"Excellent."

Tom hoisted the new acquisition to a wide ledge where it would not be bumped into or knocked about, and the two men took up their usual chairs: Tom behind the desk, Allam keeping an eye to the entrance.

"The Tuesday past," said Allam, speaking precisely—was he disappointed that he hadn't been asked?—"I could not come because my *fambly* had a celebration. Birthday of husband of my daughter. Small *fambly*, small celebration," he added. "At a bistro. My grandchildren, two girls, one boy, were present. Is that correct? The sound is not right, I think."

"Family," Tom told him. "No *b*. Though I can see how the word can be heard that way."

"Thank you, Toe-mas. I need to learn the small things about language as much as the big."

"And how was your dinner out?" Tom hid his surprise at the sharing of personal news.

"The food, yes, fine. But tell me, Toe-mas, why must pork be pulled? Why must peas be smashed before they take their place on a menu in a restaurant that is said to be special? I am happy to be in this country, but smashing peas and pulling pork . . . well. I did not order pork, Toe-mas. I did not order smashed peas."

"But you did eat something?"

"Arctic char, excellent fish. I did not complain about pork and peas. Those I read from the menu. We drank to the health of my son-in-law. I told stories to the children. Laughter on all faces is good. But later, after we returned to my daughter's home, after everyone was sleeping, I sat by myself in the kitchen and thought of my father, how he roasted lamb outside, over a firepit. How he told many stories. That was long ago, in our village when I was a boy. Later, we moved to Aleppo. My father died there, age eighty-three, before the present troubles began. There have been many periods of trouble in my country's history. When I was a child, my father showed me . . . things he wanted me to know."

Allam looked toward the ceiling and rubbed the back of his hand beneath his chin before he went on.

"He showed me how to make the fire, how to slaughter and

roast lamb. How to negotiate with others. To believe that learning is important. To know and remember the past. How can we go to the future if we don't know our past?" Allam extended his arms as if the past might swoop in and land on his open hands. But the hands pulled back. He closed his eyes. "I was blessed to have a good father who lived many years. Others from my village were not so fortunate."

In companionable silence, the two men contemplated their separate pasts.

"He taught me *steelth*, Toe-mas."

Which Tom interpreted as "stealth," recalling how silently and abruptly Allam came in and out of the shop.

And just as abruptly, with no prompting, he found himself sharing the only story he owned about his own father. The one first-hand story he had to tell.

"My father was a soldier during the war. He was sent off for training just before I was born. Any detail I knew of him was from a single photograph. Brown and white . . . well, sepia, actually. My mother told me that my father left Wilna Creek on a train, and later in the year, he embarked on a ship in Halifax to cross the ocean. He did not return home after the completion of his training. She told me no stories about him, no history. The only clue to his existence was the framed photograph of him in uniform, propped on my mother's bedroom dresser. All this seems strange to me now, of course. We boarded in behind Ross and Main, with an older friend of my mother's. I suppose I didn't think about other belongings that might have been, or perhaps *should* have been, in the two rooms that were ours. My father had been born in northern England, border country, and we never met any of his family. As it turned out, they didn't know we existed.

"I had never seen this man except in the photograph, which I looked at with occasional interest. Few of my friends had fathers at home. I knew the man in the photograph was 'fighting overseas,' because that's where men disappeared to during the war. They were invisible, but they were 'fighting overseas.' The families on our street were made up of grandparents and mothers and children. There were old men and teenage boys, but hardly any men of fighting age.

"And then, on a sunny day in October 1945, when I was six years old, everything changed. I remember leaves whirling through the air. I remember the sun's warmth—even in the crispness of fall. Much like weather we have here in Wilna Creek. Golden leaves were scattered across the grass and along the edges of the sidewalk. When the leaves were spread out like that, I shuffled my way through them and told myself I was walking on the sun. The leaves had to be raked—that was a boy's job, my job. I see the outline of the leaves now; I see everything so vividly. I recall this detail because in the midst of the scene, a tall man, a stranger I had never before laid eyes on, walked into my yard. He was wearing a uniform, and he picked me up and held me high in the air and said my name. He put me down again and reached into his tunic pocket and pulled forth two gifts. Both were for me. One was a brown leather wallet. The other was a crinkly package of Planters peanuts. He put these gifts in my hands and told me he was my father.

"I was awed by the presence of this man called Father, by the gifts, by his sudden appearance, by the uniform. And then I remembered the photo, which wasn't exactly this man, but maybe almost like him. I went running and jumping down the street, kicking through the leaves, shouting out to my friends who were playing in their front yards and on the sidewalk. 'My daddy's home! Come and see what he brought me! See my wallet! Look at the bag of peanuts, Planters peanuts!' Everything, every detail of that afternoon, is imprinted on my memory. And when—or if—I think of this, the scene is always enacted as if it took place only moments ago.

"My father was home for two days before he disappeared a second time. He went away, left us—my mother and me—and never came back. The wallet, the peanuts—these are my sad, my deep memories. Running down the street, kicking aside the leaves, shouting out because my father had miraculously appeared. I did not know that within days, he would just as miraculously disappear.

"There was another woman. Of course, another woman. A second family in another country. England, as we found out. Maybe he had other children, I don't know. I might have had— might still have—brothers and sisters. I never saw him again. Nor did my mother. She had to try to get support; that's the way she found out about his other wife. Things like that happened during the war. I learned about similar situations later; these were not unheard of. But we never talked about this out loud. My mother was bitter, angry. I was not permitted to say his name, to ask questions."

Tom remembered finding his mother in the kitchen with two other women from the street, all three slumped on hard-back chairs in tight-lipped silence when he entered the room.

Allam was listening closely. "You have told this story to others?"

"Only Ida, my late wife. There wasn't much to say. The memory was painful. *Is* painful."

"Yes. There would be pain. Our fathers are important."

"I knew, if we ever had a son, I would be present in his life."

"You have a son?"

"Yes, in Edmonton. He was here a few weeks ago. Ida and I named him Will, after my mother's father. My grandfather, William Murray, was an honourable man. He was strong, and he was protective of my mother and me. Every summer, we spent time with him and my grandmother in Nova Scotia. He set an example as a father figure. I was determined that I would do the same when the time came. I knew this from childhood; that's when I made up my mind. At seven years old, I decided that not only would I find myself a wife when the time came, but I would have a family and be a father. I intended to be a good one. I thought about this for a long time when I was a small child. Even at seven, I was considering how I might find a wife."

Both men smiled at this.

"You were learning to measure your decisions, Toe-mas. A good sign."

Allam got up from his chair and wandered about the shop for several minutes. He returned and placed both hands on the desk.

"I have been thinking about an idea. A question I would like to ask."

"Fire away."

"What do you do with ordinary items that people use every day? Items that have little value in an antique store such as this."

"In the shed around back. At the moment, it's more than half full. Sometimes I'm forced to purchase an entire lot when I'm at an estate sale. A lot of the items are just memorabilia, not antiques. Do you have something in mind?"

"There are newcomers to this city who have not many belongings. Have you thought of donation?"

"I've donated in the past. Actually, I'm no longer buying or accepting large furniture because I have only my Jeep, out front. It holds more than you'd think, but not really large items. I used to own a small truck, and that was pretty useful. After I reduced the size of the shop, I had no further need. The Jeep transports pretty much everything."

"I could tell you of a place where there is a need for ordinary items—what you call memorabilia."

"If you bring in finds like the old chair over there"—Tom gestured—"I'll be happy to join you in emptying the shed from time to time. As well as paying a commission when you find such beautiful pieces—if I can sell them. Or if you bring in a buyer. That, too, might happen."

"That sounds good, Toe-mas."

Allam headed for the door.

"And by the way," Tom said, "take the second key with you."

# A Normal Life

ADDIE

Before leaving for work, Addie sipped at her coffee while listening to Haydn's First Symphony. She was thinking about what she had walked into at Cassie's over the past several weeks. And willingly. She enjoyed talking to the people who turned up at the meetings. Each person so different. She just wasn't convinced that she belonged. She liked Hazzley, the organizer. Capable, experienced, someone who'd been through ups and downs across a span of decades. She liked Chiyo, in whom she detected wry humour, an alertness that appealed. A woman unafraid of her own feelings; someone older than her years, who could take action when action was called for. She'd probably had to assume family responsibilities at an early age.

Haydn's tempo was too quick so early in the morning, and Addie's ears objected to the overabundance, the surfeit of intent. In her mind's eye, she saw courtiers flinging themselves in circles, violinists racing on tiptoes, horns blaring, the entire Haydn assemblage making unexpected stops and starts. An assault on her revved-up brain. She switched off the radio. Felt the sudden collapse into silence. Good.

Peace was good.

She would make a quick omelette for breakfast, no toast. She liked breakfast, needed to eat before starting her hospital day. But she had to lose weight, too. One egg or two? She began to bargain, accustomed to inner debate. "I'm not the kind of person who eats whites only or yolks only," she said aloud. "That seems extreme, even bizarre. Eat the egg or don't. No, this is a question of quantity: one egg or two. Fat content? Eggs are a wonder food, aren't they? Like blueberries, wild sockeye salmon. Don't forget the vitamins in one egg. Oh, give it up. Whisk two eggs and be done with it." She pushed away the idea of diet, but only for the moment. She had made a promise to herself and would honour the promise. Maybe.

She checked the time, turned up the heat under the pan, looked through her kitchen window. The smoker was on her balcony, puffing away in her blue-black pyjamas, a fixed bruise on the side of the building opposite. Exhaled smoke was spirited away by errant gusts of wind. One balcony below the smoker, a pair of armchair rockers made of cocoa-coloured cane tipped back and forth in tandem, an empty-chair dance. At ground level, a bright-yellow crosswalk, painted across pavement, resembled a ladder laid out horizontally, tapered at one end. A vanishing point perceived from above.

Addie looked off in the distance toward a silhouette of undulating hills. Clouds had gathered in a moody, broody sky. September and October could be unpredictable: windy, sunny, sometimes cool, sometimes sweltering. Tom, at the most recent Tuesday meeting, had lamented the humid days of summer they'd all endured, and then he'd quoted Keats. Addie had learned the same poem, "To Autumn," at school in Quebec, long ago.

*Where are the songs of Spring? Ay, where are they?*
*Think not of them, thou hast thy music too,—*
*While barred clouds bloom the soft-dying day,*
*And touch the stubble-plains with rosy hue.*

The hospital wing where Addie worked was air-conditioned, but she'd walked home in the heat one evening, along Main Street, in an effort to be serious about exercise. She remembered her clothes being soaked in perspiration, the sensation of wading to her thighs in a warm, soupy sea. Without thinking, she'd kicked her right leg out to the side to disentangle her twisted underwear. Having done this, she looked around, knowing that if she'd been seen by anyone, she'd have been judged comical, unfeminine, unwomanly. Why should she care? Well, she did care, she reminded herself. It's just that she couldn't care right now. During that same humid spell, she had been out on her balcony after dusk one evening, sipping at a glass of Scotch, thinking about Sybil, thinking about work. She wondered what people in the building opposite saw—or imagined they saw—when they looked across or down at her. A doughy specimen with arms and legs, stuck to the side of cement like a flat figure on a felt board. The specimen raising one arm in strong drink. "Oh, don't be so hard on yourself," she said aloud.

She stepped back, away from the window. She wasn't so plump, surely. She had to get a grip on her life, that was all. She tilted the omelette onto her plate and, still standing, dug in with a fork. She took a last sip of coffee and admitted to herself that there were days and nights when she wanted to call Tye. Come back, she would say. I need to lie beside you, talk, tell what is important to me right now. I need to be close. But Tye didn't know about the weight she'd put on. She'd have to lose a dozen pounds before any meeting with him. Buy a couple of flattering outfits. Stop worrying about her thighs sticking to chair seats in summer heat.

How could any of this matter? Tye was in Montreal and she was in Wilna Creek, and there wasn't going to be a meeting. She was running on overload: she had information about new privacy laws to disseminate, meetings, obligations, departmental concerns about security of staff and patients, long drives back and forth to Greenley. The utter and complete responsibility for Sybil's care on weekends. Not to mention the way Sybil's mother looked to Addie as if she alone could save Sybil. And of course, she could not.

Addie had not lived a normal life for a long time. She had to dig back in memory to think what that might mean. Life as normal, before everything was put on hold while she began to help care for her friend. Nothing she did anymore added up to what she was used to—her routine, she supposed. But what exactly was on hold? Maybe the days she was putting in did add up to normality of sorts. Working, holding meetings, managing staff, being on call, driving, waiting for news, bracing herself for one more request by phone or text.

She thought of her late mother's professional life. What about that norm, the parental norm? Leaving home every day to work on a locked ward where an obsessive-compulsive man stuffed his pyjama pants with toilet paper every half hour, was chased out of the ward bathrooms, only to duck back in behind a stall when the nurses were occupied so he could refill his pyjamas again. Where a man hanged himself in the shower on an evening shift. Where a female patient in a manic state threw a brass sculpture at the wall of her room, creating a dent the size of her head. Where one of the permanent night nurses, as disturbed as the patients she cared for, gave up all pretense of practising her profession and slept behind a glass cage at the nurses' desk through most of her shift. She neglected everyone and everything but her need for sleep, chin propped on a stack of phone directories, reference texts and a thick vademecum, the total of which held her head upright so that the night supervisor, passing by at the end of the corridor, would see, through a narrow barred window in the door at the end of the hall, the nurse's profile and believe she was hard at work over her charts. The supervisor did have a key to the locked psych ward, but she refused to enter because several months earlier she'd been threatened by a patient with a gun. And though the gun turned out to be a plastic toy, the supervisor would no longer do her night rounds directly inside the ward. She'd had quite enough.

Those were some of the stories Addie had been told. Her mother took the work conditions in stride and carried on. She was used to dealing with danger, with the bizarre and unexpected. Addie recalled how her mother had always been positive, searching for ways to help. An optimist, because she could make things happen. She was trusted by people around her, and she was tough.

But her mother had also puzzled over ordinary moments, over normality. Addie remembered how she had talked about her basic nursing education, about living in residence for three years.

"Just before Christmas," her mom told her during one of their drives home at the end of the day, "the head nurse on the ward I was assigned to for three months happened to mention that she'd be spending her holidays with a group of yodellers. She was unmarried, about fifty. I was eighteen years old and couldn't reconcile what I saw as her two lives. All that starch and poise on the job. She was strict, demanding. And there we were, in a structured, dignified setting governed by rules and decorum, always with people's lives on the line, and she was going off somewhere at Christmas to yodel and bellow and holler, or whatever yodellers do. I never saw her in quite the same way after that. My eighteen-year-old and obviously limited imagination couldn't grant her a separate private life. I thought the image of her yodelling was preposterous."

Addie was aware of the fact that her mother had not been ordinary in the slightest. She was sturdy and strong, could roll up her sleeves and do what had to be done. That was her legacy to Addie. *Do what has to be done.* Addie secretly believed that her mother charged headlong into fraught situations because she knew that if she had to, she could wring someone's neck as easily as she could wring water out of sheets in the laundry room when the mangle was broken. If anyone even used a mangle anymore. Apparently, her mom had, because she'd mentioned mangles more than a few times.

She had also held strong opinions about issues of personal cleanliness. Under the parental eye, Addie as a young child was frequently reminded: "Scrub those dirty elbows." Even now, close to fifty, she sometimes found herself pointing her elbows at the mirror after a shower and checking for unlikely grooves of dirt. As for the navel, her mother insisted, "There's no such thing as a child with a clean belly button." All the same, despite the demands for cleanliness, she'd been a caring and loving parent. Capable, Addie thought. My mom was entirely capable. She could be relied upon. My God, how I miss her. And Father somehow created a balance to all of that. He loved her, too. He missed her after she died, I know he did. Maybe he still does, even though he has a new wife. All the possibilities. Maybe Tye and I should have had children. We talked about adopting, but never did.

At that thought, Addie fought against the urge to contact Tye, to pick up the phone. Tye was aware of Sybil's illness because

Addie had informed him after the initial surgery in January. She could provide him with an update; that could be her excuse to call now. She watched her hand reach for the receiver. Willed it back.

She was on a difficult path. Headed toward—whatever lay ahead. Sybil was not going to get better. That was a certainty. Maybe, just maybe, belonging to this small group at Cassie's would be helpful. Addie reminded herself that the others believed Sybil was dead. Too late now to correct her story, and maybe the order of events wasn't going to matter anyway. What she was dealing with was the tragedy of Sybil losing her life. Tragedy for Sybil. Tragedy for Addie, who would lose her. Was already losing her, because Sybil was turning away, turning toward something only she could see.

But what could she tell the others in the group if she did admit that Sybil was alive? That versions of grief had been stampeding through her head during that first meeting?

Grief was complicated. People grieved when they fought with siblings, when grudges were held, when they didn't receive an expected inheritance, when they finally understood that their childhood years could never be set right. They grieved severed relationships, marriages that broke down or were abandoned. They grieved loss of hearing, of eyesight, of damaged or missing limbs. They grieved for hundreds, thousands of reasons—as many as the human brain could invent. And what about refugees who'd recently moved to Wilna Creek? Over the past two years, fourteen Syrian families had been sponsored by local citizens. Addie was a member of one of the sponsor groups. The Syrians had been forced to leave relatives, villages, towns, their entire culture. Some admitted to grieving openly when they left the refugee camps, even though they'd lived an uncertain and dangerous existence. They had become accustomed to being in limbo. Later, they grieved all over again when they arrived in Canada, even though they were glad to be here and to be safe.

Addie was grieving because Sybil was suffering. She was doing her best to face up to the difficulty of looking to the near future and imagining life without her dearest friend. The travellers on this journey, all the travellers—Sybil's mom, her brother and his wife, Addie, other members of Sybil's extended family—had begun a slow march toward some sort of open pit that would be created by Sybil's absence.

She thought of the letters again. A more relaxed time during her friend's "good" period—a heartbreakingly short remission.

*For the past month, I have been a lady of leisure. My blood work is good. My stamina improves daily. I firmly believe that the capacity to treat this disease lies within my own body. My responsibility to my body is to mobilize resources and allow it to cure itself.*

*Addie, it truly is a new experience not to be under the stress of work all the time. Even though I was aware of pushing myself continuously, it had never really occurred to me just what that meant. My life has changed dramatically. Absolutely no pressure—and to be honest, not a situation conducive to productivity. Some days I believe that if I were any less productive, I'd cease to be classified as human.*

Addie checked the time, irritated to realize she'd be late for an early morning meeting. This was going to be a long day. She had to leave directly from work in the afternoon to drive to Greenley because Sybil was being moved from her mother's home to the palliative care wing at the health centre. Addie had promised to be there to help her take that step. The family needed support during the transition.

Some of us really are perpetual caregivers, she thought. Do these roles land on us because they're predestined? Is there a gene that doles out instructions for caregiving? Because I have certainly noticed that caregivers make up one strip of society. The needy lean. Heavily, at times. If one caregiver turns away, a replacement will be found. Because the needy will always be . . . well, needy. But caregivers seldom turn away. We allow the leaning because we are perpetual caregivers. And we are mostly—but not always—women.

Despite being entirely worn out, Addie could not imagine herself turning away from Sybil's needs. She could not remember a time when she'd walked through her days with so little energy. Thinking about this, she recalled a Cambridge study that had moved across her desk earlier in the year: about genes playing a role in empathy. Sure enough, several months later, an Oxford study contradicted. Neither one was going to alter Addie's course at this particular moment.

She glanced at the clock one more time, scooped up her papers and, in double time, headed for the car. She checked herself, and slowed deliberately. She was thinking of Tye again. *Vaut mieux arriver en retard qu'en corbillard*, he'd once warned. Better to arrive late than in a hearse.

Madame Levesk. She still enjoyed the title. She and Tye had made an effort to learn Portuguese phrases from their building superintendent in the early years of their marriage. The man had enthusiastically shared his language, and Addie could still haul up a few words and expressions: *Como vai?*—How are you? *Adeus*—Goodbye. *Tenho saudades daqueles tempos*—I miss those times. *Desculpe*—I'm sorry.

Who was sorry? She. Tye.

Tye carried on with his life, as did she. The last time Addie phoned, a woman answered. For heaven's sake, she told herself. That could have been the voice of a neighbour, friend, cleaning woman, landlady. And so what if someone else lives with him now? Is that my business? *Qui va à la chasse perd sa place.* Move your feet, lose your seat.

Addie had dated a man named Henrik after her split with Tye, but briefly. Henrik told her he was a scientist and had to leave the city during the summer, to conduct fieldwork. His project at the time was to determine the population of mice in certain wooded areas. So he went off to do his fieldwork counting mice, taking an assistant with him. He carefully explained the procedure to Addie before he departed. He and his assistant spread peanut butter on small plywood boards that were then set on the ground around trees and undergrowth in a given area. A day later, the two returned, collected the boards and counted tiny turds so they could estimate the population and tabulate results. The woods were divided into sections, and each of these had to be accounted for, given the known range of the movement of mice.

Addie learned that peanut-butter-smeared boards weren't the only ones Henrik set out. After another absence from the city, he confessed that he was a Stompin' Tom Connors fan and made stompin' boards from plywood, and then—uninvited—presented the planed and polished boards to the singer at his dressing-room door. That is, if Tom happened to have a dressing room. Some-times he did, sometimes he didn't. Sometimes the stompin' board was presented before, sometimes after a performance. Henrik was a one-person groupie.

Their relationship ended fairly quickly. She'd confessed to Sybil that she couldn't deal with the obsessions of Henrik, whom she'd begun to think of as Plywood Man.

Now, after several years of separation, Addie still dreamed of Tye. In the most recent dream, her father had entered from the side, knowing she was upset but unable to comfort her directly. He stood with shoulders drooped, wearing slippers, a kind of shuffling position. Not at all the way she pictured her energetic father in Spain. In the dream, he would not or could not face her directly. She knew that he cared for her and Tye, and that he was sorry the marriage had not survived. The morning after the dream, she phoned her father in Sitges but didn't mention Tye or the dream. Had she done so, her father might have thought she was losing control.

Control was necessary, yes. She'd learned control long ago from her capable mother. Addie had inherited the caregiving role. It had definitely been passed on through the genes. But what was she to tell the Tuesday night group about Sybil?

Nothing, she decided. For the moment, she had enough to face on her own.

# Backroom at Cassie's

**B**efore the discussion started, they purchased drinks in the main part of the café—group decision—and carried them to the backroom. This week, there was an air of familiarity, the mood slightly jovial. Perhaps, in part, because of the extra person. At the second meeting, Tom had mentioned a friend who might be joining, and he'd been encouraged to bring him along.

Tom was wearing grey tweed, a steel-blue sweater under his jacket. His glasses needed cleaning. Allam, with ceremony, with solemnity, shook hands and repeated each name as he was introduced.

Gwen, in a shapeless black turtleneck over black pants, no jewellery, no adornments, sat at the table with her decaf latte and silently admired Cassie's centrepiece of oak leaves circling a small but brilliantly orange pumpkin. How did nature manage a colour so perfect for the waning season of fall? She wondered about Rico's response to colour. Was he attracted to orange? In her search for information, she'd read that certain parrots refused to eat any food that was red. Others refused food chopped a particular way. Like humans, parrots had idiosyncrasies, likes, dislikes. But surely they had colour vision; eyesight was their prime feature. Why would they be adorned with spectacular shades of their own if not to attract one another, mate, stake out territory, be seen? She would do more reading in that direction. Her thoughts continued to drift.

Allam, the new person, was seated beside her. She looked over and then away. He was almost the same height as Tom, who had introduced him, but Allam was slightly wider in the shoulders, bulkier. His hair was dark and thick at the back, but with whorls of grey. He slipped off his jacket and Gwen was certain she could smell autumn wind on his sleeves as he draped it over the back of the chair. She wondered how Layamon the priest would have described autumn wind in 1200. Maybe he had, and another chronicle was lying in a monastery somewhere in England or France, still undiscovered.

Addie was looking around at the others and thinking, Let's stretch our boundaries, push into ever-widening circles. She liked the way Allam joined in with a tone of earnestness that could not be feigned. Each word spoken as if it was of vital importance and equal to every other word. She wondered if anything Allam expressed would ever be considered lightweight. Probably not— but then she thought better of this. Why wouldn't he have lightweight thoughts, the same as anyone else? She wondered if he was from Syria. She didn't recognize him from the sponsoring group with which she was affiliated, or from any social gathering at which new Syrian families had been present. Not that she'd attended many. At the last, held at a church hall, she'd watched five or six children laugh and shout as they took turns riding a bicycle in circles around a small courtyard. Inside, she'd spoken with a group of women who surrounded her, ambushing her with questions. They were perpetually trying to make sense of new ways of doing almost everything. Addie was recognized as a problem-solver, partly because she'd managed to persuade the hospital to hire two Syrians: a man, a woman. They were doing basic jobs—laundry and kitchen—but they had full-time hours, a foot in the door. *Four* feet in the door.

Hazzley, delighted to have a sixth member seated at the round table, was reminded of the weekend crossword: *idiolect, speech habits peculiar to a particular person.* She listened closely to Allam's purposeful pronunciation. "I am honoured to be part of this company," he announced as they took their seats. And from that moment, he referred to the group as "the company." No one thought of themselves as a member of a company, but no one objected, either.

Company of Good Cheer, Tom said to himself. Or more correctly, Order of Good Cheer. He called up history, Champlain's tedious and difficult winters at Port-Royal in the early 1600s. Champlain—or someone in his company—must have come up with L'Ordre de Bon Temps to fend off bad times, sad times, confinement magnified to a state that could lead to madness. Alleviated, supposedly, by the bountiful supply of moose and woodland caribou and small game; by storytelling, singing and merriment after the meal. Maybe those men four hundred years ago had a handle on events in life that were worthy of celebration. Maybe there was that much contrast between cheer and the stark conditions that threatened survival.

Tom was feeling cheered for another reason: the day's transactions at Rigmarole. After some delay, the couple he'd contacted about the papier mâché chair had arrived that morning and purchased both chair and tray, two substantial sales. He was sorry Allam had not been present to see the appreciation on their faces. He wondered now if his friend would pull out an interesting fact or two for this group—this company. The man had an unending supply.

Chiyo was thinking, Tragic hero, *Letters from Iwo Jima*. The new member of our "company" is about the same age as Ken Watanabe. Allam has tragedy written all over him, but he's not a brooding presence. She and Spence had gone to see the brooding Watanabe in the recent film *Bel Canto*. Some scenes were difficult to watch. When violence was portrayed, she closed her eyes.

A company, Gwen said to herself. A pandemonium of parrots. She knew how much racket one parrot could make. No surprise that a company of parrots was also known as a pandemonium. Maybe someday, she would be fortunate enough to see and hear a company of parrots in their natural habitat.

Not very likely.

She had nothing to contribute. She waited for the discussion to begin and looked to Hazzley, who was ready to take up the reins of leadership.

"We're glad to have *your* company," Hazzley told Allam. "Tom probably told you that the reason we meet is because all of us have experienced loss of some kind recently. Grief in our lives. Though that's not the only topic we discuss. We talk about anything, everything."

Allam nodded. "Yes, Toe-mas has explained."

"Do you live in this area, Allam?" This was Addie.

"Close enough to walk," he said. "But tonight I am in the car with Toe-mas. I have been in Wilna Creek not yet one year, and I live with my daughter's family. They arrived three years past, and together we rent a house. The house is having an extra bedroom, even for me. Someday I will have my own place. I can't forever live with my daughter. Of course, she would not ask me to leave." He tossed his head back and laughed as if the idea were preposterous.

"At my daughter's, we have more space than we have known before. I was in a refugee camp in Turkey, near the border. I was sponsored by my daughter, who left Syria before me. She went with her family, also through Turkey." Allam shrugged. "Life is good now, but in the past, not so much. And we don't forget the people left behind. In camps—thousands, hundreds of thousands. In Lebanon, close to one million Syrian people are registered with

UNHCR, the agency for refugees." He stopped. "Many more would leave if there was a way of doing this."

This was more information than he'd previously shared. Perhaps Tom hadn't asked the right questions. But he had respected Allam's privacy, believing that a man said what he had to say when ready to speak. And hadn't Allam also respected Tom's privacy? The two men did not approach subjects head-on. Information was gleaned in small bits, like the stories about their fathers. Knowledge was built incrementally. Sometimes facts were given, sometimes not. And yet, knowledge was what Allam was all about. Before his life changed in ways he couldn't have imagined.

"In Syria, people disappeared," Allam was saying, his voice rising. "People I knew most of my life. Not seen again. During the worst fighting, when I was in Aleppo, we heard rumours about a body lying face down in the street. Or maybe three bodies in sprawl somewhere. Someone saw this, or spied through ruins of a building or through a doorway before running to get away. Rumours spread house to house, one family to another. The bodies disappeared. Some were never found. Many in our area were killed when barrel bombs were dropped from helicopters. No one was safe. My grandchildren stopped going to school. We had no electricity, no running water. People left quietly in the night. They passed through checkpoints, sometimes paying much money, and escaped to another country. My daughter and her family arrived at safety. I was glad when word came to me from Turkey."

There was a long pause, and everyone sat quietly, waiting.

"My wife," he said softly. "Killed when a bomb destroyed the building where she visited to help a neighbour. Her body was one that disappeared. Before my daughter left the country. Now my wife does not exist. We gave up our hope of finding—as you say—the remains of her." He looked at no one. He stared straight ahead. "After that, there was nothing left in that place for me."

Hazzley saw effort, intention. He had spoken these words of loss before and stowed them away. As he did now. Deep sadness, private place, private space. But he had shared that much, and shared with strangers. Hazzley thought of the capacity, the reservoir each person carried inside. She turned the idea over in her mind. With no warning, up from the deep well, up from the reservoir came grief.

Allam broke his own silence, his voice strong again.

"My daughter is speaking English," he said. "She is speaking well because she studied English in university, before the war. Now, in our new country, she works, but she reads at the noon meal or after her children are in bed. She and friends at her work talk about books they borrow and lend. She told me about a book by a Canadian woman. A friend gave her stories to read about one family. In the stories, when a man dies, after the funeral service the women roll down the hill by the graveyard. Not the men—only women, when one of their men dies. Each woman lies flat and crosses her arms over her chest and rolls. Over hard earth and rock and stone and sticks, whatever is there.

"Sometimes I think of that story my daughter told me from the book. I would feel better some days if I could do something like that. Better than having no one to bury, better than having hope that dies. I am sorry." He looked around the table and shrugged. "I am sorry to be saying sad things. Maybe when the women roll down the hill in the story, also they laugh. Or they cry. This is not something I have seen with my two eyes, and maybe it is rare and maybe it is invented. I try to imagine a good storyteller writing this. My daughter told me and now I share with you."

He smiled and the others smiled, too, each creating a picture, each imagining the ritual, finding the nearest slope—if the graveyard didn't have a hill of its own—and rolling, whatever the season, whatever the weather.

"I'd like to read that book," said Gwen, speaking softly and for the first time this evening. "Next time we're here, will you tell me the title?" As if someone else had made the request, she stared at the pumpkin again.

"Yes."

"I'd like to roll down a hill," said Hazzley, thinking of what such an act would release. She would get rid of the bottles, then find a hill and roll down. Or roll the bottles down. That would be the end of them. Except there'd be broken glass at the bottom of the hill, a lot of glass. Not a solution after all.

"Sounds like a great ritual," said Addie, thinking that sadness imposed by grief would be heavily tinged with relief while rolling down a hill. "I'd like to meet the woman who started this."

"This ritual, these women in the story," said Allam, "they give strength one to the other. There is a place in the world for ritual. Not everything is a bad story, sad story. I know we must look ahead, not forever behind.

"Another ritual I have learned—not about humans—is the dance of the cranes. In Hokkaido, red-crowned cranes were hunted until on the edge of extinct. Is this understood? On the edge?" The others nodded, and he carried on. "In the last century in the north part of Japan, only thirty of these beautiful creatures remained. Now they are protected, valued, hunted no more. When the numbers became bigger, the old meaning of cranes came back for the people, for the culture of that place. Beauty, long life. The dance of one pair of cranes declares territory, but the dance also makes the cranes strong, one to another."

"I hope to see dancing cranes someday," said Chiyo. "I've never been to Japan, though it's the land of my ancestors. Plenty of ritual in that country, I'm sure." She paused for a moment. "Here's something that isn't exactly ritual. Or maybe it is. About a week after my mother died, I was home by myself. People had come and gone and the funeral was over, and I was in the living room alone and sun was shining through the window and I lay down on the floor in the middle of the room and curled up and wept."

"You did that?" said Hazzley. "I did exactly the same—though I didn't plan to tell anyone. After Lew died, when everyone was gone and I was alone, I wandered around the house for a while and kept thinking of what people had said at the funeral: that he'd had a good life, a useful life. He'd been dead only a few days and already he was being summed up. And what if I didn't agree? There are so many facets to a person's life, so many incidents and turns and adventures and insights and loves and joys and likes and dislikes and regrets and embarrassments—well, now I'm out of breath. But how can we choose 'good' or 'useful' as if together those two adjectives make up a life? Finally, trying to put this all together, I wrapped a blanket around myself and curled up on the floor in the family room and cried my eyes out."

Chiyo and Hazzley looked to the others. Gwen was nodding. She had something else to say. "I cried so hard when my boys—the twins—left after the funeral," she said, "I stayed on the floor the entire afternoon." She did not say that there had been days when the only feeling she had was the recognition that her life energy had gone out of her. She had been deserted by her emotional self.

This was Gwen's first mention of children, let alone twins, but no one had a chance to comment because Tom jumped in. "The floor was hard," he said. "There were moments when I felt like doing that, but the floor was merciless for these brittle bones." He had stood at the window and cried for Ida and for himself, but he didn't mention that. Nor did he mention that when he cried, tears flowed only from his left eye. One more condition to report to his ophthalmologist, along with the occasional difficulties he was having now with depth perception.

"You know something?" said Hazzley. "It makes me feel better to hear that others have done the same. But what on earth is comforting about lying on the floor? The act, I suppose. The prostration of self. The giving over. The discomfort. The abandonment to grief. Comforting in some way. But done privately in our culture. Not *actually* visible to others. Not like rolling down a hill. Though I suppose one could roll down a hill when no one else is around."

Allam slid back in his chair, watching, listening.

"There are so many things that aren't apparent," said Addie. "Things we keep private. Not necessarily about grief, and I don't mean to change the topic—that is, after all, what has brought us together—but . . ."

"Things that aren't apparent." This was Chiyo.

"More or less invisible. We could take this in any direction."

Gwen was thinking about how she was able to become invisible while hiding in plain sight. She still hid occasionally, even though she lived alone. She didn't actually hide, but she felt that she was hiding. Old habits. After Brigg died, after the funeral, after her sons left to go back to their families in Texas, after she'd curled up on the floor and cried herself out, she picked herself up and opened a bottle of red wine and sat on the stoop at the back of the house, where she was sheltered from prying eyes. She drank one glass of wine. Another. She smoked two cigarettes she'd blatantly lifted from a package one of her sons had purchased while staying with her. She tried to inhale. Blew smoke gracelessly into the air. No grace, no elegance, no charm. Finished the first cigarette, stubbed out the butt, lit the second. Drank a third glass of wine and felt a sense of accomplishment. An act of defiance against the dead. Dead Brigg. There was no summing him up. No sirree.

Allam looked over. The woman beside him, the woman intro-duced as Gwen, was trying to erase herself. He knew this instinc-tively.

"Let me tell you something that has been out of sight in my family," said Addie, who'd definitely decided to keep the lie about Sybil buried. Sybil was alive in Greenley, but barely, in a single room in palliative care. Rails on her bed to prevent her from falling out; family members taking turns sitting in a chair at her bedside, reading, staring out the window or falling asleep under a borrowed hospital blanket. Taking their cues from Sybil's level of consciousness. Nurses came in and out of the room. Not sadly or tragically, but not cheerily, either. They did what had to be done. Drugs were administered for pain. Addie had the feeling that all of them, including her, were managing to "support" and "sustain" Sybil. Collectively and with enormous effort, they were holding her frail self together. They reinforced her human dig-nity, her right to breathe, her right to existence, as long as these rights endured. Who would give the signal to let go? Would it come from one of them, or from Sybil herself? Maybe her friend was ready to die and they were all standing in the way, blocking her exit.

She continued, switching tracks in her mind. "Family funerals, though very much a reality, have become almost invisible in my extended family. In the past, I'd heard rumblings about unresolved disputes among my mom's relatives. Grudges. I suppose there are disputes of varying proportions in all families."

"There isn't a family I know that doesn't have a few members who don't speak to one another," said Hazzley.

"True enough," Addie said, and continued. "Relatives can make demands. Or feel they're in a position to criticize. The grudges in my mom's family started out as personal quarrels among aunts, uncles, in-laws, outlaws, even cousins, nieces, nephews. My late mother had a large number of relatives, many of whom are still alive. Here are some of the tales that were reported: a brother snubbed a sister in a Walmart parking lot; an uncle sent a letter to a brother-in-law that the recipient found insulting; a sister told her brother he smelled like boiled meat; someone offered to help put up storm windows but didn't show up; another was accused of 'ugly' behaviour when he drank too much rum at an anniversary celebration and refused to go home; an aunt flirted with her sister's husband; there was a misunderstanding about a ring. I didn't hear the entire range of behaviour. I only know that the sum of all the grudge-holding was magnified out of proportion to the initial disputes. Everyone was getting old, moving along the continuum, and no one knew how to fix things. Now when someone dies, nobody is notified. The immediate family holds a private funeral, and two or three weeks after the burial, an obituary is placed in the local paper. The relatives, including sisters and brothers, are not given the opportunity to attend or participate in mourning rituals. This has happened four times that I know of. Does this help anyone involved? Of course not. It only adds an extra layer to the existing grief."

"As an only child, I've always wished for sisters and brothers. I tell myself I'd heartily accept grudges and all," said Hazzley.

"You might want to reconsider what you wish for," said Chiyo. "One of the complaints I've heard more than a few times from participants in my classes is that out-of-town relatives who drop in for a few hours or a few days to visit are the first to criticize the primary caregivers. They go away believing they can do better but don't bother offering to share the load. They often have no idea how bereft of spirit—how bereft of energy—the responsible persons really are. Well, who knows, really? I, too, am an only child." I needed help, she thought, but I had no idea whom to ask or how to ask. I'd already been swallowed up by the role.

"I *was* lonely sometimes," said Hazzley. "Though I did have cousins. After I moved to Canada, away from my parents and their extended families, I stopped hearing about daily events." She nodded to Chiyo. "I can see how complications could arise when blood relatives live within shouting distance. Same village or town, same province, even same country."

"Grudges are not so amusing when you've heard the litany of baggage relatives tow behind them for half a century," said Addie. "Though I've laughed at some of the antics in my family. When I was a student in Montreal, I used to visit one of my favourite aunts, who lived near Dorval. She was skilled at doing crafts and started up a joint venture with her closest friend, who was considered family. They created sturdy baskets using a variety of materials, and local gift shops were happy to carry their creations. My aunt was not in great health and couldn't get out to drive, so her friend did the driving to the craft stores to purchase supplies. My aunt paid exactly half the cost of the materials, but she refused to pay half the cost of gas. There was a dispute, an actual fight, and they stopped doing crafts together, which was a great shame considering how much they enjoyed the shared activity. They remained friends and continued to see each other from time to time, but never again discussed the basket-making. That was the elephant in the room."

"Elephant in the room?" said Allam.

"A problem people don't want to talk about," Tom offered.

"Ah, the fact that is refusing to be ignored."

"What my aunt's friend didn't know was that my aunt continued to make baskets," Addie said. "She hid them away until someone else could collect them to be sold in a different set of shops. I was at her house one day when her friend arrived at the door unexpectedly. My aunt hissed at me to gather up the baskets and materials, run them down the hall and hide them on a top shelf in her bedroom closet. 'She'll never go into my bedroom,' she shouted after me. And then arranged herself to greet her friend." Addie shook her head. "What a family. Invisible funerals, invisible crafts. After that, my aunt lived in fear of being caught out by her closest friend. Even so, she carried on creating baskets for several more years."

"Fear," said Tom quite suddenly. "Fear can be hidden, out of sight ... sometimes. After 9/11, no one wanted to fly—at least not right away. My wife, Ida, said she was staying put, but I booked flights and began to take trips, several trips. I realized later that I did so in the spirit of trying to cheat death. A bad thing had happened. An unthinkable event. An unthinkable *series* of events. I told myself: I will board a plane; I will fly without fear. Could this horror possibly be repeated? I flew to visit our son, Will, in Edmonton. After that, I flew to New York to see a Rockwell exhibition at the Guggenheim. With that trip, I was showing solidarity with our American friends. But I did not fly without fear. Many of us who flew during those early days after 9/11 were frightened. But we were watchful, too. We were on the lookout for odd behaviour. In airports, in rows of seats on planes. You know what I mean? I could see others watching. Trying not to be obvious. Men were sizing each other up—including me."

"I do know what you mean," said Addie.

"I didn't fly until several years after 9/11," said Hazzley. "I lost all desire to travel."

"A whole range of feelings was experienced during that time," said Tom. "So much was public, but much was also kept private. I never discussed my feelings about this with Ida."

What he did not say was that there were other things he hadn't discussed. Nor did he say that Ida had been the most honest person he'd ever known. When he'd occasionally learned, after the fact, that he'd paid a price that far exceeded the value of an acquisition, did he tell her? No. She'd have been upset. So he'd fudged the accounts once in a while, to save himself an argument. Oh, it was all small stuff. But truth needed a break every now and then, he'd told himself. He had wanted to tell that to Ida, but the circumstances were never quite right. How would he have started such a conversation? So he told occasional lies, but only when necessary. Didn't matter; she never knew.

Or did she? Did she expect him to reveal every fib he'd ever told, no matter how tiny? One truth he was certain of was that Ida had loved him. And later? Had she loved him later in their marriage? The way he loved her? They were together many years, and they'd done all right. They'd been friends, real companions.

"I'll tell you something that wasn't obvious to me, at least not at first," said Chiyo. "And this has nothing to do with 9/11. I suppose you could call it a moment of overwhelming emotion. A few years ago, I learned that a rerun of *Snow Falling on Cedars* was coming to the repertory theatre in town. I had never seen the film—I was in my early twenties when it first came out—and asked my mom if she wanted to see it, and she surprised me by saying yes, though she rarely went out to a movie. She preferred to watch DVDs her friends brought to the house—a lot of them were films from Japan. I mean, maybe she and my dad went to movies when I was a baby, but I kind of doubt it. I did tell my mom a little about David Guterson's story because she hadn't read the novel. I knew she'd be interested, and I asked if she wanted the book from the library. But she said no; she didn't feel the need to read it in advance.

"So we went. And at the end of the movie, after the last credit rolled, neither of us was able to move. We just sat there. My mom could not rise up out of her seat. The lights came on and the other patrons wandered out, but the two of us stayed. No one came down the aisle to ask us to leave, which was a good thing because I don't know how my mom would have reacted. I believe she was physically incapable of standing during those moments. She showed no outward emotion. We just kept sitting. I'd never seen her like that before. Her feelings about those memories were so deeply hidden.

"After a long silence, my mom spoke, but she did not turn in my direction. She was staring straight ahead. 'I know some of those people,' she said. She motioned with her chin in the direction of the dark screen. 'People in that movie. Actors, extras in the crowds—do you remember the part? When the families were forced to leave their homes? Some of the people who acted in this movie were in the camp with our family. I recognize them even after all this time. Part of it was filmed in Canada. It had to be. One of the scenes was Greenwood; I know that place, old mining town. We moved there for a short time after we left the Fraser Valley at the end of the war. I think one of the boat scenes, too, was filmed in Canada. Did you see how helpless those families were when they were taken away? What were they supposed to do? They had to follow orders, just as my parents did when I was a child. We were ordered out of our home. We were allowed to take only what we could carry. That was British Columbia, where I was a Canadian citizen. But this is an American film, what we just saw, *ne?*'"

Chiyo stopped there. The credits had run up the screen quickly; she hadn't been able to spot every filming location. She looked up the information later. Her mother was correct: several Canadian locations were used. But her mother had looked so helpless sitting in semi-darkness in the theatre. Reliving what her parents had gone through. Reliving what she had gone through as a child in the camps. Small and helpless.

Addie had seen the film, as had Tom. He remembered the year, 1999. He and Ida took the train to Toronto and managed to get tickets for several films at TIFF. They were both moved by the film. They had read Guterson's book in advance. Tom had never met anyone directly related to someone who'd lived in one of the camps, and he was interested in what Chiyo had to say about her mother's reaction.

Hazzley picked up the war-movie thread.

"*Hope and Glory*. I watched that in Ottawa with my daughter, Sal. The setting was the Second World War, and the film was pretty darned accurate about capturing the experience of children in London—some children, anyway. I was young during the actual war, but for me the film evoked the years that followed, when there was so much rebuilding to do. Parts of *Hope and Glory* were amusing, downright funny, despite the seriousness of the times. Ian . . . Ian . . . the grandfather?"

"Bannen," Chiyo prompted.

"Yes, that's him. Ian Bannen as Grandfather George made me laugh out loud, every scene he was in. But you know, at the end of the film—after taking it all in—I, too, just wanted to sit there in the theatre. For a long time. Let those years wash through memory."

Chiyo was still thinking of her mother. Small. Helpless. But the image of the brown bandage, the knot at the side of her head— the death knot—slipped in and replaced the earlier image. Now it refused to let go.

"All of these," said Allam, "are good stories to hear. The stories we tell about our lives. And the lives of the ones who are gone. Everything changes when we lose someone. But we—the ones who are left—we have to choose life."

Cass came into the backroom to see if anyone wanted a refill, and Hazzley stood with glass in hand. Tom pushed back his chair. The mood shifted. Everyone decided to take a break.

As Gwen rose, a single grey hair loosed itself from among her ginger highlights and rested on the shoulder of her black turtle-neck—unnoticed by everyone except Allam and Chiyo. Allam leaned forward and delicately removed the hair, flicking it away. Gwen made no acknowledgement, but looked up at him briefly.

Cass turned back at this moment and happened to see the expression on Gwen's face.

An exchange.

I predict, Cass thought. She carried on into the café.

What Chiyo saw was an exquisite and delicate move. *Approach, step up and grasp*, she said to herself. An intimate but silent act. Two wounded people advance in very small steps.

# Wall at Your Back

GWEN

The moment she entered, she heard scrabbling, followed by sudden silence. Perhaps not terrified silence, not this time, though she wondered if she was intuiting correctly. She shut the door, aware of her presence filling the space. She heard no further movement until she walked into the family room. She turned off the radio, which she'd left on during her previous visit. Rico hopped to the front of his cage, stared, dipped his head down, up again, down.

Progress indeed.

Maybe this was the day to let him out into the room, but how? Cecilia Grand had provided no details. Gwen went back to the instruction sheet in the kitchen to ensure that nothing had been missed.

*After several days—and only if you feel confident enough—let him out of the cage for brief periods.*

She decided to get to it. She would let him out, clean the cage, change the water while he was strutting to the tune of freedom.

She walked slowly, talked slowly, opened the cage door with as little noise as possible. No fuss, no hullabaloo.

Nothing happened. She took six steps back, until she was halfway across the room. No sudden gestures; nothing to startle. Now she stood entirely still.

Rico observed every one of these actions. He dropped to the floor of his cage. He regarded her with interest, and then looked away. He hopped onto one of the lower perches and pecked listlessly at a puzzle-toy that was no longer a challenge. Crumpled paper, the half shell of a coconut, a set of interlinked plastic cups to turn. He'd already turned the cups, found and extracted the cashew in the deepest labyrinth. She'd have to hang something new, insert a fresh treat.

"Are you coming out, Rico?"

No sign.

An idea came to her. She stretched out both arms to the side, shoulder level. He made a sudden move. So sudden, she was taken by surprise. She lost her balance and rocked back on her heels. He was already perched on her lower arm; she felt his toes take hold as they gripped her right sleeve. *Opposable digits. Two toes forward, two toes back.*

He needed a place to land, and she had provided one.

She couldn't stand in the middle of the room all day. She had to prepare his chop and clean the cage. She walked slowly and deliberately in the direction of the kitchen. While moving forward, she lowered her arm and crooked it slightly, broken-wing position. Here I am, she thought. With an unlikely passenger, a parrot with a crimson tail, coming along for the ride.

In the kitchen, she sat on a chair and rested her right arm on the table. Rico worked his way sideways along her ulna/radius and stepped onto the back of her hand. The sensation of parrot feet. Soft cool pads on her skin. One of the notes on the back page of the instruction sheet read: *Rico is on his feet 24/7; feet never at rest. If a tender spot breaks down, bacteria could enter. To prevent bumblefoot, hygienic practices must be followed, especially wiping perches.*

Bumblefoot! That was all she needed.

"Don't start getting bumblefoot," she said. "I am not going to be responsible for that."

Rico glanced at her as if imparting a casual message, and then moved from hand to tabletop. Once there, he began to investigate. A pad of paper lay on the table, along with a ballpoint pen. He bent forward and grasped the pen in his beak. With natural ease, he tilted the tip of the pen toward the page. For a moment, he looked as if he intended to write a note outlining his needs. The ones she wasn't satisfying, no doubt.

Fine. Let him make his list. She got up and turned her attention to preparing fresh chop. Later, she would figure out some sort of roosting place where he could land when he left the cage.

She set a container of water on the floor, and he dropped the ballpoint and hopped down to drink. He was entirely at ease in the kitchen. When the Grands were home, he was probably in this room with Cecilia much of the day. Pooping every ten or fifteen minutes, which is what he seemed to do. She bent forward and wiped up.

"Look at me, Rico. I'm a birdkeeper. Who would have thought? Today you'll have beets and carrots in your chop. And bok choy and radish and turnip and herbs. You'll even have cherries—no pits. How about that for a treat? Along with all those supplements you get in your pellets."

Rico did look at her. She wondered what he saw.

"I'm sorry your family hasn't come home. Maybe they'll never come home. I guess I shouldn't say that. You need your family. I need mine. I have two grandchildren I rarely see. Girls. They live in Texas. Maybe I can convince my boys to start bringing them for visits. Maybe I'll fly to Texas to visit them."

Rico was behaving in a more friendly manner now. She could intuit the difference, intuit the bird. She was beginning to believe she could read his mind, his tiny brain. Or was it his behaviour she was reading?

She managed the chores efficiently; she could be quick now that she had a better grasp of what she was supposed to do. She had also noticed a large jade plant in the bay window at the end of the kitchen, and she decided she'd better do something about that. Cecilia Grand had made no mention of caring for the jade. There was no other plant in sight. The jade was spindly, rooted in a large clay pot. At that moment, a wide beam of sun shone through the window and illuminated one side of the plant, ennobling it some-how. Yes, it took on a noble look, and in that instant, Gwen saw its beauty. She poured a measure of water to the dry cracked soil, and with that nurturing gesture, she took on the care of the jade.

Rico continued to wander around the floor of the kitchen, poking his beak into corners. She brought out her sheets of paper, her mother's manuscript, and sat at the table again.

"Listen up, Rico. I'm back to Layamon. You like to listen; I know you do. Where else can such beautiful language be found? I've already told you about my mother writing this paper long ago. She was a clever woman. She was curious about the vicissitudes of history. Someday, Rico, I'm going to travel to a rocky, windy place in Cornwall called Tintagel Castle, in the land of King Arthur. My mother never got there, but I will. Yes, I will."

Rico's head pivoted at what appeared to be an awkward angle. He looked toward the ceiling and feigned indifference.

She realized, after telling Rico about Tintagel, that she did, in fact, have the money to go there. The money Brigg had been hoarding was now hers, and she could do with it what she liked.

"Okay, Rico, I've just made a decision—a big decision in your presence. Now let's get to it. In this passage, King Arthur is bat-tling the treacherous Mordred. I don't think you'll be bored. Think of the heaviness of all that armour. The knights were doomed before they stepped into it. Or however they dressed. Maybe somebody fastened it onto them, or over them, in sections."

She began to read: "They encountered . . . and smote on the

helms. Fire outsprang. Spears splintered. Shields gan shiver. Brave Arthur saw knights in their armour, drowned in the water as steel fishes, their scales like gold-dyed shields. Shafts brake in pieces. Heads were split . . . the sword at the teeth stopt."

Gwen was not a violent woman. She thought about the words "sword at the teeth stopt" and admitted that in the past, she *had* imagined, *had* considered violence. She'd imagined violence being done to her, and she'd imagined herself committing violence. But that was before, when Brigg was alive. The interminable days and nights during which she'd been fragile, close to the edge where he had pushed her. She would have—if someone had placed a sword in her hand—she would have liked to smite Brigg through his skull until the sword at his teeth stopt.

She shuddered. Let the man rest in peace. She didn't want to think of him again. Ever. But thoughts had a way of returning, whether you willed them away or not.

"'Smite' is a glorious word," she said to Rico. "Think of the act of smiting. Woodcutters, for instance, in fairy tales. Woodcutters were always poor, honest and helpful. Witches were wicked, woodcutters kind. I've always thought of woodcutters as having immensely satisfying work. If a woodcutter has an enemy, he has only to imagine a face on a block of wood and split it down the middle. All part of life, Rico. A giant soap opera is what it is, even for kind woodcutters, I expect."

Rico, unenthused, wandered away, two dark smears of droppings on the floor in his wake. If Gwen were asked to describe the colour, she'd say green-black. *He will not soil his food; he will not soil his water.* He soiled the floor instead. And the colour had been consistent since the first week of parrot sitting, so she must be doing something right.

She followed him into the family room and watched as he easily flew into his cage and stared out at her through the bars. The positioning of the cage was necessary for Rico's safety, for his *feeling* of safety. *A parrot will never rest properly in a round cage. He needs security, a wall at his back.*

"Got it," she said. She fastened the cage door. "You've had enough of the kitchen, enough of King Arthur, enough of open spaces, enough of life as a soap."

He cocked his head to the left, his preferred posture, stayed like that for a moment and said, in a calm, quizzical voice, "Whatsamattah?"

These were the first meaningful words she'd heard from him since the day he'd called out, "Save me!"

Now he was on a roll. He straightened his head and ordered, in a deeply low male voice, "Pick it up." He made beeping sounds as if punching keys on a speakerphone, and then, in her voice, in Gwen's own speaking voice, he said, "Hello," and added a word that sounded, in a different octave, like "smite."

"You—are—astonishing—Rico!"

He puffed his throat and replied with a series of clicks and whirrs as if in perpetual dial mode, this time on an old-fashioned rotary phone.

He began to eat the chop, paying her no attention. As for Gwen, she experienced the short-lived satisfaction of believing she had done something well.

November

# Remember, Remember

## HAZZLEY

**M**onday morning, her birthday, Hazzley looked out at giant flakes of falling snow, a scene of luxuriant beauty. She began to strip the bed while thinking of Guy Fawkes.

*Remember, remember!*
*The fifth of November.*

She could almost hear the chant in the street, the shrill and deliberate voices of children calling out, "Penny for the Guy?" No fireworks, no bonfires during the war years, when she was a child, but she recalled in detail the excitement of 1945. That year, her fifth birthday coincided with her father's returning home after the end of the war, a war he did not discuss. Ever.

He'd been home a couple of weeks, weary but in good spirits, assuring her that a bonfire and fireworks—her first Guy Fawkes celebration—would be held especially for her birthday. She had already tagged after a few of the local boys, up and down neighbourhood streets, while they wheeled the Guy in a broken-down pram, begging for a penny. Her family had helped with rag-and-straw stuffing and contributed a pair of oversized trousers. The boys painted the Guy's face on a stuffed paper bag that served as head. Someone's grandfather proffered a worn fedora and a pair of holey socks. Another donated scuffed boots. Hazzley's father, at the boys' invitation, added the final touches: a buffoonish Hitler moustache drawn with charcoal under the Guy's large nose, and a puny and distorted swastika on each cheek. And then, the event itself, a long procession of flaming torches through the blackest of nights.

In an open space that backed onto a row of bombed-out flats and amid great cheers, the effigy burned atop a pyramid of wood scraps, boxes, crates, old mattresses and broken furniture. For days, the people in the surrounding area had been tossing these onto the growing heap. When Hazzley thought of it now, she realized that the pile must have been fifteen or twenty feet high, the blazing fire even higher, flames shooting straight up into the night air. A memorable birthday, yes.

After the fire was lit, after potatoes were thrown into coals around the edges, the fireworks that had been purchased with "pennies for the Guy" were set off. Empty milk bottles had been lined up to hold rockets; Catherine wheels were tacked in place; there were Roman candles, bangers and squibs. Ah, it was all so much fun. Especially the Catherine wheels, spinning in a frenzy at the end. Sometimes an occasional wheel disappointed and fizzled out, but that still wasn't quite the end because the potatoes, now black and charred lumps, were prodded from the coals with gloved hands and peeled—a mess of dirty potato skin and ash, to be eaten with enormous pleasure. Of course, Guy Fawkes Day and the bonfires went on year after year, but Hazzley's first was the standout memory, never to be repeated in quite the same way.

FROM THE SECOND-STOREY WINDOW, she saw that the falling snow was now caught in an updraft, as if released from earth rather than sky. Surely this small storm wouldn't amount to much so early in November.

Having thought of Guy Fawkes in postwar London, she remembered a partially gutted building not far from her childhood home, a three-storey affair that had been hit by a German bomb. Any surviving occupants had been moved, the remains of the building condemned and cordoned off. But this did not stop her and one of her pals, a girl named Dorothy, from squeezing through a barricade at the rear. After crawling through a shattered window and climbing unstable stairs to get to the top floor—steps missing or swinging from a single nail—she and Dorothy created their own secret space within a ruined kitchen. Here, inside a cupboard that still had doors, they stored their prized finds: a tortoiseshell comb studded with rhinestones, two teacups, a cracked plate, one bent spoon, one partly melted knife, a doll's head attached to its shoulder and left arm, two pieces of twisted shrapnel (one of which had German markings). Much of the roof was destroyed, and rain frequently dampened their play area. One afternoon there was a light snowfall, which caused the blackened kitchen floor to sparkle magically, but only for a moment because the snow melted so quickly. It was a wonder the whole structure hadn't collapsed on top of them. Their parents didn't know they were there, and how would they? Hazzley and Dorothy were entirely free to play in the bombed-out streets.

Where was Dorothy now? Last time Hazzley had seen her was when they were thirteen years old and Dorothy came to say good-bye because her family was moving to Liverpool.

THE WIND HAD INTENSIFIED, and snow was slanting to the left. Wind and snow on her birthday. Not a real winter storm—not like the ones in January that went on for days. Prior to real storms, she stocked the pantry shelves and stayed indoors. When it was necessary to go out again, she and her neighbours emerged like bears stumbling from dens. The roads were always a mess of ice and slush, and Hazzley was not fleet of foot in those conditions. Even though she wore boots with grips and rubber soles.

She also knew that this early snow wouldn't last. Rarely was there snow on her birthday. As of today, she was officially seventy-eight. She never asked herself, as she sometimes heard others say, Where did the years go? She knew exactly where the years had gone. She could call up various periods of her life in stark detail. Whether the memories were accurate . . . well, that was another issue.

She looked sharply toward the doorway to the hall as if glimpsing the sudden movement of someone close by, but no one was there. Her past, probably. Her past was all around.

Slightly unnerved, she sat on the edge of her mattress. Lew had been dead for three years. She had mourned grievously immediately after his death. A part of her still mourned. There were unresolved issues during the last part of Lew's life—she couldn't deny that—but she had loved him. One of her widowed friends told her, soon after Lew died, "You know, Hazzley, it took two years for my brain to start functioning fully again after my husband died." At the time, Hazzley didn't know what her friend was talking about.

She had a better understanding now. The ashes, for instance. Lew had been vague in his instructions about what to do with them after his body was cremated. "Just spread them somewhere," he had told Hazzley and Sal. He was laughing; those were the good times. "Throw them into Spinney's Ravine, or into a fast-moving creek that leads to a river that leads to an ocean."

The ashes, after the funeral service, had come home with Hazzley. First in a plastic bag. After that, they went into a ceramic urn she and Sal chose together. It seemed preposterous that a body could thus be reduced, and though she hadn't exactly decided what to do with the cremains—she hated the word—the urn sat on the floor in a corner of her dining room, behind the door.

On a day when she was particularly stressed, she felt she had to have some part of Lew with her when she went out to deal with a lawyer and all the demands that had to be met. She opened the urn and looked around for a small container. A near-empty plastic pill bottle was on a shelf in the kitchen, and she grabbed at that. Lew had been prescribed prednisone for something or other; she couldn't remember what. An inflammatory flare-up of some sort, probably. Hazzley dumped the few remaining pills in the trash and filled the prednisone bottle with some of Lew's ashes. She kept the bottle in her purse when she went out that day and forgot to remove it when she returned. Part of Lew travelled with her for weeks until she remembered to dump his ashes back into the urn. She was not about to tell Sal any of this.

Another day, she backed her car into the closed garage door. Five days later, she left the driver's door open and backed out again. Two trips to the dealership in one week; her brain had deserted her.

While at home one evening, she turned on the hot water tap in the kitchen and left the room to get a clean tea towel from the linen closet. The plug was in the drain. Water filled the sink and spilled over the counter and onto the floor. She was oblivious because she'd been sidetracked. She returned to the kitchen ten minutes later and slipped in a layer of water that covered the entire floor. She went down fast, falling sleekly, smoothly. What a surprise, she thought, as her body went into its reflexive curl. The fall *was* a surprise, the way accidents are—a slippery-eel surprise.

She didn't break a bone, but she might have. She worked for hours sopping up the mess.

Her capacity to concentrate had been shredded. She was dealing with the after-effects of death. She didn't want to read, interact with people, do much of anything. There were days when she didn't want to get up in the morning because what was the point? She attended a political meeting just before the local election and had to clench her fists while she fought off the impulse to stand up and shout, "Don't you realize that my husband died only a few months ago?!" She didn't stand up and shout, but she wanted to. She was angry. She was indignant.

Sal and the grandchildren did not give up on her, even though they were in another city and busy with their lives. The first Thanksgiving after Lew died, she drove to Ottawa. She planned to arrive at Sal's an hour before Sunday's dinner was to be held. She planned to stay overnight and return home Monday.

When she drove onto her daughter's street and approached the house, she broke down without warning. She began to cry—she was sobbing—and put her foot to the gas. She kept on driving and passed the house, slowing to a crawl only when she was on another street. She circled the block. Mopped at her eyes. She tried again. Drove past, still crying. This was the first year Lew had not been with the family for the Thanksgiving celebration. Hazzley pulled onto a street several blocks away and parked the car and wiped her eyes and blew her nose and sat there for ten minutes, trying to compose herself. The third try was successful, and she parked in Sal's driveway and rang the back doorbell. No one seemed to have seen her car go by the house twice. No one mentioned her slightly reddened eyes.

When she was home again, she mustered enough energy to sound normal when Cass called to see how she'd made out at Sal's. But Cass wasn't buying normality.

"There's more, Hazzley. Something you're not saying."

"No, not at all." But Hazzley broke down again, and Cass was on her doorstep in thirty minutes. She'd brought a giant pizza and a bottle of wine.

"Rice will pick me up later," she said. "We're going to sit here and eat and have a glass of wine, and you're going to tell me what's going on."

And Hazzley did tell her. About how she'd fallen apart and then pulled herself together, doing her best so she wouldn't upset the entire family.

But every one of them, she'd told Cass, had been aware of the person absent from the Thanksgiving table.

HAZZLEY FOUND HERSELF watching more TV in the evening. She was thankful for Trevor Noah in his new role as host of *The Daily Show*. He could make her laugh out loud, and she needed laughter. There were times, she admitted, when it was difficult to decipher the absurd, as if absurdity itself had been coded.

During the daytime, she made an effort to be at her desk. Her contacts in the magazine industry continued to send work. She stared at herself in the mirror one morning and said, "Hazzley, this is the life you have, and you are going to move it forward. Alter the fine points, if necessary. Allow yourself to embrace your future life. Whatever it's going to be." She didn't totally believe she could, but she knew she was gathering her forces. She carried on.

Part of another year went by before she posted the notice on Marvin's bulletin board. Now she was emptying the house. But only three rooms, so far. Maybe she should move after all. Give up this big house and live in an apartment. A small condo, perhaps, with all rooms on one level.

Not yet. No, she would take her time. Fortunately, Cass had not been to the house since Hazzley had begun to empty the rooms. Usually, they met before or after hours at the café. If Cass did find out, she'd want to help. Define the problem and fix it. Fix Hazzley. But Hazzley was trying to repair herself.

THE SNOW HAD STOPPED abruptly; the yard was cushioned in a layer of white. Hazzley thought of a poem she'd once read, though she could not remember the name of the poet. She wondered if Tom might know. At the first meeting of the company, he'd said quietly, as if hoping no one would hear, that he wrote a bit of poetry. He'd quoted Keats at the same meeting. Maybe he would recognize these lines:

*Snow drifts to the trees, settles*
*And I think of you, my love*

*As I look over the*
*White and soundless world.*

Whose love could be thought of? Were days and nights of love over for her? She thought of her unplanned tryst with Meiner in Toronto. "Tryst" must be Middle English, she thought. Or maybe French, from *triste*—but that would mean sad, sorrowful, glum. She kept dictionaries both upstairs and down, and she smiled when she looked up the origin of the word and was surprised to have to consider an appointed place in hunting.

She gathered the heap of bed linens into her arms and headed down to the laundry room. She had put a load of towels in the dryer earlier, and she pulled these out now and folded them, wrapping a bath sheet around her shoulders so the warmth of it wouldn't be wasted. While at Marvin's on Saturday, she had purchased two blueberry scones for her birthday, and she planned to heat one and lace it with melting butter. She would add a chunk of Dubliner cheddar. She'd work on her crossword and the daily sudoku and eat breakfast while she stood at the kitchen counter. She would relax over strong continental coffee. There was nothing else to compete for her attention on this day. No obligations, no appointments. Sal would call later; the grandchildren had sent cards. Hazzley's plan was to have a quiet day at home. She might drag a rocking chair into one of the empty rooms and stare out at the snow before it melted away.

She and Cass should sign up for dance classes again. They'd

enjoyed the swing lessons and had talked about taking line dancing next. One new thing Hazzley had learned was that in Wilna Creek, there were plenty of people who wanted to dance.

Tomorrow, the *company* would meet again. She refused to think of it as *her* company. Knowing that any topic might erupt, she wondered what would come up for discussion. And wasn't that the attraction? No one, beforehand, had any idea of the direction of conversational flow. What was helpful was having others around. Others who had been through similar experiences and understood implicitly why each of them was present. Comfortably so.

# A Small Party

Tuesday evening, Hazzley arrived early to check the table and chairs in the backroom. Not necessary because Cass, with her usual efficiency, had seen to everything. Cass was good at organizing, directing. She had also fancied up and was wearing a double strand of pearls over a sparkly top. Her late father was a jeweller in town after the war, and he'd designed the necklace himself, a gift to Cass's mother, Georgie. The pearls were Cass's now; they'd been modelled after pearls owned by Queen Elizabeth and were known fondly, in the family, as "Lilibet's pearls." Cass's mother and Queen Elizabeth were born the same day, April 21, 1926. Georgie had been invited to Buckingham Palace for the Queen's eightieth birthday luncheon twelve years ago, but that venture had not turned out as expected.

Cass returned to the front of the café, and Hazzley followed. A circular cake with creamy icing, candied lemon wedges artfully arranged across the top, had pride of place on a shelf behind the counter. The cake was on a pedestal plate under a clear dome. Unusual at this time of evening, because cakes and pastries in the café generally sold out by mid-afternoon. Cass reached over, lifted the cake and carried it to a side table in the backroom, where she'd already placed dessert plates, forks and wineglasses.

"Fabulous! What's the occasion?"

"You're joking, right? The cake is for you! It's your birthday."

"That was yesterday."

"I know that. But I didn't see you yesterday. I thought your birthday would be a good excuse to serve dessert to the group tonight. Tom will be pleased."

"I think he's been suppressing his longing for cake. He'll love this one, for sure. What kind? Lemon?"

"Hold your curiosity, madam. Leave room for one surprise."

"All right, all right. But you're the one who always says: 'Be not ignorant of any thing in matters great or small.' I love Lilibet's pearls, by the way. Always have. They're great for a celebration."

"Thank you, my friend. Thank you."

"You know," Hazzley said, "these little celebrations make us pause and reflect, don't they? Whether we want to or not. Yesterday, I got to thinking about my childhood. After the war, in 1945, a Victory Party was held on our street. I wasn't quite five, but I can still haul details out of the past. The entire neighbourhood was involved in this huge street party. Wooden tabletops were set up on supporting trestles. All of us—children of every age—sat facing one another. And our mums, bless them, laid white tablecloths over those joined tables that stretched right down the middle of the road in the shape of a long, narrow V. Maybe the women had been saving their precious linens to unfurl at the end of the war. I know they had hopes of normalizing our lives and theirs. Everyone longed for ordinary, and ordinary we got! Fish-paste sandwiches. But for dessert, vanilla ice cream scooped out of a deep tub. What a treat! The best part was the cake. That's what we wanted most, even on rations, even if it had to be cake with no eggs. I'll never forget the cake. As I gobbled it up, I looked over at the mums, who were standing together in a subdued group once the children were settled. Every one of them holding a precious cup of tea—tea was rationed, you know, right through to 1952. And there was my mum, crying silently in the midst of this scene, tears rolling down her cheeks. For the sheer relief, I suppose, of the war being over.

"A few months after the Victory Party, my dad returned home. After that, we celebrated my first Guy Fawkes Day, also my fifth birthday, on November 5, 1945. Bonfire day! I've told you about that already."

"You have. It's wonderful that you remember the celebrations. But you remember the bombing, too. You've told me about that."

"When I returned to London with Lew ten years ago, we visited the Churchill War Rooms, the underground complex that was once the command centre. Every detail was interesting to us: a combination of Cabinet War Rooms and the Churchill Museum. We were acting the part of tourists and took our time because we wanted to read every word of explanation that accompanied the displays. But at one point, while listening to sound effects of the period, a chill went through my body. I feel it even now. What I was hearing was the sound of a doodlebug, the V-1, the buzz bomb. I was completely unnerved and thought I'd have to run out of the museum. The recapturing of sound from the past was just too much. It was as if an airplane was flying close at that very moment. Abruptly, all noise ceased before the bang was heard. We knew, during the war, that if you were lucky enough to hear the bang, you were safe. In that command centre, my body remembered the reflexes it had learned, even though I was very young when doodlebugs fell on the city. At that time, the V-2 rockets were still to come. It's difficult to bring this back, even now."

"We won't discuss it further. Tonight we are celebrating your day-old birthday. The others will be here soon, and we'll have a toast. Is everyone coming?"

"As far as I know."

"How about Addie? Is she okay?"

"I'm not surprised you've noticed a change," said Hazzley. "I've been wondering myself. She's been tired out. Last two meetings, I was certain she'd fall asleep at the table. Still, she keeps showing up. She wants to be here. I'm just careful about intruding, you know? Don't want to push hard. Don't want to push at all."

"Grief can be unrelenting," said Cass. "We never know when it will take us by surprise. I've been through this and so have you. Maybe the loss of her friend is eating her up."

"All the more reason to have people around her. People who care. And have you considered this? When we lose someone close, we begin to think of our other losses. When Lew died, I mourned my parents all over again. My mum, my dad."

Chiyo arrived just then. "Something special going on?"

"Hazzley's birthday," Cass said. "I'll join in for a bit of cake, if no one minds. Rice told me he'd help out in the café. If things aren't too busy, he'll bring his guitar back here and play some jazz for us later."

"Sounds great," said Chiyo. "I've heard him play and he's wonderful. Happy birthday, Hazzley. We're due a celebration."

She took her coat to the side of the room and hung it on a hook while thinking of friends and relatives whose birthdays she and her mom had celebrated during her childhood. They'd be invited for lunch, maybe dinner. Everyone ate a hearty meal: beef teriyaki over rice, maybe stir-fry with noodles. Sometimes salmon tempura was on the menu, if fresh salmon could be found and, more crucially, afforded. After everyone had eaten, the table was cleared. The men and boys went outside or into the living room, while the women and girls washed the dishes and stacked them in the cupboards. As soon as the place was cleaned up, the Japanese teapot was pulled out. Green tea, *ocha*, was poured. Instead of plain green tea, *genmaicha*—popcorn tea—was sometimes served. That was Chiyo's favourite because roasted brown rice was added to give it a nutty flavour. But that wasn't all. Colourful bowls were filled to the brim with various kinds of Japanese crackers, *arare*.

Sometimes a tray of leftover sushi was unwrapped. Dishes were set out—smaller dishes than those used for the main meal—and everyone drifted back to the table. All of that before the birthday cake was served.

Where were those other girls now? For sure, they wouldn't have lived with their mothers until they were forty.

The rest of the company had arrived, Addie looking weary, downcast. She cheered up when she saw that they'd be celebrating Hazzley.

Cassie brought matches to light the candles, one for each decade of Hazzley's life. "She'll have eight the year she turns eighty," she said. "This year and next, she gets seven."

"Do not rush to push me forward," said Hazzley. She recited:

*Because the birthday of my life*
*Is come, my love is come to me.*

She blew out the candles with one breath, and the company applauded. Thick slices of cake were served. Wine was poured, a toast given, and then Cass returned to the front of the café to help Rice.

"Was that Rossetti you were quoting?" Tom wanted to know. He'd finished his slice and come back to Hazzley for seconds.

"Christina, yes. I don't know why those lines came to mind. Strange, really, the remnants of other times, other periods in our lives, the way they're linked in our brains after half a century."

Allam had picked up his wineglass and was moving toward the round table where they usually sat. The others remained standing, and he seemed surprised by this. He balanced his wine in one hand, cake plate and fork in the other, and returned to the group.

"Does everyone eat standing up?" he said to Gwen.

"People who live alone, maybe. I do, some of the time," she added. This came out awkwardly because she wasn't used to being part of the main conversation. She wouldn't have dared explain the complex emotions that smouldered when she sat down to eat in her kitchen and stared at the empty chair across from her. She had never wanted to look Brigg in the eye.

She could look this man in the eye, though. This man who had set down his drink and now stood beside her, eating Hazzley's birthday cake. She could look him in the eye because he seemed to receive whatever was in the room. This was difficult to explain, or even to understand. He didn't send out from himself; he took in. When the company met, he sat next to her at the round table. Everyone took the same place on Tuesdays, because of habit or routine, or for comfort, or whatever the human explanation.

"In Syria," Allam told her, "we sit for a long time at small tables in our favourite coffee house. Drink tea or coffee, smoke from the water pipe—*argeelah*. Sometimes we play cards or chess or backgammon. Sometimes we discuss books or history, whatever is going on in the world. For all this, we do not stand—we sit. I miss that. The coffee house was a place where I met my friends. Also, there are famous cafés, especially one in the old city of Damascus, where a *hakawati* in traditional dress sits on a platform and reads through a microphone the stories of ancient times. The way the story is read and told is a special art, a way of telling that makes people want to listen to tales of sultans and warriors, of the Baibars, of the Mongol invasions. Now"—Allam shrugged—"with war, it is not easy to say if storytelling carries on in public places."

Gwen was thinking of the many hours she'd spent at a table right here at Cassie's, reading the tales of King Arthur. Never looking up. A lone activity. An activity of aloneness.

Hazzley had overheard Allam speak about storytelling cafés. "I hope the practice doesn't come to a halt, Allam. I'm also thinking that this might be a good magazine topic. Especially as many Syrians have come here to live over the past few years. All cultures have traditions of sitting around the fire, the hearth, the table, the stone circle, passing stories from generation to generation. But the cafés you describe sound unique. Maybe I'll suggest this to the managing editor I usually work with. As for standing for meals, I confess that I'm one of those who stands at the kitchen counter to eat breakfast while watching the birds in the backyard. These days, I seem to stand more than sit, though I don't give either much thought. After Lew died, I guess I began to stand for meals while doing my daily puzzles. No one to talk to, you know?"

Hazzley thought of breakfast that morning. How she had looked out and felt an enormous rush of gratitude for being alive. This had come on so suddenly: she was grateful for being able to open the window, breathe the November air, watch the sun's rays sparkle on the remaining patches of snow. She followed the flight of chickadees as they darted back and forth, trees to feeder, feeder to trees. She resolved to keep a good supply of black oil sunflower seeds on hand for the feeder, right through to next spring.

Addie spoke up. "I eat standing up while I look out over the city," she said. "From my condo window on the fifth floor. But I sit when I drink tea. Most of the time. Not always. Sometimes." She couldn't seem to decide. Occasionally, she ate a can of tuna while facing the lone smoker who was always on the balcony of the building opposite. Addie didn't tell that to the company.

Tom said he ate standing up sometimes. He preferred to sit, though he could hold his plate in one hand, fork and serviette in the other, and still manage. He kept an eye on the neighbourhood from the side window of his kitchen, and the table allowed the view; that's why he preferred to sit. He didn't mention that he sat in what used to be Ida's chair. As a matter of fact, he still considered it to be Ida's chair.

Chiyo never stood to drink or eat because she was always reviewing schedules, updating records, keeping track of her hours, replying to student queries, answering texts. She ate with her phone at hand. "Sitting is definitely my mother's influence. She'd have had a fit if she saw me standing to eat."

Addie was wondering what her own mother would have made of standing for meals. If she'd been around to comment, she'd have had something to say about digestion, relaxation. Her mother had connected just about everything back to health, physiology, good body practices.

Hazzley changed the subject and suggested that since she was in front of her computer much of the time anyway, maybe it would be a good idea to compile a list of people's addresses and phone numbers or emails, whichever way they preferred to be contacted. She could distribute the list next week. Only if everyone agreed.

Everyone agreed.

"Great," she said. "I'll take the information home and give out a contact sheet next Tuesday."

Rice entered the backroom just then, and Cass was right behind him. This time, everyone sat and pushed back their chairs and fell silent while Rice played his jazz guitar. Something recognizably Django-like. Soft and mellow, but at the same time, plunky and fast. The melody was a favourite of Hazzley's and had been a favourite of Cassie's mom's. Both Cass and Hazzley were thinking of that.

# Ways of Listening

TOM

In the afternoon, Tom carried the bronze sculpture of the geese into his store. He set it in a prominent place, with no plans to sell. He liked the piece and wanted to be around it during the workday. It reminded him of his early days with Ida in their first apartment. The surface was sleek and smooth, with an attractive brown patina. Tom positioned the sculpture to face the entrance, hoping to create the illusion that the pair were about to take flight, through the door and up into the sky.

Allam arrived and expressed appreciation. "This is beautiful," he told Tom. "For me, it is also symbolic of my new country."

The two men walked around to the shed behind Rigmarole and opened the double doors. Tom flattened the rear seats of the Jeep and they began to load: bedside table, desk lamp, chair, child's dresser, storage baskets, radio, collapsible shelving unit, two cast-iron frying pans, a box of dishes and a hall runner.

Everything crammed in tightly. The men had two stops to make.

At the first intersection, Tom paused for a red light. A man holding an empty Tim Hortons cup in his left hand, a sign in his right, ran into the road with determined agility and threaded his way between two lanes of cars, cup extended. He was wearing a white hoodie with a fifties peace symbol painted across his back. The hood, more grey than white, was pulled up, and a single brown antler jutted out horizontally above his forehead. The stuffed cloth antler was held in place by the hood itself, or perhaps by an out-of-sight headband. His printed sign read: Help a Dear in Your Headlights. Tom wondered what Allam thought of this, but Allam, though always observant, remained silent. As they drove on, he continued to point the way until Tom pulled up to a small warehouse, nothing on the outside to indicate that people were within.

Tom was somewhat familiar with the area because he'd once purchased items stored in a locker along the same stretch. A woman in her nineties had hired a mover to store some of her furniture in the locker when she downsized, sold her house and moved to a retirement home. After a year and a half, she faced reality and admitted to herself that the extra furniture was never going to fit into her new quarters. She offered Tom first choice of the stored belongings. He purchased six or seven items: a lap desk she had used in her youth, a smoker table with a hinged door, an elegant nineteenth-century mirror. The woman had told him how difficult it was to part with these items, even though she hadn't laid eyes on them for some time. She added, with sly humour, "But not one of my friends has towed a U-Haul behind their hearse, and I guess I won't, either." She and Tom had a great laugh over that. He remembered her well; he remembered her spirit, her energy, her dose of reality.

He followed Allam now as they left the car. The entrance to the warehouse was in semi-darkness, but voices could be heard—the chattering voices of children. A bright light shone at the end of a long corridor. Allam continued on to double doors that opened into a gymnasium-sized room that had high windows covered in wire mesh. Long, low tables had been set up at one end. In the centre, tables of standard height were arranged irregularly. Seated at the low tables, some kneeling on their chairs, were about a dozen children between the ages of four and eight. A meagre supply of materials was stored on open shelves along one side of the room. Paper, paints, pastels, crayons and coloured pencils had already been carried to the tables. The children were eagerly and earnestly bent over their creations. Two adults, a young man and woman, circled the room, moving from table to table, offering encourage-ment. Everyone called out greetings to Allam and then settled again after Tom was introduced.

Allam swept his hand toward the shelves. "We are always trying to raise funds for supplies for the children. Toys and games, also." He guided Tom to the far end of the room, where there was a doorway that led to a galley kitchen. He poured hot sweet tea into small glasses, and Tom sat across from him at a corner table.

"Is this where you come in the afternoons?"

"I work here part of the week, not every day," said Allam. "The place is sponsored by the city. These are the youngest children. They finish school early. Older children arrive later. The schools are near to this place. We have students in high school, middle school, and these young ones. All come to play and draw and paint and talk to one another—and to me and our workers and volunteers. We teach them about Syria because it was their country, which they had to leave. It is good that they learn stories of their first culture and the history of their land, an old civilization in the world. The volunteers help them with English. Sometimes we play a trivia game. I prepare my questions about places and things in the world. Like the pangolin, its entire body covered in scales. Who has been hearing about that, Toe-mas? This mammal lives in Asia and Africa, south of Sahara. It is on the edge of extinct because of greed, illegal traffic, poachers. Why? Because foolish people want the scales for healing. These small animals wobble on their hind legs. When I show the children a photograph, they think it is an anteater."

Tom knew nothing of pangolins. He had never heard of pangolins.

Allam continued. "The children come here because we are kind to them. This is one more place where they can belong. We are hoping, too, that they will let us know what is in their minds and their memories. But only if they reveal in a natural way. Some have lived sadness, sorrow, tragedy. Each has a different story.

Some have seen violence, even extreme. Some have no parents and now live with uncles, aunties. Here at this place, they must feel safe. We want them to *know* they are safe. At first, when new children arrive, they don't join in. But always they are looking around. They see smiles, they hear laughter. This is like watching baby birds learn to fly, Toe-mas. Flap and flap again, the bodies sink through the air, and then, before the final moment, a flutter and somehow they are saving themselves. Or they plunge to the ground and don't get up again."

"And no one wants that."

"Correct. We want them to get up again, and they are learning. How to have new lives. Here, in this small city, in this big country."

Tom was thinking of the considerable effort his friend was making while trying to carve his own new life in a different—as he called it—system. The Canadian system. Always new things to figure out. Even the smallest things, Tom was realizing.

He stood now, and followed Allam back to the main room.

As they passed the tables where the children were drawing and painting, Tom looked over the shoulder of a boy of six or seven who was hunched over his art. With coloured pencils, he had drawn a woman lying on her back, her mouth open. Her dress, a Western dress, was torn, one leg awkwardly bent. Maroon-coloured blood was seeping from her head. Odd-shaped bombs were falling from the sky over the roof of a building. The boy was slashing strokes of grey rain over the entire scene.

The young woman in charge was suddenly beside the child.

She pulled up a chair, lifted him onto her lap. The boy closed his eyes and allowed himself to be rocked.

Allam was frowning and gestured to Tom to follow. The young woman sang softly while she continued to rock the child.

"Once in a while," said Allam, "a certain kind of story comes from memory, what you see here. We hope the children will express what they must, but with no one forcing." He shook his head in sadness. "After a time—short or long—maybe this same child will come someday here and draw a house, a big yellow sun, green grass, a bird. Like a normal child. It is what we hope for when the children are healing. We try to pass on hope."

Tom examined the paintings and drawings pinned to a board as they walked along the side of the room. What interested him was the way the children drew rooms, beds, private spaces of their own, damaged or not. Backgrounds depicted both Syria and Canada—it was easy to tell which was which. A jagged hole in a house showed a bed against the wall of a shattered room. A stuffed elephant lay on its side beside broken furniture. In another, the entrails of a house without a front were blatantly exposed. In the same drawing, a mattress hung over the edge of the floor in a child's upstairs room. A stick child was holding a blanket and peering out. Tom could not help thinking of Will's childhood and how privileged it had been. He wondered if Will realized this, too.

AFTER LEAVING THE WAREHOUSE, he drove the Jeep to a different section of town. Again, Allam gave directions; he really did know Wilna Creek's streets and turnoffs. The items they'd packed into the car were to be taken to a three-bedroom bungalow that was being prepared for a sponsored family scheduled to arrive the following week. Allam had a key to the front door, and he and Tom began to unload. Tom immediately saw that there was still a need for small items: coat hangers, bedside rugs, glasses, extra chairs. He had two TVs at home and would bring one with the next load.

While he was unpacking the box of dishes, a Syrian couple arrived. Allam greeted the man and woman, and Tom was introduced. The community helped out when a new family arrived, Allam explained.

"The family, when first in this country, is not familiar with any part of the system. Men and women will nod their heads as if understanding when a Canadian talks to them. I know, because I did this in the past. But much of the time, we don't know what is said. Part of our job with new families arriving is to explain. My daughter, she is good at this because she speaks and understands both languages. Sometimes she has to explain words to me. But I signed up to be a student at a night class. Did I tell you? The class is about learning to listen."

Tom was intrigued, never having considered a course in learning to listen.

Allam shrugged. For him, this was his usual state of affairs, a deficit he was addressing. The class was helping him deal with everyday life.

While driving back to the store, Tom asked Allam to tell him about the class.

"This takes place Wednesday only, every week. We talk about how to identify the topic when people speak fast. Try to separate words when sounds stick together. That is the hard part for me. Someone once asked me, 'Izzeebizee?' I could not reply. Another said, 'Jeetyet?' I did not understand the meaning. My teacher explained: 'Is he busy?' 'Did you eat yet?' No one has said the same things to me again, so I don't know if I will recognize them next time. There are many sounds missing. People say 'Wouldja?' and I must think about this. Or 'Couldja?' Again I must think. For my ears, 'ship' sounds like 'sheep.' Sometimes I am slow to answer. In class, we learn how to focus, how to predict."

"When I hear you talking about this," said Tom, "I realize that maybe I speak too quickly. Maybe we all do."

"You I understand most of the time, Toe-mas. Because I am used to your way of speaking. In class, the teacher asks what we have been hearing the past week. She helps to separate meanings and words and how to pronounce. She teaches us not to listen word by word. We learn to listen for what she calls *chunks* of words. Better to understand. Sometimes, too, we talk about the idiom. Like raining cats and dogs. Like apple of my eye. Like burning bridges. These are amusing and we have the equivalent in our own language, but now I must learn in this country if I am to understand. In class, we also learn songs. Songs help us to understand words that clump together."

"But you do remarkably," said Tom. "This must take enormous effort."

"I am always learning, Toe-mas. Every day. Last week, I heard someone on the bus saying 'whole 'nother level' and I did not understand. In evening class, I looked in the dictionary for 'nother' but was confused. I went to the teacher and she explained."

"That's something I hear around me, for sure," said Tom. "It might be very old, might have been around for a long time. Or maybe it's just modern jargon."

"No matter," said Allam. "I feel that now I am reaching for a whole 'nother level in this language."

"This is impressive, Allam. I don't think I would do nearly as well as you are doing."

"Thank you, Toe-mas. But I think you would. If you found yourself in another country, you, too, would learn the language of that place."

Allam was grinning when Tom dropped him off.

# Keeping Vigil

## ADDIE

L ate Friday afternoon, Addie had a couple of hours to fill. Maybe she should play the *Emperor Concerto* and dust. Or wipe out the fridge. Carry out quotidian tasks that required no thought. She couldn't shake the feeling that she'd lost touch with something vital, significant. Her present life had narrowed to a singular context. The way Sybil's had, but without the accompanying illness. Immediately, she regretted making the comparison, knowing what Sybil was facing. Or trying to face *down*.

Even so, Addie's life as it had existed only months ago could scarcely be imagined now. She was functioning at work, that was true, though she wondered what staff members said about her among themselves. Maybe they didn't discuss her at all. She couldn't remember if she'd told them about her friend's illness. Five days a week, first thing in the morning, she showed up at her office. Five days a week, she disappeared when the day was done.

She assumed, but wasn't certain, that she was bumbling through the requirements of her job. Weekends, she was in Greenley. At least two evenings a week, she was back in Greenley again.

She could take a leave of absence. She'd considered this before. But then what would happen? She'd sit in her apartment filling the hours until it was time to drive to Greenley. Sybil weighed less than ninety pounds, but she wasn't ready to let go. Not yet. She was still in her single room, and her mother, her brother and his wife were there most days. Occasionally someone pushed Sybil out to the sunroom in her narrow hospital bed or—if she could sit without pain and discomfort—in a wheelchair. That was something Addie could do, and did, when Sybil had the stamina to both contemplate and withstand being lifted, pushed, wheeled. Addie talked; Sybil preserved her strength and listened. Sometimes the two laughed quietly together, remembering a detail of Sybil's earlier life—before cancer. Sometimes they told stories to each other about places they'd been.

"Do you remember the thief in Geneva? He was gaunt and shabby. Baggy pants, old clothes. He'd have been fifty at most. Probably stealing for his family. He ran out of a corner pharmacy holding a shopping bag, a trail of people after him, and we were on the street gawking, trying to see what the hullabaloo was about. He dropped the bag and lost a shoe and kept running, but he was nabbed by a pair of policemen who pursued him on their bikes. They dragged him back and the pharmacy owner was shouting, and the crowd made a huge circle with the thief at the centre.

Humiliation made public. You, Sybil, broke through the ring around the desperate man and handed him his missing shoe. He looked so downtrodden and pathetic with a shoe on one foot and a sock on the other."

"The crowd was silent when he leaned forward to put on his shoe. He took his time tying the lace, a simple everyday gesture. That's what I saw: a small moment of human dignity." Sybil smiled at the memory and winced. Even a smile required effort.

"When he stood up, both shoes on, the shouting and accusations started up all over again."

They looked at each other. What they could no longer do, these two problem-solvers—as they'd always considered themselves— was define the problem, consider possible solutions and choose the best one. This problem was in another category, one beyond resolution.

ADDIE DECIDED that the dusting could wait. She would make herself a pot of tea and eat a square of dark chocolate. One of her bargains with herself was about rationing the number of squares she permitted herself each day. She used to eat six, and then she cut back to four. Now she was aiming for two. She ate only Ecuador, 75 percent cacao. While trying to cut down, she had tried 90 percent because those bars were so bitter. Too bitter to sustain, so she went back to Ecuador and was still on four squares a day. If she were honest with herself, five.

She made the tea and poured a cup and decided that she should give herself free rein to eat as much as she liked—four or five or six squares, even the whole bar—because she had the drive to Greenley ahead of her and a long night where she'd probably be awake in Sybil's room. On Sunday, she'd go back to rationing. Sunday was face-the-music day, the day she hauled out the bathroom scale, checked her weight and made decisions about the week to come. Of daily rituals are we made, she told herself. Do not introduce drastic changes into your routine at this time of your life. Remember what you've learned about dealing with stress.

The bargaining side of her replied, But it's also stressful to be overweight.

To compensate, she walked the five flights down to the lobby to check her mailbox. Another of her resolutions. She hadn't started walking *up* the five flights, but that would happen next week.

Maybe.

In a few hours, she would be driving to Greenley to take over the late-evening and all-night shift. The family liked to have someone with Sybil all the time now. Sometimes on weekends, Addie took the day shift; sometimes the night shift. For tonight, she decided to bring her own small travel pillow, her own shrug. She'd be able to stretch out on the chaise the nursing staff had set up in Sybil's room for family. Vigil. Where did the word come from? Probably Latin. Hazzley would know. Hazzley, of the Tuesday meetings, displayed a quiet but expert fascination with words. The point of keeping vigil was to stay awake; Hazzley would agree with that.

Addie would have to take along something to read. She was sorry she hadn't been buying new books these days. She'd bring along a spy story by le Carré. Maybe one of the early Smiley novels. There were a couple she hadn't read. And hadn't George Smiley been revived in his later years to star in a more recent book? She'd check that out. All the le Carré novels were in her apartment, taking up a shelf in her bookcase.

Or perhaps she'd grab something by Gardam. Another complete shelf. Jane Gardam could keep her awake with her signature humour and love of life. Not to mention her insights into human behaviour.

Addie returned to her apartment by elevator, a flat padded envelope in hand. Who had sent a CD in the mail? That's what the package felt like. Printed label on the outside, no return address. She ripped open the envelope and a small card fell out: *I remember your love of music. This might help.* Unsigned, but Tye would know she'd recognize his writing. Tears filled her eyes quite suddenly. Tye knew how difficult these days would be.

The recording was one Addie knew about but hadn't heard. Max Richter's *Three Worlds: Music from Woolf Works*—the ballet. She hadn't seen the production; the music must have filtered down from the original performance. She glanced at the insert while putting the CD in the player and kept the pamphlet in hand so she could follow along. Three books had been chosen for the work: *Mrs. Dalloway, Orlando, The Waves.* The piece began with Virginia Woolf discussing words in a 1937 BBC Radio broadcast.

Richter chose a passage one minute long from the only known extant recording of her voice.

Addie played the opening minute twice, straining to hear individual words. *Incarnadine. Multitudinous seas.* That would be *Macbeth.* She settled into her chair, put her feet up on the jute ottoman and listened to the entire recording. The mood was that of a threnody. Contemplative, wavelike, urgent, haunting, reminiscent.

She didn't know how to respond to Tye. Perhaps it would be best not to. Right now, she could deal with only one large issue at a time. He had sent this as an act of tenderness, of kindness, she was certain. And the music, not always soothing but appropriate, did help her mood. She was immensely grateful that someone in the world knew her well enough to understand how much this would mean to her.

She gathered up her things: pillow, shrug, books. Gardam and le Carré both, for good measure. She headed to the parking level and her car.

# Changes

GWEN

Snow had fallen again in the night, enough to cover the lawn. The world sparkled in morning light, and Gwen was cheered by the sight. The earlier sprinkling hadn't lasted, but this snowfall appeared to have every intention of staying. The real beginning of winter. A season she used to dread because extreme cold and deep snow meant she'd be locked indoors with Brigg for long smothering stretches without escape, especially to the impassable backyard—unless she spent half a day shovelling, which she sometimes did. Especially when the twins were young. She and the boys made snow caves, which the boys called quinzhees, though the word wasn't entirely accurate to describe their creations. The three of them sat inside, backs to the curve of wall, marvelling at the way sound was muffled, the way ordinary noises of the street were kept far off. They ran their mittens down hard-packed inner walls and gazed out through the arched entrance, which faced the hedge at the back of the yard, never the house. Gwen provided hot chocolate, which they drank solemnly, passing the thermos cup, their winter quinzhee ritual.

She wondered if the boys ever thought of the caves, sitting inside those temporary shelters. She wondered if they had conversations with each other about their childhood. She would forever wonder if she had protected them enough. Not a question she could ask. Not now.

The parrot-sitting job had not come to an end as agreed. Cecilia Grand phoned Gwen at home to say that she and her husband had been obliged to extend their visit to LA. Could Gwen continue to go to the house until the last week of December? They'd definitely be back before New Year's Eve. For the moment, their daughter still needed them, and they couldn't abandon her, not at this time. Not before Christmas; they just couldn't. Cecilia assured Gwen that she had booked a flight for the twenty-eighth; reservations were definite. She was counting on Gwen's goodwill to continue caring for Rico.

Gwen had already put in more than the seven weeks she'd initially promised, but she wasn't upset about the extension. She knew she'd miss Rico when the owners decided to come home, if they ever did. Bury the thought, she told herself. I am not taking on a full-time parrot. Parrots bond, so an owner can't very well pass one on to someone else. Rico and I have a tentative bond, but that might be pure luck. And parrots can outlive their humans;

some live sixty, even eighty years. No, I'll carry on with the job until the end of December, and that's it.

"Face up, Gwen," she said aloud. "You know you're fond of Rico. You have admitted him to your life."

SHE STOOD AT THE KITCHEN WINDOW and wrapped her hands around her coffee mug. Allam, too, had been admitted to her life—in a tentative way. He was becoming her friend. It had been a long time since a man had come calling at her door.

A few days after Hazzley distributed the contact list to the company members, Allam phoned Gwen and asked if he could stop by to drop something off. He arrived at her front door on foot and told her he often walked through her neighbourhood, just hadn't known she was there. He presented her with a gift, a slender paperback. He'd ordered it from the bookstore because several weeks ago she had asked about the title. It was a book of stories, the book his daughter had told him about: *Holy Days of Obligation.* He announced this slowly, and held the book so that she could see the cover. It was by a writer named Zettell.

Gwen was surprised and pleased. She remembered asking about the title, but she hadn't expected him to order a copy for her. She invited him in, and they sat across from each other at the kitchen table and drank tea. Allam told her about his long walks through different areas of the city, and how he and Tom were working together on a couple of projects.

"Toe-mas is a kind man," Allam told her. "I visit him at his shop.

We are like good brothers, getting along." He told her about two new Syrian families arriving in the city, and his involvement with the refugee community.

She talked to Allam about books she liked to read, how she was almost finished *TransAtlantic* by Colum McCann. He listened while she described the way the writer presented his characters— sometimes direct and face-on, sometimes coming in from the side. McCann mixed things up, she said. He kept the stories interesting. As soon as she was finished *TransAtlantic*, she would start *Holy Days*.

Allam asked about Gwen's name, its meaning. "I like to know the beginning, the background," he said. "I like the story of words."

"Gwendoloena," she said. "It means 'white-waved' or 'new moon.' My late mother decided that would be my full name, though Gwen is how I'm known to everyone."

"Gwendo-leen-ah." He spoke her name into the air several times, adding the *h* at the end like a sigh that hovered in the room.

"And yours? Allam?"

"It is a word about knowledge, learning. My ancestors moved back and forth between Syria and Turkey, Egypt, Iraq. One of my great-uncles owned—maybe his family owns now, I am not certain—a large antique stall in the market. I visited when I was a boy. He sold beautiful objects: mosaic, copperwork, glass that is blown, textiles—all made in the area. Information was always exchanging, passing along. Learning was given value. Also travel."

After Allam left, Gwen walked through her house, room to room to room. It was as if every window had been opened. And why was she surprised that she had not felt threatened—not in the least—while he was there?

TWO DAYS AFTER Allam's visit to her home, Gwen began to make changes. She decided to move back into the main bedroom from the spare room. She resolved to take possession of what was, after all, her own space. After Brigg's death almost eight months earlier, she had shut the door of the master bedroom, wishing its contents away. Of course the room was still there, and one double closet was full of his clothes.

The first step was to get rid of the marital bed. Brigg died in that bed, she reminded herself. She gritted her teeth and phoned the town junk remover to have the mattress and box spring hauled away. She donated the bed frame and two dressers to Helping with Furniture, a charitable organization that did good work. Just before the truck left, she asked the driver to wait. She ran back up to the bedroom and removed a painting from its hook on the wall and donated that as well. It was the one she'd been given during her retirement dinner at Spice. Brigg had liked it and insisted that it be hung in their bedroom. Gwen hoped that Helping with Furniture could find a use for it. They placed donated goods in homes they furnished for refugees, for people who had no homes of their own or had been caught up in unexpected circumstances. Maybe the scene of rolling hills and placid lake would be a peaceful setting for someone who had come to Wilna Creek from a place of violence or unrest.

Next, she went shopping. She purchased a thick queen mattress, a platform frame, linens, pillows, a new comforter in muted golds. She enjoyed spending every dollar. She presented her credit card with no pangs of fear or regret. She bought the deluxe line of linens because she could. All was matching, all was new. The large items were delivered by two men, and she showed them exactly how she wanted everything placed.

The following day, she walked into a gallery and bought a painting called *Shimmering Forest* by Quebec artist Louis Hughes, carried it home and hung it on the empty hook. The wall came alive with movement and colour.

After that, with neither nostalgia nor remorse, she bagged every suit and tie and boot and shoe and shirt and sweater and jacket that Brigg had ever worn and dispatched them to a shelter for the homeless. Her closet space doubled. She had shelves, baskets and dividers installed.

She dismantled a sectional living-room bookcase, carried it up the stairs herself, piece by piece, and put it back together against one wall of the bedroom. She unpacked the last few book boxes and filled the shelves with her mother's library and with purchases of her own from the town bookstore.

One surprise was a large box of books from her childhood, thought to have been damaged by water from a leaking pipe. Her mother had salvaged these, packing them separately, probably while Gwen was away at university. The box had not been labelled, so Gwen didn't know that her earliest books had been saved. She spent three happy hours sitting on the floor of the bedroom, her back to the wall, handling each book, leafing through old memories: *Maggie Muggins*, *Just Mary*, *Harold and the Purple Crayon*, *Charlotte's Web*, *The Chronicles of Narnia*, *The Secret Garden*, a child's version of the *Aeneid*, along with Greek, Celtic and Roman mythology—the influence of her mother. There were early novels by W.O. Mitchell and Gabrielle Roy and—again, gifted by her mother—*King Arthur and His Knights of the Round Table*.

The discovery of her books, the unexpected opportunity for self-indulgence, the renewal of old friendships, provided an afternoon like no other. She decided to take her time finding a good home for each one. Some she would give away. Others she would send to her granddaughters in Texas. Some would be kept for herself; these she wanted to re-explore, and would take her time doing so.

When the book boxes were unpacked, she went out again and shopped for a chaise longue. She had it delivered and hauled upstairs and placed near the bookcase, at an angle from which she could see the new painting. As soon as the delivery men left, she stretched out and began to read the book of stories Allam had brought to her house.

The refurnishing of the bedroom was complete.

ALLAM PHONED AGAIN on a Friday morning. He suggested that they walk together, perhaps go to a coffee house. But Gwen could not.

"The timing isn't right," she said. "I'm on my way out the door; we'll have to meet another day. Or maybe at midday. Today—well, every day—I go to a house to talk to a parrot. This is a job I have for a few months. A temporary job. The parrot's name is Rico, and I keep him company twice a day. I provide him with a social life." She laughed.

Allam laughed, too; he was interested.

She told him about Cecilia Grand's detailed list. She told him about her experiences with Rico, and how she was learning about parrots. How she sometimes read passages from Layamon's *Brut* aloud, and that she had successfully coaxed Rico out of his cage, terrified that he might not go back in, and how grateful she was when he returned to the cage on his own. How he'd flown up and in and hopped onto his widest, thickest perch so that he could watch while she shut the cage door and locked him inside. She told Allam that when Rico spoke, she detected something like sarcasm in his voice. Or irony. She wondered if she was imagining those attributes. Was Rico mimicking her? He'd already demonstrated that he could speak in her voice. This was entertaining, but also unnerving. Then she wondered if she'd blurted out too much.

Allam listened to all of this. "I would like to meet the parrot Rico," he said.

"I'll introduce you," said Gwen. "Some afternoon, I suppose you could come with me. He might be hostile at first, because you are unknown to him. If you're patient and allow him to vet you in his little parrot way, he might be at ease in your presence. I'm not sure about this, because he might also have personal likes and dislikes. I only know that you have to endure his investigative behaviour."

For her, Rico no longer shrieked when she parked her car in front of the garage. His alarm calls had ceased. That bit of information, outlined on the instruction sheet, had been disconcerting from the beginning: *He'll send out his alarm call when anyone new comes near.*

After hanging up with Allam, Gwen remembered, as she drove away from her house, that Rico, clearly upset one day in September, when she'd first started caring for him, had clung to the side of his cage and beat his wings so rapidly and for so long, she was afraid his little parrot heart would explode while she stood helplessly by. She was concerned, felt badly, did not know what was wrong, kept trying to divert him. She spoke soothingly, calmly. Eventually, she spoke not at all. He quieted and began to behave as if nothing had happened. Perhaps he'd had a stab of pain in his little bird intestine. Who knew?

Or maybe, like humans, he just needed his own silent time.

# The Floodgates

After breakfast, Chiyo began to select the playlists for winter classes that were about to begin. She liked to introduce new music, but she was careful, too, or tried to be. Whatever she chose had to suit the type of class, age groups involved, tempo required, beats per minute. No breakup music, no music that would remind of grief, nothing too sad or emotional. She was aware of the lyrics in every selection and tried to imagine feelings the words might evoke in the class participants.

Much to consider.

For tai chi, no music. Tai chi was about meditation. In her opinion, participants achieved more without music for that particular class. Other instructors might use music during tai chi, but Chiyo did not. She taught the moves and the language of the moves until the two came together in a kind of music of their own. She did not tamper with what had been created a thousand years ago. *Swallow*

242

*skims water. Dragon creeps down. Lying tiger listens to wind.* Why would she heap anything on top of that? Anything added would only take away. She wondered again about the overactive Hopps, who was slated to be in the new class. She hoped he'd be able to settle in, settle down. A challenge for her, and for him, too.

For yoga, the music she chose had no lyrics. Her playlist included flute, oboe, *koto, shakuhachi*, occasionally harp or violin. She preferred wind instruments to start off the class, ending with violin or strings of some sort. Classes were forty-five minutes in length, all classes. For stretch and strength, the participants liked Elvis, the Everly Brothers, "Stand by Me," the inimitable dusky voice of Cher and always ABBA. For young groups she sometimes used top-forty lists. For all, she mixed in Spanish music, Latin, more oldies. There was plenty of choice. She could tell when students were responding and enjoying themselves.

The selection process, however, required effort, not to mention time spent on purchases, permissions, downloading from computer to iPod. Along with even more time listening and eliminating. Something she expected to be suitable for yoga might turn out to be busy, plinky, not soothing at all. One piece she listened to began with sounds of tranquility, a soft wash of waves. Without warning, the waves uttered a hoarse croak. Well, not exactly a croak; it was as if a pig and a goose had found themselves in an ocean, and gave off a combined honking snort of surprise while being tossed by the same wave. As for the busy section, the sound of raindrops falling softly suddenly turned to hail bouncing off a tin roof. Chiyo had learned the necessity of listening to the end of every selection.

She thought of Addie, who'd confessed that she played the *Emperor Concerto* while she dusted. Chiyo had never considered a connection between Beethoven and a dustrag in someone's hand, two centuries after the composer's death. Good way to get through mundane chores.

She looked around the room. Staying on in the small bungalow was convenient, but it was work. All in all, positives outweighed negatives. Her taxes were low. She was getting used to living on her own. She had privacy. Spence could and did visit. They were considering merging their two households but hadn't come up with a workable plan. Not yet. But they would; Chiyo was confident they would.

She would like the group at Cassie's to meet Spence sometime. *The Company of Strangers*, she thought. A quirky film she'd come upon in the library and brought home to watch. The members of the company at Cassie's were strangers no more, but she wondered how long they would be connected to one another's lives. She liked Addie, a person who had also spent much of her time caregiving. Maybe they could go out for a meal sometime. She had also begun to think that the group wasn't about grief at all. They were linking up, talking things through, telling stories. Each was discovering how to start anew. Maybe even learning that there was a selfishness to grief. Chiyo considered her own experience. How, for a time, she'd thought that grief belonged only to her. And then she was forced to acknowledge that others were in the same place. We're not allowed to have it to ourselves, she thought. Grief will not be contained and owned. It spills out and joins streams and rivers of grief that are already out there, heading for an ocean of sadness that never makes its way onto a map.

It was not going to go away. Not completely. Had her mother ever stopped grieving Chiyo's father, even though he'd died decades earlier? Maybe there was some tucking-away place where grief was stored. A tucking-away place that permitted you to carry on, pull yourself up and out of that river or stream. She and her mother had never talked about anything like that.

Look at what had happened early this morning. She got up as usual, stepped into the shower and began to shampoo her hair. She was thinking of nothing in particular when a wave of sadness rolled through her and she found herself crying hard. The floodgates were open and everything was spilling out. Good thing she was by herself in the house. But even as she cried, some part of her knew that almost eight months after her mother had died, she was treading the same waters. She'd lost some part of herself, and there was no one to blame. Like some of Pina's dancers, she was out of balance. But unlike the dancers, Chiyo was determined to get back up.

WHEN ALL THE MUSIC was chosen to her satisfaction, she checked the time and decided to walk to the Anglican church she used to attend with her mother. One day a week, a noonday service was held, and this was the day. She checked the website to be certain. She didn't go to church regularly and hadn't been inside since the Anglican minister had conducted the service for her mother's funeral. There'd been a small group of people: her mom's friends, her own friends. Maybe thirty in all.

As had happened with every other church in Wilna Creek, the congregation of Anglicans had shrunk over the past decades. Chiyo wondered if anyone even bothered to attend church in the middle of the week. She supposed the midday service was timed for workers who were on their lunch break and wanted comfort or reassurance for whatever was going on in their lives. Or maybe they were just seeking the communion of fellow worshippers.

She pushed back the heavy door and entered as the organ was starting up. The minister was at the front, and he recognized her and smiled. He motioned toward the two front pews, where five people had stood to sing, but Chiyo held out a hand as if to ward him off and slid into a pew the second row from the back. Just in case she needed to bolt. All the pews between were empty.

She unbuttoned her coat and dropped it to the pew and set her purse beside her and pulled out the Book of Common Prayer she'd brought from home. This had belonged to her mother and to her mother's mother in the camps; it was old and small, the cover softened from use. Chiyo found the correct page and joined in for the opening hymn and prayers. She heard the minister say something like "heads are bowed with . . ." She thought he said "woe," and maybe he did. But no, that couldn't be. At the same moment, she heard a rustling noise behind her and glimpsed back quickly to see a woman about her own age in the pew behind. The woman had entered the church soundlessly and had taken Chiyo by surprise. A long arm was reaching over the back of the pew just as Chiyo turned. A hand had almost grabbed her wallet from her purse.

This was so unexpected, she didn't realize for a second or two what was taking place. The woman had come in to rob someone, and she intended to grab the wallet and run. Chiyo immediately placed her hand firmly over her purse, zipped it shut and placed it directly on her lap, gripping the strap. She slid over to the right so she could look to the side and keep the woman in her peripheral vision. But the woman behind her slid over, too. Chiyo knew instinctively that the woman would try again, this time perhaps to grab the entire purse. Chiyo held on with a fierce grip and heard the woman give an exasperated sigh, as if she was giving up. Whatever the minister was saying had to be ignored because Chiyo had to be on her guard. The service was mercifully short. She heard the words "by the grace of our Lord," and then the minister was walking down the aisle during the final hymn. He was carrying the silver collection plate close against his body, one of his large hands covering any money that lay within. The collection plate had not been brought to the back rows during the service.

He went directly to the woman behind Chiyo and said, in a calm, knowing voice, "Claudine, you took money from the collection plate last week, didn't you?"

247

The reply was a sucking in of air and then a plaintive "Yes."

"You needed the money for drugs?"

"I'm sorry, I'm sorry. I didn't know what else to do." Claudine's voice was hoarse, as if she'd been chain-smoking for days, weeks.

Chiyo put on her coat and fished a twenty-dollar bill from her wallet and dropped it into the edge of the plate, which the minister was still holding protectively. His palm moved quickly to cover the bill. Claudine's eyes stared greedily and hard as the money moved from wallet to plate. Chiyo nodded to the others, who had grouped around the minister and the woman. They all seemed to know one another; they'd been through this before. Collective counselling, of sorts.

Next time, she told herself. Next time—if I ever return—I'll leave my purse and any other bag at home. She stepped out into the street. As she walked, she thought about her own life. So many people had problems worse than her own. There would always be people who were badly off. She had resources, an education, work that she loved. She had so much more.

Maybe she should be offering a free class of some sort in the church basement one evening a week. Maybe she could start showing up at the winter soup kitchen, giving a hand. Maybe she should move beyond her own safe borders, with or without her mother's ruling hand. And what would her mother say about all of this? About Chiyo picking up her own life? *Now, Voyager*, indeed.

# December

# A Foot Steps

GWEN

As agreed, Allam waited in the car a full five minutes while Gwen went inside to test the mood.

"I don't want you to be upset, Rico. I want you to be on your best behaviour. Have I done anything to injure your body? Your psyche? Have I? Ever? Well, then, be nice to my friend. DO NOT SOUND YOUR ALARM CALL. I'll be offended if you do. For good measure, I won't read out loud today. Enough of King Arthur for now. Talk only, one-on-one, you-me. Well, you-me and my friend Allam."

In response, Rico offered indifference. After that, he hoisted his wings like sails gathering air, lowered them, shrugged his little parrot shoulders, puffed up the sails again. Held. Lowered. Bobbed his head sharply several times. Stepped from his perch to an adjacent branch in the cage.

He began to call out several seconds before Gwen's ears heard the front door open. He did not flap wildly against the bars of his cage. He paced back and forth on the branch. Ran a few steps and then clambered over to a rope perch. Wrapped his bird toes around it. Two toes forward, two toes back, she reminded herself.

"Settle down, Rico. Settle down. I'll let you out today," she half sang. "You like being in the kitchen; I know you do. You had a grand time exploring last time you were out. Remember?"

Rico stopped and stared. Allam had entered the family room silently, no sudden movement. Rico conducted a rapid but complete inspection. Continued to stare hard. Ran back and forth. Grabbed at the perch with his toes. Became silent and still. Pupils contracted to pin size.

"Don't wear yourself out, Rico. And don't try turning yourself to stone. This is Allam. He will not hurt you. I promise."

Rico, used to hearing her voice, feigned disinterest again and turned away. He glanced back now and again to reinspect. Curious? Gwen couldn't tell. She, too, was curious; there were many things she didn't know about Allam.

In good time, she reminded herself. In good time. There is much that Allam doesn't know about me, either. For the moment, let me do my job. Introduce man to parrot. Or parrot to man. Not sure which direction this goes. Both, I guess. And remember Rico's peripheral vision. Sight is his strongest sense. He's watching, every second. Even when he pretends to turn away.

Allam, unobtrusive by instinct, stayed back. Gwen went to the kitchen, washed a pellet bowl, began to prepare chop, returned, changed the water, hung a new toy. Rico continued to check Allam's location from time to time.

"Okay, Rico. I'm going to let you out now. I'll clean the bottom of the cage and sweep the floor while you're exploring the kitchen. As usual, you've done a great job as a seed splatterer. Didn't your parrot mom and dad teach you any manners? Or is this some vestigial grand plan to propagate new growth in the forest?"

As soon as she'd spoken about parrot parents, a thought winged into her brain: not one person in our company has a mother. Not a living mother. Not that anyone has spoken about.

She turned to Allam. "Is your mother alive?"

"Yes. She is eighty-nine and lives with her youngest sister in Beirut. Not a refugee camp. An apartment. She has lived there a long time and wants to stay with her sister. Even so, I am concerning myself about her. I talk to her on the phone one day each week."

Gwen opened the door to the cage. She walked to the centre of the family room and stood with arms outstretched. Rico barely hesitated. He flew directly to her and perched on her right arm, the favoured arm, or so it seemed. She felt his toes grasp. Allam observed this and muttered something. He backtracked in silence and went out through the front door. Gwen heard the latch click behind him. Rico echoed the sound with an identical click of his own.

She moved slowly toward the kitchen while Rico made his gradual descent toward her wrist. She sat at the table, and he hopped over to the tabletop. From there, he flew down to the floor. He seemed to want the extra step while travelling from cage to forearm to wrist to table to floor.

Gwen was watering the jade when she heard the front door reopen. Rico, in explorer mode in the kitchen, raised his head and stared in the direction of the noise. He did not sound his alarm.

Allam came into the Grands' kitchen carrying a sturdy branch he'd liberated from a tangle of prunings at the side of the garage. He had stripped off the bark and any protruding twigs. The branch was slightly more than two feet long, its diameter ideal for a perch.

"I will find a way to set this up in the room," he said. "So he will have a place to land when he leaves the cage." His voice softened. "After that, you will not be the human cross."

*Sacrificial.* He had seen her as sacrificial in that moment. She hadn't thought about self-immolation. Was that a condition that lay under the surface of her life? Maybe some women were better at self-immolation than others and she took the grand prize.

She wondered what Rico used to land on when the Grands let him out. Perhaps he flew straight to Cecilia with no fanfare at all. No arms outstretched, no perch. Or maybe a quick left turn through the air to the kitchen.

If so, he had never done that with Gwen.

SHE AND ALLAM DROVE BACK to her house in the late afternoon. The thin layer of snow had hardened over the surface of the lawn, but there hadn't been a huge snowstorm so far. They took off their boots and jackets and headed for the kitchen. Allam had been in her home several times now. They always sat in the kitchen, and now, while she filled the kettle to make tea, he pulled two mugs from the cupboard and set them on the table. He'd been telling her about the class he was taking and about the teacher, whom he respected because she was good and she was committed to helping students navigate the ins and outs of speaking *Canadian*.

"What about Rico?" he asked Gwen. "Is he speaking more than at the beginning, when you first met him?"

"Yes, he is. And no matter what he says, I'm always astonished to hear human sounds coming from his hooked beak. What I actually know, language or not, is that Rico and I communicate."

"When first I entered house, I watched to see how he would react. I think he is comfortable with you, so he gave me permission to be there also," Allam said. "And when you let him out, he travelled first to arm, then to wrist, to table—and then floor? I saw part of that from the window outside. Many unnecessary steps along the way."

"He might have those particular quirks. There have been so many changes in his behaviour since September," Gwen said. "He's more relaxed now. At the beginning, I couldn't help but be aware of filling the room, of filling the whole house with my presence. He was wary of me for days."

"Your presence maybe does fill the house when you are alone with a parrot, but when you are in a room with people, Gwendo-leen-ah, you disappear," Allam replied. "This I have seen with my two eyes.

I understand, because I also know how to disappear. How to let myself in and out of places silently. With *steelth*. But I can fill a room with my presence. Maybe not a whole house, but a room. When I am choosing to do this."

It was her turn to listen. To understand that he had his own ways of knowing things about her.

LATE IN THE EVENING, after he left, she considered how it had come about that they had travelled up the stairs of her house together. How she had allowed herself to let down her guard.

They'd finished their tea and stood to gather the dishes. She had faced him, surprised and not surprised. He took her by the hand. Both waited a few moments in silence. Weighing what was to come. She wasn't exactly certain about what happened next. Maybe she leaned in. For certain, he maintained his grip on her hand. And led her up the stairs, where he had never been. She took the lead then and brought him to her room.

After they made love, they talked for a long time.

"Why did you come here? Why to me?"

"A foot steps where it loves," he answered. "Where it desires to love. And to be loved in return." That was all.

Why did she trust him? The way he behaved, the formalities, the way he listened carefully. It had been a long time since she had trusted. She found herself telling him about Brigg, about sewing up all the pockets before taking his clothes to the funeral parlour. She told Allam the reasons why. She had never before discussed the true nature of her marriage, the kind of man her husband had been. The bullying that had gone on for decades.

Allam pondered the sewing of the pockets and said, "The action suited the situation." And held her tightly because she was shaking; her entire body was shaking. He instinctively knew that they should speak of other things while she allowed herself the realization of having shared a part of her story—never before told.

"When I am walking in this town," he told her, "I walk sometimes at night and hear the sound of Canada from the skies. In September, October, even to late November, from the dark sky comes the sound of geese in migration. For me, this is Canada's sound. If a window is open in my daughter's house, I hear and go out and stand in the yard to listen while geese are calling. Sometimes I cannot see them in the dark. And why do I go out and stare up at the night sky? Because for me, this is important in my new life. The sound is a symbol of something. Freedom? Beauty? I do not yet know."

"But you miss your own country." Gwen was feeling only relief. I can speak of ordinary things to this man, she told herself. Maybe we will be able to say anything to each other. Talk and listen. Listen and talk.

Even so, she spoke softly, as if a third presence in the room was also listening.

"Yes, I miss," Allam told her. "I miss my mother, who is in Beirut; I miss my cousins, my aunts, my uncles who are still alive in Syria. I miss the pomegranate tree in a special garden near the place where

I lived. I miss the souk, the barter and confusion and colour. I miss the spices, the coffee house where I met friends many days and played chess. I miss the stories of my friends. I miss the dry and dusty street, the broken cobblestone beside my door that my foot tripped over every day. What I must understand and admit is that much of my city, once beautiful and ancient and full of history, is now white stone, rubble, a tragedy in this world. Many things are gone from me, Gwendo-leen-ah, but I am finding ways to live this new life. Also, to live in a colder climate is not easy, but this can be done. Where I lived in Syria could be cold some of the time, but not like here. Not thirty-five degrees below zero, not forty below some days. But we come here and see Canadians living in winter, playing in winter. We say to each other, 'We can do the same.' Especially when we know so many Syrians are living in shelters with no heat at all."

Gwen considered what *she* was missing. Her twins. Her two granddaughters. She wanted to be part of their lives. She would definitely contact her sons and make arrangements to visit them in Texas. Maybe next summer their families would agree to come to Wilna Creek. They could stay at her house. She would find room for everyone. She had two spare rooms. She had a basement room that could be painted and furnished. She could introduce her sons to Allam. She wanted them all to meet.

She closed her eyes, remembering. She realized that she had never been spoken to so tenderly. If she never saw Allam again, she would not forget the feelings that were now hers to keep. She would not forget the two of them naked in her bed. Allam above, the sound of spine, rising, falling. The weightlessness. The space beyond touch . . . yes.

# Desperate Measures

At the next meeting—no planned agenda—the company began to talk of their experiences of taking on executor and trustee duties. Almost everyone had something to say. Allam listened with his usual curiosity. Addie sat back, trying to take in information. She still held power of attorney for Sybil, but she would not be executor when the time came. That duty remained within the jurisdiction of Sybil's family.

Allam and Gwen had arrived together in Gwen's car and parked on Beamer Street in front of the café. This was witnessed by two members of the company and by Cass, who was standing at the cash register near the front window at the time. In the backroom, the two sat side by side at the round table, as always, and made no effort to explain the frequent exchange of glances. There was no ignoring the current between the two. There was no ignoring the solicitous attention he bestowed in her direction.

Gwen wore a bit of colour—a silk scarf atop the usual browns. The scarf was printed with images of butterflies in a blend of colours against solid backgrounds of green and indigo. A sight to behold. Gwen fingered the silk as she sat, her thoughts elsewhere.

Chiyo, taking in every detail, said to herself: *Jack Goes Boating*. Philip Seymour Hoffman as Jack, Amy Ryan as Connie. Awkward at first—shyness from one, then from the other, not always at the same time. They're suited, maybe for the long run. Or as long as they can make the run last. Chiyo smiled to herself and then felt like weeping, not because of a possible Gwen–Allam alliance—that should be celebrated!—but because of the tragedy of Hoffman's death. She and Spence would have to pull out some of the dozens of Hoffman DVDs and watch them again.

Hazzley was laughing with an edge to her voice, telling the story of lineups she'd endured at Service Canada counters. A huddle outside the building before the door opened first thing in the morning. No sign of a queue. The crush to get inside to tear off a number-strip. So many people needing passports, child or disability benefits, Canada Pension Plan death benefits, job-search assistance, on and on and on. "Sadly, some officials behind the wickets—not all, thankfully—don't have their first cup of coffee before they start the day."

"One of the people I encountered while dealing with my mom's estate looked stunned, as if he'd been punched in the head," said Chiyo. "For sure he hadn't had his caffeine fix. To stand on the vulnerable side of a counter facing him, to be the object of disinterest, indifference, irritation—all of that was so seriously disheartening I can scarcely talk about it. Maybe some people in these jobs no longer connect with their clients because they're forced to repeat mind-numbing tasks ad nauseam. Some people arrive without the required documents, some without a full grasp of the languages of the country and some without any idea how to proceed. Others have every document in hand, to the nth detail. But everyone is treated with the same grim glare of disdain. It's downright demoralizing."

Gwen liked Chiyo's descriptions because Chiyo wasn't afraid to say anything in front of the company. Well, Gwen could talk comfortably to Rico, couldn't she? But that was different. Rico was a private audience, his tiny bird earholes covered protectively by auricular feathers. Letting in human sounds, the ones he wanted to hear. Was he capable of selective hearing? Probably not. Someone might know the answer to that.

"Too much tapping at keyboards," said Hazzley. "Think of the steady diet of lacklustre communications, day in, day out. Multiply that by months, years. It's unfortunate the way figures of authority get to utter decrees that alter people's lives. Actually, not everyone behind a counter has been there for years. One day my number was called by a young woman in her twenties who had painted her lips so purple, I couldn't take my eyes off her mouth the entire time she was speaking. I stared and stared, hardly heard what she was saying. She was used to drawing attention, and my staring didn't bother her one bit."

Tom chipped in. "It's a wonder, with all the paperwork we're required to submit—death certificates, copies of wills, affidavits, proofs—it's a wonder we don't have to bring in photographs of our late relatives in their caskets."

"I remember something," Hazzley said. "When I was a child in England, during the war and after, my mum used to rhyme off a little chant whenever a hearse or an ambulance passed us by in the street: 'Hold your collar, touch your toes. Don't want to be in one of those.' And we did just that. We stood still and held our collars, or whatever was at our neckline. After the hearse went by, I don't think we touched our toes, but I recall seeing others around us holding their collars, too. It's queer, really. An old custom that goes back to the time of the plague, I expect. I don't know what made me think of this."

The others instinctively reached for their collars, as if experimenting.

"Anyway, Tom," Hazzley continued, "you're right about the paperwork. Unfortunately, it goes on for a couple of years. I had to keep supplying extra copies of the death certificate and the will. You might also be asked for notarized copies. Sometimes it seems there will be no end to demands for proof of death, joint ownership, inheritance. I am finally free of the paperwork to do with Lew's death—I hope—but that was a long, difficult period." She thought of Lew's ashes in the ceramic urn behind the door in the now-empty dining room. Maybe her daughter would deal with them. She added, softly, "Not to mention the number of times I sat in the car and cried after one of those dispiriting encounters with an official."

"Exactly," said Chiyo. "That's what I mean. When we're vulnerable, we can easily be undone."

"Tears can be close to the surface, for sure," Gwen offered quietly. "The slightest word from someone else—even a stranger, even on an unrelated topic—can trigger a completely unexpected reaction." Woe came upon the people, she said to herself. And remembered how hard she'd cried in the chair next to Rico's cage.

Chiyo remembered her mother's tears—and her own. "And while we're sorting through paperwork, we're pulling out photos, aren't we? Spreading them around at home. A natural thing to do. Someone dies and we begin to sift through envelopes and boxes. Or create an album as a tribute. A woman in one of my fitness classes told me she covered an entire wall in her den with photos of her late husband, ceiling to floor. I thought that was so sad, but maybe we all do the same in more controlled ways. We might move a framed photo from a bedroom dresser to a prominent living-room shelf, where it can be seen while we wander aimlessly around the house." She was thinking of the photo she'd framed, now on her kitchen shelf. A head-and-shoulders shot of her mother, who'd been in her forties at the time, glistening black hair, eyes watchful, challenging the person behind the camera. Chiyo had no idea who had taken the picture.

Others were nodding, but not Gwen. No framed photo in my house, she was thinking. Any photo of Brigg that had once lain around was disposed of after the boys left, the day I sat on the stoop and smoked two cigarettes. Gone. Every photo went into the trash. I hold enough of him in visual memory to last a lifetime. Maybe someday, I'll be able to create one kind thought about him. Or even two. Maybe I have to start thinking of kindness. Of why I married him in the first place.

Not now. Maybe not ever. All the reasons, all the reasoning, so tangled up.

Had Brigg hated her? Had he hated himself? The only place she had been safe from his shouts, from the summoning clang of the bell, was on the toilet seat in the downstairs bathroom. She stifled a sob, thinking of this now. She hadn't been able to get away from him, but she had learned how to get away from his voice and the bell. And somehow, he excused her when he demanded to know why she hadn't come immediately and she told him she'd been in the bathroom. What he didn't know was that she took a novel in there and sat on the toilet seat and read half an hour at a time. If the novel was well written, she was able to forget him during those thirty minutes.

Allam caught her change of mood and looked at her quizzically. She looked away. Eventually, if he wanted to hear, she'd share that, too. But why bring up every detail? Maybe she really could move on. Step away.

"What about groups?" Addie asked, quite suddenly. "Did anyone join groups? Besides this one, I mean."

"Not really," said Hazzley. "But there are other groups out

there, let me tell you. Two women I know belong to a widows' group. When the Greenley Orchestra came to town a few years ago for their annual performance at the Belle, I sat alone, four rows behind the widows. I could hear them laughing, and I longed to be part of their group. But I wasn't eligible because Lew was still alive. He was supposed to be with me, but he bowed out at the last minute. I ended up going alone because there was no time to contact anyone else. The situation was bizarre, now that I think of it. There I was, next to an empty seat, wanting to sit with the widows. I couldn't because my husband was dying but not dead. I felt so guilty about thinking that. But they didn't even know I was there. Most of them didn't know me anyway. We're so human, so damned vulnerable. That's what I was at the time. Vulnerable."

No one was judging her, she could feel that in the room. What she didn't tell the company was the real reason Lew didn't go: he'd had so much to drink that day, he couldn't be roused when it was time to leave for the theatre. She shouldn't have purchased a ticket for him in the first place. She shouldn't have had expectations. She thought of the enormous cache of bottles in the basement and shuddered. Out of sight under the tarp, pushed into an enclosed corner that once was the coal bin of the original house. She had no idea how many boxes there were.

Addie was nodding her head, content with being present. Pretend you're listening, she told herself. Listen or pretend to listen to anything that will take your mind off what Sybil has asked you to do.

THREE DAYS EARLIER, late Saturday afternoon, Sybil had reached out to Addie with a startling request. She told Addie she had asked her brother to bring her iPad to the hospital. After he'd gone, she ordered a variety of herbs and teas and powders that would help cure her cancer. These were to be delivered directly to her room on the palliative ward, and she was to pay cash. Sybil did not want her brother, her mother and especially her doctors and the nursing staff to know about the order. Her purse was on the lower shelf of the bedside table. As she was too weak to reach for it, she asked Addie to remove her wallet and go downstairs to the entrance to intercept the package. Delivery had been timed to take place during Addie's shift.

Addie had no way of knowing who would be delivering, how large the package would be, whether the person—man or woman—would wear an identifying uniform. Sybil was adamant that Addie stay downstairs in the lobby until the package arrived. That way, no one would learn of her determination to treat herself with the new remedies.

"Don't judge me," she told Addie in her weakened—horribly weakened—voice. "Conventional treatment hasn't worked, has it?"

Addie did not judge her friend's behaviour, but she was over-whelmed with sympathy because she recognized this as the desperate measure it was. Reluctantly, she took Sybil's wallet downstairs and stood in the lobby, watching every person who came through the front entrance. Every person who might have a package in hand.

After waiting a full hour, Addie returned empty-handed to Sybil's room. There, on the bedside table, was a flat opened box, which had been delivered shortly after Addie went downstairs in the elevator. The delivery person must have been in an elevator on the way up while she was in a different elevator on the way down. Addie returned the wallet to Sybil's purse—luckily, there were bills in a zipped fold of the purse, and Sybil had been able to pay for the remedies herself.

But Sybil was in a rage and blamed Addie. The staff had most certainly found out what was going on because the man who'd arrived with the package went directly to the nurses' station to ask permission to access Sybil's room. The staff did not confiscate the supplies, and why would they? Addie thought. The box probably contained completely harmless tea leaves or who knew what. Dozens of Cellophane packets of herbs and powders and leaves were tucked neatly inside the box, each one folded and stapled and labelled.

Sybil, having exhausted herself in rage at Addie's failure to intercept, fell asleep. She was pitifully thin, and Addie looked at her despairingly but held her tongue and did not respond to the anger. She stayed at the bedside until Sybil was awake again, hoping her friend had calmed down. Sybil, racked by weakness and discomfort, was still angry when Addie left, shortly after nine.

SUNDAY NOON, when Addie returned, Sybil told her she had made another decision.

"All these powders and herbs and leaves are bullshit." Her voice was a harsh, accusing whisper. "You know that as well as I do. How could they possibly help me at this stage?"

Addie had to agree, but she was not prepared for what Sybil said next.

She wanted Addie to help her with a medically assisted death. Just the two of them present.

Was Addie hearing correctly?

"You know I can't do that."

"You can," said Sybil, and this time her voice failed completely. She waited several moments before she tried again. She turned her face away and stared out the window. "I can't bring my mother into this. She would never accept such a decision. It would break her heart. I want to die, and I want to die now. I can't go on. I absolutely cannot. I have to do this while I'm competent to make the decision."

"What do you suppose I can do? You have to initiate the process. I can let the staff know; I can do that much. They can get the paperwork started. Two doctors have to be contacted. All this will take time. The laws are more relaxed now, but there will be paperwork, signatures, a ten-day waiting period."

"I can't wait." There was a long silence. "I can't go that route because my mom must never know."

"But what on earth can I do? Think of what you're asking."

"Bring morphine," Sybil said in a new hard-edged voice. "You work in a hospital. You can get some in Wilna Creek. You have access to drugs."

"I don't have access to drugs. I work in administration, remember? And even if I did—"

"You're in contact with people who do. You're resourceful. I'm already taking the drug. If I happen to take more, no one will even notice."

Addie had nothing further to say. She didn't want to fight with her friend. But Sybil wasn't giving up.

"I'm asking because you are my closest friend. Closer than any family member. I'm asking you to respect my wishes. You know there's no one else I can turn to. Please, Addie, please. Won't you do this for me? If you asked the same of me, I would agree in a minute."

Addie recognized emotional blackmail when she heard it. She recognized utter and total despair when she heard it. The conversation required so much energy on both their parts, the two of them ended up in tears.

And that was how Addie had left Sybil on Sunday.

She'd had a slow drive back to Wilna Creek because the temperature had dropped and there were patches of black ice on the road. Along the way, she momentarily considered how she might put her hands on extra morphine to help her friend die. Then she banished the thought.

In two days, Sybil had see-sawed from spending heaven knows how much money on a box filled with powders and leaves she hoped would keep her alive to begging for help to end her life. She had convinced herself that Addie would come up with a solution. Addie was supposed to be the problem-solver. Oh yes.

Oh no. She could not and would not end her friend's life. A life that was going to end soon without intervention.

In the evening, when she had finally arrived home, she parked the car and made her way upstairs and collapsed in her chair and put her feet up. She had no appetite. She skipped dinner. Her muscles ached, her limbs ached, her eyes were so heavy her vision had blurred. Caregiving was relentless. Over the past weeks and months, she had tried to be positive, tried to support Sybil, tried to keep up the spirits of Sybil's family. But her own spirits were down. The support part, the raw fact of being on call, of giving and giving, was more exhausting than any of the physical care, or driving back and forth between cities. The only outside activity she kept up now was getting herself to the Tuesday evenings at Cassie's to meet with the company—her new friends. She would not give those up. Even so, a feeling of hopelessness prevailed. Hopelessness weighed so heavily, she sometimes felt she couldn't rise from her bed in the morning.

She'd been in desperate need of music that evening and had lifted herself out of her chair long enough to put on a CD of Chopin's nocturnes. She dropped back down, sank into a soothing lull and allowed the amazingly delicate fingers of Fou Ts'ong to calm her for a full hour until she was finally able to go to her bedroom and sleep.

". . . GUILT," someone said now. Addie caught only the last word.

A cognitive emotion, said her reflexive self. Socially, culturally constructed.

She had no idea what they'd been talking about. The company was indulging her; she knew that. No one was asking her to pay attention. They all thought she was grieving the loss of Sybil. And she was, she was. It was just that Sybil was very much in the present, not in the past.

She saw a cup of tea in front of her on the table but had no recollection of it being placed there. Maybe she had dropped into sleep for a few moments. That was frightening. Not being aware of the last few moments—whole minutes? But here was Chiyo beside her, reassuringly ready for whatever might take place. Addie reached for the tea.

"Other emotions get mixed in. Maybe you feel obliged to do something you're asked, and you go ahead and do it, but you're seething with anger at the same time." That was Chiyo.

"A wasted emotion if someone else dumps it on you—guilt."

That's what she'd heard: *guilt*. Who said that? Addie had black spots before her eyes.

"Guilt," she echoed. But this was the only word she spoke. The others were looking at her with kindness. Where had they been taking this? Wake up, she told herself. Wake up and allow guilt to fill the space.

THE SWEDE, Hazzley was thinking. And quickly brushed Meiner away. She had no regrets. At the time, she had wanted nothing more than to break free and live a normal life. Was normal achievable, or was it a myth, a state no one experienced? She had come to believe that there were many different and undefined ways of being normal. Whatever it was, she sometimes felt herself outside the conversation.

For instance, while Lew was alive those last couple of years, she was prevented from living the way others did. The way she thought they did. Lew's drinking had prevented that. Don't blame everything on Lew, she reminded herself, but don't start feeling guilty, either. *Schuld*, she said to herself. German for "guilt." But *Schuld* also means "debt." Surely, surely I am not carrying a debt load at this stage of my life.

IDA DIED AND I'M ALIVE, Tom thought. Why did life turn out that way? Why should I be the one to live? What better reason for guilt? He thought of her receiving oxygen, telling him she was thankful for the life she'd lived. He lowered his head, stared at his hands clasped together on the table.

CHIYO ONCE AGAIN SAW the brown death knot at the side of her mother's head. "Help me," her mother cried out. Her mouth shaped the silent words: *Help me*. But Chiyo could not help. She had been unable to keep her mother from dying. She had not been capable of staunching her mother's fear. And now she was trying not to feel guilty about moving on, about taking up the reins of her own life. She and her mother had both been born into the concept of *on*, the concept of *giri*. The limitless obligations that bound. Why did she think now of *Amour*, the one film that had caused her to become undone? The lowest point in the film was the scene that would not be forgotten: the old man, the old woman, the pillow over the face because love had been pushed beyond its breaking point. The director had been wise enough to call the film *Amour*. No, Chiyo told herself. I have many strengths. And I am already carving out a new path.

WE HAVE SUCH IMPERFECT LIVES, Gwen was thinking. I hated the bell. He made me hate everything about him at the end. What kind of horrible human am I to feel that way, to hide on the toilet seat and read while he was upstairs clanging the bell, giving orders that had to be followed? Well, folks, if you want to hear the ultimate guilty thought, there were times when I wanted him dead. But surely he'd have possessed his own version of dignity. A dignity that was lost to him because of the damage done by the stroke. I couldn't see that at the time because all the other feelings got in the way.

ALLAM HAD ONE THOUGHT ONLY: I could have stopped her from going to help the neighbour that day. Conditions in Aleppo were too dangerous. If I had stopped her, she would be alive. Who could say which of the buildings would be bombed? We should have left long before that; we should have left our country when our daughter did. Our now-broken country that once we loved.

ADDIE KNEW THAT CHIYO was hovering, keeping watch. Chiyo could be trusted. She felt Chiyo's hand rubbing her shoulder soothingly. But Addie had gathered herself. I'm fine, said her inner voice. I need sleep, that's all. Lots and lots of sleep.

Cassie walked in with a tray that held a rectangular cake decorated with white icing, candied green leaves, red berries. It was December, after all—the festive season. A small and brightly decorated tree had been placed on its own table at the side of the room. Everyone looked up blankly, greeting Cass as if she'd bounded in off the surface of a cream-cheese moon. She set the cake in the centre of the table and looked around at the faces.

Good timing, she said to herself. Definitely good timing.

The members of the company roused themselves and ordered a round of drinks, and then made short work of the cake, which had the slightest hint of rum in its December icing.

# On His Watch

T O M

Tom was thinking of dragonflies in Nova Scotia, jewel-like neon colours, violets and purples, greens and blues, flashes of silver wings. How they flitted toward him and away, abruptly changing direction while going about their business. During one visit, his grandmother had told him that dragonflies were the devil's darning needles. Grampa Murray scoffed and tried to offset superstition by explaining their usefulness and worth. "They eat mosquitoes and blackflies, for a start. We have dozens of species right here in our own province," he told Tom. "Dozens. They're here for a purpose. Part of the life chain."

While Tom waited for Dave in the roundabout at the entrance of the Haven, he recited softly three lines he'd written during that childhood visit to Nova Scotia. He was fourteen years old and writing poetry even then. He and his grandfather had taken the rowboat out early in the morning, fished for an hour and a half, caught their breakfast, released a few.

"Put your hand under the belly, keep it underwater as much as you can. Don't lift it by the tail; you'll damage the spine."

Later, when Tom was alone in his upstairs room, he pulled a small notebook from the pocket of his suitcase and wrote:

*beside us*
*wide-winged dragonflies*
*stared with big bead eyes*

The only lines he could remember. Much water under the bridge since he'd written those. His was the work of an amateur, he knew that. But he kept on, worked at the poems anyway. And continued to read poetry, whatever he happened to lay his hands on.

The door of his Jeep was wrenched open, and Dave hitched his barrel body into the passenger seat. Was Dave thinner? Seemed that way to Tom. As if staves of weight had dropped from his skeleton overnight.

They were on their way to Greenley for Dave's cancer treatment, and as he was the only passenger scheduled this time, they both knew they could relax, didn't have to make polite talk. Later, on the way home in the afternoon, Dave would be worn out; he and Tom would drive back in relative silence. Lots of energy on the way there, however. Dave, despite his weight loss, was raring to go. He had stories to tell about the inmates. Tom assumed the listener's role and didn't mind one bit. He was ever aware of the fact that he did not have to deal with what Dave was dealing with.

"Dumbasses," Dave said. "Pardon the language. First of all, this morning, the guy in charge of the kitchen set everyone off. This guy has sleek black hair, wears a two-inch ponytail at the crown of his head so it sticks straight up. A silver bauble on an elastic holds this frickin' little ponytail in place. He's good in the kitchen, this guy, but tough on his staff. Well, he was ranting at top pitch about needing more carafes of decaf, and that voice of his got everybody off on the wrong track. After that, when the plates were cleared away, there was a fuss about toothbrushes. One of the inmates needed a toothbrush and wanted the tuck shop unlocked, but it's closed early in the day. So a predictable flare-up, another crazy man shouting down the hall. I tell you, Tom, people around here don't have enough to think about. The joke of it is, when you talk to this guy who wanted the toothbrush, you can see three teeth and that's it. If he throws his head back and laughs—not often, because he's a complainer—you see that he really does have a mouthful of teeth. With gold caps on his molars. Or maybe they're crowns. I don't know the difference."

Tom pulled out of the roundabout while Dave tugged at the seat belt, adjusting it gingerly around what he referred to as the chemoport implanted in his chest. He'd showed it to Tom one day and Tom had felt sadness, seeing it.

"All that fuss for a lousy toothbrush," said Dave. And went silent.

Tom thought about Ida and how, after brushing her teeth, she used to rinse her mouth with lukewarm water. She had sensitive teeth or gums, one or the other; she couldn't rinse with cold at all.

What a thing to think about now. He'd teased her about it once, and she had flared up. They'd been in their thirties at the time, maybe forties. Turned out it wasn't only her teeth that were sensitive.

He had told himself before and told himself now: we had a good marriage, sensitive teeth and all.

Dave was starting up again. "A few of us walked up the hill to McDonald's for supper last night. A change from the dining room, you know how it goes. After that, with full bellies, it was downhill all the way." He laughed at his own joke. "Anyway, we had a yearning for fast food. Too much healthy food in an institution wears you down after a while. Well, there was someone in the lineup ahead of us and she had stovepipe legs, I tell you. I'm not kidding. I never saw the like. No fat, just solid legs shaped like stovepipes. Big. She was a young woman, maybe about thirty, short overalls that stopped at the thigh, rubber boots to the knees, arms akimbo, and she stayed like that the whole damn time she was in line. Daring anyone to say a word. To top it off, she was wearing a railroad cap. What an outfit! And at this time of year."

Tom tried to picture this and got as far as the thighs.

"So we sat down and one of the guys I was with—he's in his eighties if he's a day—started in on a story about his youth. How he'd saved a man from *drownding* once. I tried to pay attention to the story but kept thinking he'd made a mistake about the word *drownding*. Sure enough, he said it the same way, over and over. Never mind, the story was a big deal for him because he'd saved this fellow's life. Turns out he never learned the guy's name, never found out, because after he hauled him out of the water and did artificial respiration, an ambulance arrived and the man was taken away. Fishermen used to go there—the Kawarthas somewhere—to fish largemouth bass. I've fished largemouth myself. Big and olivey-coloured. Those bass like weeds, and they don't care if the water is warm. Good eating, too. Especially when you have a cast-iron frying pan right there on shore so you can cook them fresh when you bring your boat in."

Dave was going on about sex now. Back to talking about the Haven. Tom wondered what the ride home would be like. He'd have a few hours to himself in Greenley after taking Dave up to the third floor. He'd go somewhere for coffee, maybe the main cafeteria, which was off to the side of the entrance at the health centre. Or maybe Tim Hortons, same level but different hallway. Past the elevators, past the gift shop.

"Before the toothbrush fiasco, Rose, at our table, started talking about sex in her marriage. 'It was good for a long time,' she told us. Then she points her index finger straight out and lets it droop from the middle. 'After that,' she said, 'not so good.' There are six at our table, four women and two men, and the women started hooting and laughing. They'll say anything, even at breakfast. Things aren't the way they used to be. But you know, Rose is still a helluva bridge player; I gotta admire that. I like her sense of humour. Everybody in the place knows her. I bet when she was younger, she was a killer for looks. She can keep people's spirits up. She's a natural."

"Laughter in your life is good, no question about that."

"You bet it is. I used to be married, and my wife and I had some great laughs, but she died. Long time ago," said Dave. "You, too, Tom? You never say much about that."

"My Ida died last year. I've been missing her a lot, I'd say." His voice cracked, and that took him by surprise.

"There ought to be a law against it," said Dave. He stared straight ahead through the windshield.

"Against what?"

"Grief."

Dave seemed to be talked out, so Tom let his thoughts wander as they neared Greenley. He was grateful for sunny weather and a clear highway in December. Next year he'd be eighty. Before his birthday and every two years after that, he'd have to pass a vision test and some sort of in-class screening assignment to renew his driver's licence. He'd be required to undergo a review of his driving record and participate in a forty-five-minute group education session. He might have to take a road test—if deemed necessary—and he hoped that wouldn't happen. He had talked to one of his long-time friends who'd already gone through this. One of the tasks had been to draw a clock with hands pointed at a particular time. His friend drew the perfect clock face, all right, but after that, he drew the hands separately and placed them outside the clock. That was the end of driving for him! Tom didn't want to make any mistakes like that.

He thought about his upcoming eye appointment. There was

no bus service from his street, so maybe he could ask someone to drive him. He did have the option of taking a taxi. He'd figure it out when he got home. At least his ophthalmologist was in Wilna Creek. He wouldn't have to ask for a lift to Greenley. He also had to remember to tell the doctor that only his left eye watered. He wouldn't say a word about crying. What would be the point? He didn't sit around crying; he hardly ever cried. But once in a while, his left eye started tearing up. Maybe he had one dry eye. He'd heard people in his shop talk about dry eyes; they carried drops with them everywhere they went. Too bad that at his age, eyes and teeth were up-and-down concerns. Half a molar could fall out of your head, and if you were lucky—as he was—you had a caring, skilled dentist who could patch you up and tell you to chew on one side until a permanent repair could take place. Most of his peers were probably chewing on one side. On the positive side, he still had his own teeth—except for small chunks that had fallen off with no ill consequences.

Tom pulled up at the entrance to the health centre, put on his flashing lights and walked Dave to one of the benches inside the main door. He left him there while he went out again to park the car in the big outdoor lot. Dave was waiting when he returned, and Tom escorted him to the elevator and up to the third floor.

"I'll pick you up right here," he told Dave. "Have a nurse call or text and I'll be ready. I brought a book along, so I'll be in the coffee shop or the cafeteria."

"I'll send a text," Dave told him. "The treatment doesn't take

so much out of me that I can't use my own phone. See you later."
And he hailed the staff in his big voice and checked himself in at
the desk.

TOM WENT BACK DOWN to the main floor and sat for a while,
watching people come and go. All shapes and sizes, some with
deliberation and intent, some looking half or entirely lost, some
tapping at phones as they walked by. A few stood around waiting; others rushed to get to the elevators. Two young women were
talking and Tom overheard, "I was listening to the news in the
car. Their president's behaviour is so outrageous, he might be
*increached*. He hasn't been in office two years yet. My mom says
the whole world is going to hell in a handbasket."

Tom shook his head, got up and wandered along to the gift
shop. He knew Hazzley would be interested in the desecration of
the word. He'd tell her about "increached" when the company met
next Tuesday.

He looked over the gift-shop merchandise, which was of no
interest. He leafed through magazines on a rack at the back of
the store and chose one about fishing, not that he fished much
anymore. He couldn't remember the last time he'd been out in a
boat. The volunteer at the cash, a man of fifty or so, looked surly,
or maybe just sad. If there hadn't been people lined up behind
him, Tom might have asked the man if he could help in some way.
It was the kind of thing Ida used to do. No feigned empathy from
her. Tom was convinced that on the days Ida worked alongside

him at Rigmarole, customers came to the shop just so they could spill out their troubles to her. Sometimes she took them to a café down the street for a cup of tea, even if they were strangers when they'd first walked through the door. He suspected that Hazzley was like that, too. Ready to help, and with humour added in. Hazzley was a strong woman, he could see that from the beginning, from the first meeting of the company.

He decided to go outside to get a bit of exercise. The grounds of the hospital and health centre covered a sizable chunk of real estate. Several buildings were interconnected—tunnels inside, pathways out. He chose a walkway that led between trees and buildings, certain that at some point he'd end up back where he started. His sense of direction could be relied upon. A few workers, wearing coats over hospital greens or blues, were out for a midday walk. Some were wearing headphones, some tapping at small screens. Tom turned a corner and faced a biting wind. His eyes smarted and the left one began to water. He chose another path and changed direction, this time passing a staff residence where interns and residents lived with their families, a three-storey building. Two boys of preschool age were playing a serious game in a patch of grass beside the parking lot. They were arguing when Tom passed, and the taller of the two uttered a threat in his high-pitched child's voice: "You keep doing that, and I'm telling the hospital!"

Tom smiled and carried on. Imagine, he thought. Imagine spending years of your childhood in the shadow of these buildings. You'd be brought up as part of a large medical community with rules, definite rules. Your ultimate threat—your ultimate "or else"—would have to be "I'm telling the hospital!"

Once he was in front of the main entrance again, he figured he'd go to the coffee shop to buy a pot of tea and something to eat. He had another hour and a half to fill before Dave would call.

In the first hallway, he pressed himself against the wall to make way for a narrow stretcher with the sides pulled up. The woman pushing it seemed familiar, and he looked and then looked again when he was certain.

"Addie?"

Before she replied, he saw the person lying on the stretcher, eyes closed, white hospital blanket pulled up to her chin, gaunt, wasted by disease. It was patently clear that the woman was extremely ill.

Addie's face was lined with worry. She had almost pushed past him while guiding the stretcher toward the elevators.

Was she surprised—relieved?—to see him, to hear her voice called out? Tom wasn't sure.

"Tom!" she said. "I wasn't expecting to see you here. Did you drive someone this morning? You volunteer for Wheels of Hope, don't you?"

"That's exactly why I'm here," he said.

The woman on the stretcher opened her eyes when she heard Addie speak.

"This is Sybil," Addie said to Tom in a half-voice, as if she were no longer accustomed to speaking in a normal tone. "My friend

Sybil. She was in radiology for an x-ray, and I told the staff I'd bring her back up to the ward."

"Do you need help? I'll take one end."

"No, this is easy to push. I'm practised, believe me."

Sybil had followed the exchange and now freed a bony arm and hand from under the blanket, extending it toward Tom. She appeared to be too tired to speak.

What a measure of humanity we are, Tom said to himself, taking Sybil's thin hand in his own, understanding the situation. Or thinking he did.

"Here," he said, "let me take the end. It'll be easier with two."

Addie acquiesced.

"I'm filling in time while I wait for my passenger," he told her. "One of the residents"—he almost said "inmates"—"from the Haven. He won't be finished treatment for a while. Maybe, if you're free, we can have a cup of tea? Tim Hortons is on this level. Well, you'll know where it is."

Addie nodded, her cheeks flushed. "I'd welcome a cup of tea before heading home. I took the day off so I could spend the morning with Sybil. An x-ray was scheduled, and we—her family and I—try to be here most of the time. Sybil likes to have someone she knows with her. Her sister-in-law is already here to relieve me for the afternoon, though. She just sent a text from upstairs. If you want to go ahead and order the tea, I'll join you in a few minutes."

Sybil had been taking in the conversation, but when the elevator doors opened, she closed her eyes and submitted to being pushed about.

Tom left the two of them in the doorway of her private room and went back downstairs. He didn't have long to wait. He'd secured a table for two in the corner, and Addie soon joined him, looking almost as weary as her friend.

"Go ahead and ask," she said, and slid into her chair.

"There's nothing to ask," said Tom. "I'm sorry. Sorry to see your friend so very ill."

"She won't last much longer," said Addie. "That's why I took the day off; I'm not really here because of the x-ray. Fortunately, the weekend is coming up. When I come back tomorrow I can stay overnight, maybe two nights. But I have to return home this afternoon. I'll check in at work and then pack a bag so I can cover the night shift for the weekend. Give the family a break. Until. Well, until."

"If you want me to drive you anywhere—if you don't feel like driving yourself—just say the word."

She shook her head. "I'll let the company know when I'm able, Tom. But I'm glad you're here. I'm glad we met in the hall. Thank you for not questioning me."

"Addie, there's no reason to explain." Tom patted her arm and started talking to her about driving Dave. He told her about Dave's easy banter on the trip to Greenley. About walking around the hospital grounds. About the overheard argument between the two boys. He filled up the space while Addie gathered herself, and he could see that she was grateful. After that, they were silent for a bit, sipping at their tea.

Tom was going back to the counter to order a bagel with cheese and asked Addie what she wanted.

"I *am* a bit hungry. Maybe a bowl of soup? Here, let me give you the money."

"My treat," he said. "Absolutely my treat."

They'd finished eating when Tom heard the low tone of his phone and checked his messages. "Dave's ready," he said. "I have to go upstairs to pick him up."

Addie stood when he left the table. He looked down—she was easily six inches shorter—and hugged her.

"You'll get through this," he said. "Sybil is fortunate to have you as a friend. And please, Addie, don't forget that you have other friends, too. Will you be at Cassie's on Tuesday?"

"I haven't missed a meeting yet. And won't, if I can help it."

"Good."

"See you then. Depending."

Tom gave a wave and headed toward the elevators again.

DAVE WAS SITTING on a bench at the end of the hall. He had an ashen look but hailed Tom in his usual spirited way.

"I'll walk you to the elevator and down to the entrance," Tom told him. "You can wait there while I bring the car around."

But when Dave stood, he became dizzy and dropped back to the bench, his head bowed.

He looked at Tom. "Don't worry," he said. "This has happened before. Some sort of issue with balance, vertigo. Nothing serious; it won't last. Thump goes my left foot. But the sole of my foot doesn't send a message to my brain to say it made contact with the floor. I know the foot is there; I can see it. Just takes a minute, that's all." He took a deep breath and prepared to stand again.

Tom told him to stay put, and he went to fetch a wheelchair, just in case. He didn't want Dave going down in a heap in the middle of the corridor. He didn't want him breaking a hip. Not on his watch. His job was to get Dave safely back to the Haven. No fainting fits or snapped bones along the way.

# Being Present

Addie sat at the table again. When Tom was out of sight, she picked up her scrunched paper napkin and began to fold and refold, until she'd worried it down to the size of a thumbnail.

Am I prepared? she thought. Is Sybil's family prepared? We have no choice and will do what has to be done. We will be present. That is the most important thing. Sybil is loved. There is nothing more important right now. But Addie felt like wailing. Wailing through the day and night.

She considered the way Sybil had collapsed onto her mattress after being transferred from stretcher to bed. An entire body collapse into instant sleep. And what was today's hip x-ray about anyway? Was that necessary? Sybil was rarely comfortable, rarely without pain. The only time the lines and creases disappeared from her face was when she was heavily medicated—almost semi-comatose. Addie knew that the x-ray results, whatever they might be, were not going to change the final days of her friend's life. She felt resentful that Sybil had been put through all the meaningless shifting and moving.

And Tom. She felt better after seeing him. He would never accuse her of being a misrepresenter of facts. He was accepting, seemed to understand, no explanation needed, none given. None of that mattered anymore.

She stared out the window at the December sky and experienced a lightning flash of remorse about refusing to provide extra morphine to her friend, who was in so much pain. Pain that lingered as life lingered. But where on earth would Addie have put her hands on a supply? And how would she have done such a thing? No, she could not live with that.

Sybil had accepted her decision and had not mentioned the morphine again. The family knew nothing of any of this. But Sybil had turned away from them all, Addie included. She had turned toward Death. Death with a capital *D*.

Addie was finally able to move. But only as far as the counter to order another tea. She sat back down at the table for a while, until she could face the journey home. She wouldn't need supper when she got there; that was certain. Food didn't seem to matter now.

But on her way out, she ordered a ten-pack of Timbits, in case she wanted a snack along the way. She probably wouldn't eat them at all. She'd just leave them in the car.

While the Timbits were being put into a cardboard container, Addie tried to pull herself together. She had to drive home to Wilna Creek, and then turn right around and drive back to Greenley in the morning. She would pray for more than a few hours' sleep tonight.

She was uneasy. The past few days—and especially this morning—every time she said goodbye to Sybil, she'd felt a looming sense of dread, a foreboding, the world topped with grey.

And yet, even through the dread, when she walked out of the health centre into the winter air, she came to a full stop. She stood outside the main doors and pulled in a deep breath. For herself. A deep breath of life.

# Ways of Seeing

Thursday, Hazzley stood by the kitchen window overlooking the backyard. She was surprised to see a peregrine falcon at the top of the neighbour's tree. *Still like the falcon; eye like the hawk.* She waited to see what it would do. Probably keeping an eye on her. No, a falcon would be watching the bird feeder for prey. But it would be aware of her, she was certain.

She had pulled the paper in from the front step and now opened it out over the counter to scan the obituaries while she finished her coffee.

Right away, she saw the notice about a Greenley woman named Sybil who had died the previous day. A name one didn't see much these days. She was described as a professor of nursing. Addie Levesque, beloved friend, was named in the list of mourners. The funeral was to be held at a church in Greenley on Saturday after-noon. Two days from now.

Hazzley stared up at the falcon and thought of Addie. The clarity and immediacy of sorrow, the devastation of loss.

She thought of her own path over the past three years. Good grief and bad. Or maybe, she told herself, all the grief just sinks to the middle, somewhere in between. A muddle of grief.

"Look at me," she said aloud, still staring at the falcon. "I'm trying not to be at a standstill. I thought I could empty the house and change my life in some unknown way, but I got stuck after three rooms: Lew's office, the dining room, a spare room upstairs. The basement is the obstacle. I'm not even sure of what I was trying to accomplish. Maybe, in the new year, in the spring, I can face a move. Would that surprise anyone? Sal? Cass? Probably not. I could move to a smaller place that would suit me better than this great big house. First things first, however. Addie is the one who's important right now."

The falcon flew off.

Hazzley refolded the paper, put on her coat and boots and went out to the car. She placed the paper on the passenger seat for Tom. The two of them could talk this over when she picked him up at his house. First, she had to get him to his appointment. He'd phoned a few days earlier to ask if she'd drive him to his eye appointment and home again. He wouldn't be able to drive while his pupils were dilated, he said. And he wondered if she'd mind.

Of course she wouldn't mind. After she'd replaced the receiver, her memory recited: *ophthalmus*, Greek root, "eye." Her brain worked that way; she made no excuses. She was glad she could remember Greek and Latin roots. Long-term memory was a blessing, and she hoped it wouldn't go away. Keep adding to the store, she told herself.

Tom was good company. He'd mentioned that he'd be flying west to visit his son's family for five days over Christmas. Hazzley would be in Ottawa over the same period, staying with Sal. She'd be happy to catch up on the lives of her grandchildren, who would all be home. And there was plenty of snow in Ottawa. More than Wilna Creek had received so far. Hazzley decided that she'd put her snowshoes in the car, just in case.

Maybe she would ask Tom about the snow poem. Ask if he knew the lines she couldn't place.

*As I look over the*
*White and soundless world.*

His appointment wouldn't last long—an hour, maybe. She could read or do the daily puzzles to fill in the time. The clinic had a small coffee bar in the pharmacy on the main floor of the building.

She had no idea if Tom was having a problem with his eyes. The appointment was probably an annual check. Everyone their age had their eyes checked. She'd had her own appointment a while back, and as ever, the doctor had commented on the abnormally large size of her pupils—without drops. Something she never noticed in the mirror or thought of at all until someone brought it to her attention. Not that she'd ever been blinded by a blazing surge of insight. No, she thought. Insight seems to be portioned out in stages.

She had never been to Tom's home, but she knew his street because it was only five blocks from her own. She slowed until she came to an older house on a corner lot. Tom was waiting at the front door and climbed in beside her. When she showed him the obituary, he did not seem surprised. He was the kind of person, she figured, who accepted things as they were. Straight on, as events unfolded.

By the time Hazzley pulled up in front of the eye clinic, the two of them had a plan. They would return to Hazzley's after Tom's appointment and start phoning from there. They were aiming for three in the afternoon. Hazzley would make a couple of sandwiches and a pot of tea for lunch while she and Tom waited for the others. In the meantime, while Tom was in the doctor's office upstairs, she would call the café. Cass would definitely want to know. Hazzley pulled out her cell.

A SELF-SERVE SHELF for tea and coffee had been set up along the window side of the pharmacy. Three narrow tables were squeezed into a small space. Hazzley draped her coat over a chair and helped herself to a mug of boiling water from a large urn. She dropped a tea bag into her mug and paid at the cash.

A family—mother, toddler on a booster seat and an older woman (maybe a grandmother?)—were at one of the tables. The toddler had a perfect rosebud mouth and reddish hair. In fact, all three had reddish hair. Hazzley smiled at the child and he shifted his torso to a defensive position, his shoulder slanted away from her. He was in a grumpy mood. She gave up trying to be friendly. But he kept vigil because now he needed to know where she was. His mother and grandmother, oblivious to this exchange, were arguing, wrangling over something, and they, too, fell into a grumpy silence. The grandmother, who was terribly thin, shifted her arms over the tabletop as if they were weightless, as if her bones were knocking about under her skin. She stared up at the ceiling as if there was no point in going on.

There is! Hazzley wanted to shout at her. At both women, really. There *is* reason! Don't waste your time arguing with each other! Even your child looks as if he's accepted conflict as the norm!

She began to work on the crossword, and then thought about bringing Tom back to the house for lunch while they waited for the others to arrive in the afternoon.

She made another decision.

# Seeking Balance

CHIYO

It was shortly before one o'clock, and Chiyo had been behind the counter for forty minutes. She was in charge of mashed potatoes—one plop or two—a slice of meat and a scoop of gravy for each plate. The next task was to serve extra helpings, if anyone wanted more. This was Chiyo's second day as a volunteer. The previous day, when she'd arrived at the church to offer her services, she was put to work immediately; that's how short-staffed they were. She was handed an apron and assigned to soup, one bowl per tray for each of the men and women as they slid their trays along.

The soup kitchen in the church basement was open every weekday. Forty to fifty people showed up regularly for the hot midday meal. Some were hungry and in need of food. She suspected that others were there for companionship. Most seemed to know one another. There was no charge for the meal. Chiyo had made a commitment to work twice a week, on days when she was free over the lunch hour, usually Wednesdays and Thursdays. She was told that for Saturday and Sunday meals, a second soup kitchen was open at a local mission not far from the church, but that was run by a separate organization.

Communal tables had already been set up in the church basement, chairs in place, before the outside doors were unlocked. Another volunteer explained that the tables stayed up throughout the week unless the space was needed for some evening event. Tables and chairs were folded and stacked along the side of the room, as necessary. The kitchen was broad, with a high ceiling, long stainless counters on one side, spacious paint-chipped cupboards above those, a huge white table in the centre, electric ranges on the opposite side, along with two deep sinks and a large dishwasher. In the room where the food was served, the ceiling was low, pipes and beams evident. Turkey suppers as fundraisers used to be served there during Thanksgiving and Christmas, and Chiyo had attended more than a few with her mom. Over the past two decades, those had been replaced by free meals for the needy. The entire place was familiar, even welcoming. A large Christmas tree in one corner of the room had been decorated with garlands that glittered of silver and gold. Strings of multicoloured lights flashed on and off like signals from a lighthouse.

The person showing Chiyo the ropes was a woman named Dottie, assistant to the man who managed the operation. In total, there were five workers on duty. The program manager, referred to as Luther, was away in Hamilton at a conference. He was supposed to be returning sometime today.

"Luther's easy to work for," said Dottie. "He's a bit frantic—he kind of darts around and expects us to do the same. Don't be put off; we all like him, and we like working for him. And I forgot to tell you: now that winter is here, it's okay to open the outside doors a half hour early on exceptionally cold days, even though the meal is served at twelve sharp. Also, all phones are to be turned off during the meal."

Other jobs, beyond preparing and serving food, were to set out paper napkins; carry food from kitchen to serving line; refill stainless steel containers as they emptied; ensure a steady supply of coffee, tea, water and juice; wipe out the fridge; wipe the counters; wipe the tables as people finished eating.

Chiyo recognized faces from the previous day. In turn, she was greeted as if she'd been there forever. There was a kind of steady beat to this, an urgent drive to get through the work alongside the others, serve the food, do the cleaning, put away dishes, hang or stack pots and pans, and set up for the next day. While all this was going on, a steady banter with the diners was taking place. With Dottie at her side, Chiyo eased her way into the routine. Her new winter class would be starting up in the evening, and she'd have plenty of time to go home first. Spence would be coming for the weekend, and she planned to stop in at Marvin's after leaving the church to pick up a few groceries.

Just as she was about to put on her coat, the program manager arrived and came forward to greet his newest volunteer. They recognized each other instantly. Luther was no other than Hopps, the man who'd hired Chiyo as his personal trainer years ago. They shook hands, and Chiyo was welcomed to his territory. Hopps was in his forties now, a bit heavier, maybe. Same ruddy cheeks, same orange hair. He was no longer addressed as either Eldon or Hopps, he explained. He'd recently decided that he wanted to be known by his middle name—Luther.

He was laughing. "I figured I was due an identity change. What about you?"

"I guess we're all capable of change," she said. She did not add, "And I'm in the middle of the slow process of removing a mother's influence from a daughter's mind."

Luther was one of two paid members on staff, he told her; the cook was the other. On the occasions when Dottie took over managerial duties, she, too, was paid. He ran a tight ship, he added. Had to. If the program was to work, a good deal of coordination was required: food procurement and health standards, garbage disposal, finding and keeping volunteers, staff management, handling issues that might arise among the diners, making referrals, coordinating social services with other agencies. He was truly grateful that she'd come on board, he said. And wouldn't he be seeing her this evening, too? Weren't tai chi classes about to begin? Wasn't she teaching again?

They were. She was.

The entire time they were talking, Luther had been rocking

back and forth on his toes, hands moving at his sides. His normal state.

She went on to Marvin's, still thinking about Hopps/Luther. Would he be able to adjust to the slow pace of tai chi? She would see. *Box tiger's ears with fists*, she said to herself, and grinned. But no, that wouldn't be necessary. Maybe, without music, without Miley, without beat, he would respond to stillness. Maybe he would be able to stretch his limbs gently while imitating the moves.

We'll find a way, she told herself. He needs an activity he'll perceive as being less frantic than his workplace. I will present him with the expectation of stillness, of maintaining balance. Equal and opposite forces. Steady stance. Solid footing. At the same time, I'll be working on my own version of balance.

She remembered to turn on her phone and saw that she had a message. She returned Hazzley's call right away.

"I'm on my way," she said. "I'll head right over from Marvin's. Yes, I know the street. I'm free now until my evening class."

# The Company

The company, with the exception of Addie, was seated around the table in Hazzley's kitchen. If anyone had noticed the empty rooms as they walked through to the back of the house, no one ventured to make a remark.

Allam had been at Gwen's home when the call came from Tom. He'd been helping to string up some outdoor lights around the windows at the front of the house. Gwen had dug them out of the basement and decided to cheer up the place for winter. Allam didn't have to work at the community centre in the afternoon and had planned to accompany Gwen to visit Rico again. They decided to do the parrot duties an hour early so they could be at Hazzley's by three. The Grands would be coming home soon, and while Gwen would be glad to have her days back to herself, she was going to miss Rico.

Hazzley showed the others the obituary she had clipped from the *Wilna Creek Times*. It was decided that they would take two cars on Saturday: Tom and Hazzley in the Jeep; Gwen driving Allam and Chiyo. They would meet outside the church and go in together. Cass and Rice had told Hazzley they'd be there, too, and would wait in the parking lot until the company arrived.

"There's one other thing," said Hazzley. She looked down and then directly at Tom. She had poured tea, and everyone was sitting back, enjoying being in Hazzley's home.

"Something we should do for Addie?"

"Something I need help with here. In the house. Something about . . . well, taking charge of my own space. Clearing debris."

"I'll help," said Chiyo, always ready to jump in.

"And I," said Gwen, who knew a great deal about clearing debris.

The two men had already stood up.

Hazzley led her friends down into the basement. The hellhole of my existence, she told herself. But no longer. When she opened the half door to the old coal bin and pulled back the tarp for the others to see, she felt like a small child who was about to be punished. Everyone stared in.

"Lew was an alcoholic," she said, and this came out as a stutter. "These are the bottles. In the boxes. I've never been able to face up." She felt a firm arm around her—Gwen. And then Chiyo hugged her.

Tom patted her arm and went straight to work. "We can have this cleared out in no time, Hazzley."

Allam had already hoisted a box over one shoulder and was partway up the stairs.

They followed each other up and down the stairs, doing what had to be done. Carting boxes, filling the trunks and back seats of the three cars until everything was loaded. One trip was going to be enough.

"There's a bulk return location here in the city, Hazzley," Tom told her. "We'll take them there. You're going to receive a chunk of money for these, you know."

"I don't want the money. Not a bit of it," said Hazzley. "If we're paid for the bottles, let the money go to charity."

"We know of a place that needs supplies," said Tom. "An art program for young children." He looked to Allam, who agreed. "Syrian children who are adjusting to this country. The money could be put to good use there."

Hazzley led the others in her car, with Tom in her passenger seat, pointing the way. By the time they'd finished unloading and sorting and dealing with every last bottle, it was after six. Chiyo had to leave for her class.

Hazzley drove Tom back to his house.

"I don't know how to thank you," she said. "The others, too. I think I really believed I'd never clear those out of the basement. It's hard to explain how difficult that was."

"I think I do understand. Sometimes it's impossible to make a move. Even though we'd be better for it. We can all use a hand now and then."

"I'm grateful, truly."

"I'm the same way, Hazzley. I hesitate to ask for help, or don't ask at all." He got out of the car but leaned back in before he shut the door. "We'll go out for a meal together, how about that?"

"Sounds like a plan," she said.

"Good. Let's make it tomorrow night, then." He rapped the car roof as he shut the door and didn't look back as he entered his house.

Hazzley drove on to the café before going home. She might as well tell Cass what had happened. There wasn't much to hide anymore.

GWEN AND ALLAM RETURNED to Gwen's home and sat at her kitchen table having coffee.

"I'm glad we could do that for Hazzley," she said. "She must have felt the whole weight of the house tilting into that corner of the basement. She must feel a hundred years younger. Did you see the look on her face when we said goodbye?"

"Yes," said Allam. "I am glad this problem is solved for her. Maybe she felt badly that she said nothing before this, that she took no action a long time ago. It was good that she asked for help."

"Too bad the clearing out ended up being her responsibility. That was tough for her. I just hope she didn't feel any guilt."

"There was no reason for guilt. Not a bit, as Canadians say," said Allam.

Gwen sat back in her chair. "Do you remember how the conversation turned to guilt a few weeks ago when we were at Cassie's?"

Allam nodded, remembering well.

"There's something I haven't been able to get out of my mind."

"Tell me," he said quietly.

"When Brigg was alive—when he was in bed after he'd had the stroke—I had a dream that wouldn't go away. It's like a never-ending nightmare."

Allam reached for her hand while she talked.

She looked as if she'd decided not to go on, but then changed her mind.

"Okay, this is the dream. I was lying in bed and became aware of Brigg, who was somehow outside the house, two storeys up, but hanging on to the outer sill of the open window in the bedroom. Not the main bedroom, the one we'd always shared, but the spare room where I slept after he had the stroke. He was desperate to get back inside, but he couldn't, no matter how he tried. I wanted to wake up. I was fighting to wake up. I was still in bed in the dream, but I could see how desperate he was, how his fingers were curved, how his nails were ashen. I could see dirt beneath them. He was pleading: 'Pull me in.' He was trying to crawl through the window. But in the dream—the nightmare—I turned my back and my only thought was: Why can't he keep his fingernails clean?"

She stopped and looked away. "What will it take to leave those memories behind? To be free of them once and for all? What kind of monster am I to turn my back, even in a dream? I still think about him clinging to the sill, his desperation to stay alive. I'm still grieving."

"That was a dream; that was a nightmare. You did not turn your back all those years you lived with him," said Allam.

"That is true. I did not."

"Gwendo-leen-ah," he said, "you are not—I am not certain of this—but maybe you are not grieving your husband who died. Please consider. You might be grieving the loss of yourself. All those years losing yourself in that marriage. I may not be right with this thinking, but I want so much for you to be happy. Why do I want this for you? Because you are a fine person. When you were with him, when he was alive, you had bad feelings some of the time. Many people also have bad feelings. If you are able to be free of those, maybe you will be free of this man."

Gwen looked at him, taking this in. She suspected that Allam could see through the barricades she had built up around her. He could see through what had taken three decades to erect. Who else had seen—or ever known—her true adult self?

"You and I," he said, "we know how grief can whip through air like a scythe and wound a person. But you were wounded already. I was not expecting to meet you. We have this chance now, Gwendo-leen-ah. You, me."

He did understand. She was beginning to see.

He put the mugs in the sink and she reached out and he took her hand and they went up to her room and lay on top of the bed, still in their clothes. Allam pulled the new comforter over them.

He was silent after that, and they fell asleep.

When Gwen awoke, Allam was still sleeping. It was almost nine, and she could tell from the glow of the blinds that the street-lights and Christmas lights were on below. She sat up in bed and looked at Allam, who had turned on his side, toward her, in his sleep. She whispered softly: "Then blew men the trumpets, and spread the tables; water men brought on floor, with golden bowls; next soft clothes, all of white silk. Then sate Arthur down, and by him Wenhaver the queen."

But Arthur, for all his finery, had to fight on the days when he dressed in armour and faced bellicosity. Armour that was so heavy, his knights drowned when they fell into a river or stream.

She looked at Allam again. Thick, dark hair streaked with grey. Worry lines in his face. Kindness that showed, even through the worry, even through sleep.

He was no king. She was no queen. But she wanted to be beside him. The trumpets, the tables, the golden bowls would always be story, legend. She and Allam would create their own story, together.

She lay down again and closed her eyes. He stirred in his sleep, and his arm moved toward her and pulled her closer, tighter.

"Perhaps," he said, and wrapped both arms around her, "perhaps we are the perfect suits? Suited? How do you say this?"

"Perfectly suited."

"Exactly that," he said.

# Solidarity

ADDIE

She arrived early, driving through a light snowfall, and went directly to the church hall. She was drained of feeling and walked heavily. She'd never been inside this church, and saw from the outside that it was old and stone, and that it presented a particular beauty against the landscape of spreading oaks and snow-covered lawns.

The connecting hall had been added in the present century and was designed to complement the church, so the impression she had, on first approach, was that this was a scene of peace and harmony. She knew that Greenley was about the same age as Wilna Creek; the church probably dated back to the late 1800s. Sybil would have attended Sunday school here. Probably church services, too, when she was growing up in the community.

Addie knew that the casket was already inside.

She had spent much of the previous day with Sybil's family,

helping to greet relatives as they arrived at the house in Greenley, keeping the teapot full, making sandwiches, giving directions to hotels and motels. She'd met some of the aunts and uncles and cousins over the years, but the people she knew best were members of the immediate family. She had driven back to Wilna Creek late in the afternoon and managed to sleep eight hours before returning: the longest sleep she'd had in months. At least she wasn't responsible for the funeral arrangements. As executor, Sybil's brother had taken over. There would be a simple service, after which the casket would be escorted by pallbearers to the exit, where a hearse would be waiting. The cemetery was at the end of the block, and those who planned to be at the gravesite could walk there from the church. Members of the Women's Auxiliary had declared themselves responsible for food and drinks, which would be available after the service. These were already set up in the adjacent hall.

ADDIE HAD LET TYE know about Sybil on Wednesday, while she was still in Greenley, and he'd phoned her back when she was home in the evening. They had talked for a long time. He, too, had loved Sybil, but he wasn't able to be present for the funeral. He was leaving Friday afternoon for the Karolinska Institute in Solna, just north of Stockholm. He'd be attending a conference on ethics and health care.

"Addie," he said, "why don't you join me? I'm going to be there eight full days, not counting travel. Phone the hospital, tell them you need a break. They're not going to argue, especially at this time of year. You'll stay with me, of course. If you're okay with that. I'm booked at a decent hotel near the institute."

"I can't possibly; it's too sudden. I'm right in the middle of—"

"I know you are. That's why you can. Try to make arrangements for Monday. I won't be presenting my paper until the middle of the week; I could meet you at the airport. We could even stay over in Stockholm for Christmas. Why not?"

Addie began to consider the possibilities. And as Tye had said, why not? After hanging up, she spent the next hour and a half on her phone and computer, booking flights and explaining her plans to the administrator of her own hospital in Wilna Creek.

She was already thinking that she would buy a couple of new outfits when she arrived. Something in black would be best. She'd walk a lot while she was there, start losing some of the extra pounds. She had never been to Sweden. Stockholm was probably beautiful over the Christmas season. Tye had told her he'd arrange for her to attend one or two sessions at the conference, but only if she wanted to. She might want nothing more than to relax and be a tourist. She might want nothing more than to have breakfast in bed every morning.

She and Tye might give themselves another chance. Maybe they were ready. She had made the right decision. She was sure of this.

SHE ENTERED THE CHURCH from a side door near the front, walking behind Sybil's family. The church was long and narrow, the pews almost full. Sybil's family had lived in Greenley for generations, so it was no surprise that so many friends had showed up in support. Addie looked out over the sea of faces and wondered if she would know anyone apart from the people in the first two rows. Wondered who would understand what it was like: to be here, to have been with Sybil over this terrible journey—right through to its end.

And there they suddenly were, filing in, the members of her company. Hazzley and Tom and Chiyo and Gwen and Allam. They were sliding along the pew in the back row and taking their places. Cass and Rice were with them.

*They* will understand, she said silently, and felt herself enfolded by their compassion and concern. The combined strength of her friends moved through her as she took her place in the oak pew behind Sybil's mom. They had been behind her the past four months, and they would be there for her in the months to come.

The service was brief. When the officiant spoke, she didn't say that Sybil's spirit would go on. She didn't say that her consciousness, her personality, would live beyond the flesh. No. She said, "Sybil's story will survive. Though the physical body dies, the story continues. Sybil's story will carry on through the many people who knew her and loved her."

Addie was thankful for this. Thankful for having known Sybil these many years. She said her own small prayer and released a long, slow sob.

*A voice that is mine cries: Deo gratias—*
*For this awakening, for this life,*
*For these sweet lungfuls of grief.*

Everyone rose, and while the organist played Bach, the pall-bearers escorted the casket to the exit. Each row emptied in turn, everyone falling in behind the family. When Addie passed her friends in the back pew, she looked over to acknowledge them with a smile of thanks. And once again was filled with gratitude.

When the entire group of mourners stood outside on the walkways and on the lawn, Sybil's casket was loaded into the hearse for the short drive to the cemetery. The snow had stopped and the midday sun shone the way winter sun does, bestowing a sharp bright edge to each crystal that lay beneath its rays.

Addie walked over to join the company. As the hearse started up, she thought of Hazzley's chant, and her hand reached for her collar and she held on tightly.

The others did the same: Hazzley and Tom and Gwen and Allam and Chiyo and Cass and Rice. They all held on to their necklines or collars or scarves or whatever they wore at their throats. They stood this way in their own special line until the hearse passed them by. And then they began to walk to the cemetery, with Addie at the centre. They were all present for the final farewell at the grave. They were all prepared to take the next step forward into life.

May

# The Wedding

Friday morning, Tom pulled into the roundabout at the Haven and saw that Dave was waiting at the door. He hadn't seen him for a couple of months. Today's trip to Greenley was a follow-up appointment; no more treatments for the time being.

"I'm early," Dave said, and slid into the passenger seat. "I feel fit enough to run all the way."

"You've regained some of the weight you lost," said Tom. "That's good. The treatments must have done the job they were supposed to do over all those months. That couldn't have been easy."

"Nope. And I tried not to complain. But sometimes we have to go through—what the hell—we have to go through *stuff*. Bad stuff to get to the good. To get *back* to the good, I should say. Life has been good to me over the long reach."

"I'd have to say the same," said Tom. "Over the long reach."

"I'll be facing a lotta follow-up, too, for a while. The appointments will taper off gradually. I'm in competent hands, all in all. And glad to be alive."

"I'll second that."

"Tomorrow," Dave went on, "we're having a bit of a celebration, a Saturday afternoon wedding—two inmates from the top floor. Doesn't happen often around here, as you can imagine. We usually hear about the other kind of ceremony, which I won't mention because I don't want to jinx the couple. The wedding will take place in the party room, and we're all invited. Guy's name is Doug. We call him Doug the Thug—I guess he really was a bit of a thug back in the day. He's old now; he's left his thuggery behind."

Dave and Tom were both chuckling.

"Management said they'd kick in a special lunch instead of the usual fare. Everybody's pretty pumped about having a wedding at the place," Dave said. "You can stop in as my guest, if you like."

"Thanks, but I can't do that; I'm sorry," said Tom. "I'll be attending a wedding this weekend as well. Later today, after I drop you off, I have to pick up my old tux from the dry cleaner."

"Are you getting married? No kidding?"

"Not me. The tux is for the groom, a friend of mine."

"I suppose a tux doesn't go out of style."

"This one's in great shape. Retro is what people are buying today anyway. I wore it to my own wedding in 1963. I found every item separately at the Sally Ann and put it all together as a match. I always loved a bargain, still do. My friend Allam—he's the groom—came over to the house to try it on, and it fits perfectly. Twenty dollars is what I paid, and the outfit gets two men through their wedding celebrations. Not so shabby."

"Not shabby at all."

"Well, that's my story, and I'm sticking to it." Tom was laughing. "If Allam wants to pass on the tux—and the story—to some young guy someday, it might even make it to a third wedding."

"I hope this couple has a ring," Dave said. "Did you read about the woman in Alberta who lost her diamond ring while she was weeding her garden? The ring stayed in the ground for fifteen years, and one day someone went out to pull up vegetables for dinner and there it was, wrapped around a carrot. The carrot had grown right through the centre of the ring. Diamond still in place; ring okay. The woman who lost it was in her eighties when she finally got it back. I love stories like that. You wonder if you should believe them. I believe this one because I saw a bunch of photos on the internet."

"I did read about that," said Tom. "As for Allam, he told me he has a gold ring for the bride."

"That's good. I guess the weather will cooperate, too," Dave said. "We'll be out in the gardens around the back of the Haven if it's warm enough. The flower beds are kept up pretty well. We have our own gardener, and some of the inmates pitch in. Tulips are up. Daffodils are up. Seeds and plants will be going into the vegetable plot soon. There aren't any diamonds in the soil, far as I know."

Tom dropped Dave off at the health centre in Greenley and

went off to find himself a coffee. He knew Dave's appointment wouldn't take long. A checkup and blood work, probably. And then the trip back to Wilna Creek.

CASS AND HAZZLEY were in the café kitchen.

"Beat the eggs," said Cass. "I want them thick. Pass them over, and I'll put in the sugar. You measure out the flour."

"You're tough," Hazzley told her. "But you make good cakes. That's why I'm putting up with being bossed around."

"Won't hurt you for a couple of hours." Cass was laughing while she eyed the whiskey, specially ordered from Cornwall for the occasion. That was Rice's idea, and a good one. By now everyone knew that Gwen and Allam would be travelling to Cornwall in early June, to visit the historic land of the legendary King Arthur. They would tour around different parts of Cornwall, not only the area where Tintagel Castle had been built so long ago.

"How many layers is this cake supposed to be?"

"Eight. Each of the four cakes will be halved. I could make it as high as I want, but I don't want it toppling over."

"And the icing?"

"Pure cream. That goes on tomorrow. That's where the whiskey comes in—before the cream gets lathered on. As for the five children who are coming, each gets a special small cake, muffin-size, without whiskey. Easy enough to do. Same batter. I'm doing extras, in case any other children show up."

"You've thought of everything."

"It's my job to think of everything. I just hope Rice is managing by himself out there today." She waved a sticky hand toward the main room. "If he needs help, he'll come and ask."

Not only was the wedding cake being prepared in the kitchen, but Saturday's ceremony and party would be held at Cassie's as well. "Where else would we have the wedding?" Cass had said when she'd first heard the news. "We'll close up for the day—front and back—and have a real party."

A FEW PEOPLE from out of town had arrived, including Gwen's sons from Texas and their families. Gwen was both excited and anxious. They'd be staying with her for three days and would return again in August for a longer holiday. Gwen and Allam had been preparing.

When the Grands, as promised, came home before the new year, the twice-daily trips to Rico had come to a halt. After that, Gwen was restless for a few days, wondering about him. She had found herself checking the clock, thinking of his routine: he'll be having his chop; he'll be out of his cage, following Cecilia around the kitchen. She'll be chattering away to him—for Cecilia had turned out to be a chatterer. And then Gwen decided to make her farewell official. On a small sheet of paper, she wrote:

*Dear Rico,*
*Maybe your tiny parrot brain has stored some old memory of me.*
*Maybe we both worked through a few things. You listened to me and*

*I thank you for that. But I listened to you, too. We are always on
a learning curve—remember that. I understand why your owners
missed you when they were away. I miss you, too.*
Gwen

She had tucked this into an envelope and addressed it: *Rico
c/o CAGE.* And dropped it into a mailbox at the end of her
street. That was the end of that. She laughed, thinking of the
mail sorters.

After that, she and Allam had begun to fix up the house. They
did a bit of painting and prepared the two spare rooms upstairs,
and ensured that there was good space for a couple in the downstairs bedroom. When everyone arrived for the wedding, Gwen's
two granddaughters declared that they were taking over the lower
room. Especially when they realized they could have their own
space without their parents around.

When Gwen had told her sons about her upcoming marriage,
both were cautious initially. What kind of man was Allam? Now
that they'd met him, they seemed to be happy for her. Relieved?
She knew they were surprised when they learned that her friends
were in charge of the wedding. They'd never known their mother
to be a part of any group. Especially a group as involved and caring
as this one seemed to be. They'd already met Tom and Hazzley
and Cass and Rice. They were to meet the others Saturday afternoon. The group would be small, the wedding modest. A judge
who was a friend of Tom's would conduct the ceremony.

CHIYO AND ADDIE were shoving furniture around and decorating the backroom while Cass and Hazzley were making the cake. The round tables were arranged, with a vase for tulips at the centre of each. A place for the ceremony was decided, a few rows of chairs set out; two long tables end to end along one side of the room would hold the food. The two women, satisfied, stood back to survey the results of all the pushing and shoving and discussion and decision-making.

Chiyo had asked Addie to join her and Spence for dinner at Spice, for Indian food, once the decorating was complete. Spence had been invited to the wedding, and Chiyo suggested that the three arrive together the next day. Addie had been at loose ends lately, and Chiyo had noticed. She knew Tye had been invited, too, but was unable to attend. Addie had told her that much about her ex. But the relationship seemed to be on-again, off-again. And Chiyo could tell that Addie was still grieving.

Six funerals and a wedding, Chiyo thought. Look at us. Look at the friendships we've made. Maybe Spence and I are ready for a ceremony of our own. Wouldn't that make my mother happy? And maybe she already knows. Who's to say?

The company was still getting together as a group on Tuesdays, but they met once a month now instead of weekly. No one was ready to give up the loyalty and friendship, and especially the support. They wanted to keep the company together, and each of them hoped to go on meeting for a good long while.

BY MIDDAY SATURDAY, everyone was in place for the wedding. Gwen, elegant in a soft gold dress and jacket, wore a gold bracelet that Allam's daughter had presented to her earlier in the week. As the guests arrived, Rice sat on a chair at the side of the room and played soft music on his jazz guitar. Tom's wedding gift to the couple, the bronze sculpture of the geese, had been positioned at the end of one of the food tables. The geese, always about to take flight, faced the doorway leading to the main room and out into the light of the larger world.

Allam's Canadian family was present: his daughter, his son-in-law and his three grandchildren, as well as several friends from the Syrian community. Gwen was escorted by her sons from the main part of the café into the space in the backroom that Chiyo and Addie had decorated the day before. The other members of the company stood together as witnesses. Allam, in his fabulous tux, held Gwen's hand while the judge conducted the ceremony.

Tom felt his left eye tearing up and realized he'd forgotten to tell his ophthalmologist about the condition last December. He dabbed at the eye because he had to step forward to read the poem he had selected for the occasion. He'd chosen it from the book left to him by his grampa Murray.

*The sadness of the winter,*
*Which gloom'd our hearts, is gone:*
*A thousand signs betoken*
*That spring-time comes anon.*

*'Tis spring-time in our bosoms;*
*All strife aside we cast;*
*The storms were for the winter-days,*
*But they are gone and past.*
*Before us lies the spring-time—*
*Thank God, the time of mirth—*
*When birds are singing in the trees,*
*And flowers gem all the earth;*
*When a thousand busy hands upturn*
*The bounteous, fruitful mould,*
*And the heart of every poet feels*
*More love than it can hold.*

After the ceremony, after the amazing cake—fluffed up with layers of whipped cream and flavoured with Cornish whiskey—was carried into the room and served, and while Rice was once again playing jazz on his guitar and the guests were eating and clinking glasses, Tom mentioned to Hazzley: "This matters; it really matters that we know enough to pause and honour the moments in life that are worthy of celebration."

"You're right," said Hazzley. "We need these moments because they strengthen us for the ordinary times, the not-so-good and—let's face it—the downright difficult times."

Allam's grandchildren had begun to clamour for a story, and his daughter joined in. "You know so many old tales," she said to her father. "Tell us one now."

"Ah," he said. "Let me think." He sat down and the others gathered round. Gwen was by his side.

Allam looked around the room at his family and his good friends. He raised Gwen's hand to his lips.

"A story that holds love," he said. "There is room for love in the life of every person. Let me tell you now about a wedding feast that took place a long time ago."

And the others quieted, and leaned in.

# Acknowledgements

I wish to thank my agent, Jackie Kaiser, at WCA, for her friendship and long-standing support, and my editor at HarperCollins, Jennifer Lambert, for her skill, wise comments and suggestions. Thanks to Noelle Zitzer and Janice Weaver, who, once again and with expertise, have escorted me through the production and copy-edit stages of the novel. Thank you: Jim Sherman at Perfect Books in Ottawa for long-time support; Cortez Kimble for permission to use his great story of the wedding suit; Susan Zettell, who wrote *Holy Days of Obligation* (Nuage Editions, 1998); Barb and Orm Mitchell; Norman Takeuchi; Marion Takeuchi for bringing to my attention the expression *Das letzte Hemd hat keine Taschen* (The last shirt has no pockets—or, you can't take it with you!).

For discussions along the way, thanks to my daughter, Sam Itani; Catherine Hoogerhyde; Hazle Sokolich; Dr. John Martins; Susan Lightstone; Norman Jamieson; Dorothy Mitts; and Phyllis Bruce.

# Acknowledgements

Thanks to my son, Russell Itani, for information about music and the ocarina, and for the gift of an ocarina of my own—I'll be practising! Thanks to Danielle Letourneau, who brings French expressions and cake to the table. *Quelle bonne amie!* And to Michel LeFrançois, who double-checks my French. For information about Syrians who have arrived in Canada during the Syrian Civil War, I acknowledge TVO's various documentaries and discussions; these have been invaluable. Larry Scanlan, thanks for the introduction to Jamal, in Kingston. Jamal Saeed, thank you for responding to my questions about points of accuracy and helping me to understand more about Syrian culture and the experiences of Syrian refugees.

For research into the world of parrots, I am grateful to Anna Durie-Matrahazy; Pam Tallon; Sally Hawks; and Margaret Williams in Brockville, who unknowingly sparked the idea. In Carleton Place, Judy Tennant, executive director and founder of Parrot Partners (parrotpartners.org), shared her expertise and showed me around the aviary, introducing me to many parrots, including one of the African greys. This caring place provides a safe environment for relinquished parrots, rehabilitates and trains them, makes efforts toward re-homing and educates the public. I thank my cousin Joel Oliver for accompanying me to Parrot Partners, and for assuming the role of photographer. Also, thank you, Joel, for the many trips to antique markets, where we learn the trade. For the article about the goose falling from the sky, I acknowledge the *Ottawa Citizen*, February 3, 2018. Excerpts from Robert Pollok's poem "Byron" and Mary

328

Howitt's poem "Coming Spring"—the latter read by Tom at the wedding—are from *The Casquet of Gems* (W.P. Nimmo, Hay & Mitchell, 1885). Thank you, Aileen Jane Bramhall Itani, for permission to use lines from your poem beginning with "A voice that is mine," referred to during the funeral. "The Rime of the Ancient Mariner" (1798) is by Samuel Taylor Coleridge, "To Autumn" (1819–20) by John Keats. The sentences from Layamon's *Brut* (also known as Lazamon or Lawamon) are from a 1977 Middle English paper that discusses the *Arthurian Chronicles;* the Modern English translation was initially done by Eugene Mason. The epigraph beginning with "Hold your collar" is a variation on a chant in Iona and Peter Opie's *The Lore and Language of Schoolchildren* (1959). For recounting memories of Guy Fawkes Day, as well as conditions in England and Scotland during and after the Second World War, I thank Janet and David Hemings and Charles Magill. Christine Déry, you're the one who helps so many of us to be physically fit and to stay that way. I appreciate your taking time out for interviews about various classes and music selections, and about the work in general. Maria Thompson dances her way through life and makes the world a better place. Christina Cole, instructor at the University of Toronto's International Foundation Program (IFP), thank you for sharing your impressive and extensive knowledge about courses in academic listening and speaking. Until I met you, I did not know such courses existed. To my movie buddy, Fran Cherry, I express my gratitude for our never-ending conversations—always laced with humour—about human behaviour and the vagaries of LIFE! Last to be mentioned, but remembered with great measures of love: my sister, Marilyn; my close friends Jill McMurtry, Donna Wells and Helen Best.